DEATH AMONG THE STARS

ALSO BY
SHARON LINNÉA

FICTION

Death in Tranquility (Bartenders Guide to Murder 1)

Death By Gravity (Bartenders Guide to Murder 2)

WITH B.K. SHERER

Chasing Eden • Beyond Eden • Treasure of Eden • Plagues of Eden

YOUNG ADULT, WITH AXEL AVIAN

Colt Shore: Domino 29

NONFICTION

Princess Ka'iulani: Hope of a Nation, Heart of a People

Raoul Wallenberg: The Man Who Stopped Death

Chicken Soup from the Soul of Hawai'i

Lost Civilizations

America's Famous and Historic Trees with Jeff Meyer

AS SHERIDAN SCOTT

Now you Tell Me! 12 Actors Give the Best Advice They Never Got

Now you Tell Me! 12 Army Wives Give the Best Advice They Never Got

Now you Tell Me! 12 College Students Give the Best Advice They Never Got

DEATH AMONG THE STARS

SHARON LINNÉA

Arundel
PUBLISHING

BARTENDER'S GUIDE TO MURDER

Book 3 DEATH AMONG THE STARS

Copyright c 2021 by Sharon Linnéa

ISBN 978-1-933608-36-5 (Paperback)
ISBN 978-1-933608-37-2 (ebook)

First Edition November 2021

Cover Art and Cover Design by David Colón

Interior Design by Phillip Gessert

For Jamielynn,
One of the best mixologists on the planet,
Happily met over a strawberry rhubarb concoction
at a bar in Lake Placid.

Cheers!

IN THE ADIRONDACKS

ONE MORE PIECE. Or seven.

The young man took a sip of Malbec and fitted the puzzle piece shaped like a fish into the larger work that created a sitting fox. A fox with a strange, knowing grin on his face. It was a long time since he'd done a jigsaw puzzle. The rental cabin had a stack of them, all wooden, with shaped pieces. This one was close to complete.

Rise was grateful to his manager for renting this Adirondack cabin. He'd flown across country from Los Angeles three days early, to rest, re-center and dismiss any jet lag. In Los Angeles there was a pile of scripts on his desk—he'd only brought the three most promising along to read—constant calls and texts, a demanding personal trainer, and, oh yeah, four stalkers, two of whom required restraining orders.

Ah, the life of a star.

Except he wasn't a star, only a guy who'd grown up on television in three different series. Enough folks were so comfortable with him in their living rooms they figured they should be married. To him. And became violent when he didn't agree.

It had been a wonderful couple of days. His assistant, Con Allred, had laid in supplies, his favorite food, and he'd been able to cook for himself. Con had then gone ahead to join Rise's agent, manager and publicity crew to lay the groundwork for the premiere of his new feature film.

A car would be sent for Rise in the morning, his hiatus over.

The tall actor ran a hand through his golden blonde hair, snapped another piece into the puzzle and groaned. Two pieces were missing. Why would you rent a cabin and offer your guests puzzles with missing pieces?

He took another large sip of wine. The fire was burning down, a bed of orange embers lined the fireplace floor. Add another log, or let it go out?

If he wanted to be fresh and rested for the film festival, he should probably take some melatonin and read awhile, then get some sleep.

Rise drained the wine glass, washed it out and put it to dry by the sink. The cabin was made of wood with antlers everywhere. He stepped outside onto the small porch, then sat in a dark-green Adirondack chair. Rushing water of the nearby Ausable River spoke of recent rain; the piquant, calming scent of pine melded with the loam of the earth. He breathed deeply.

Back in Los Angeles, his house was a fortress, alarms everywhere. Even so, one enterprising woman, a teacher for god's sake, had left a note on his bed when he was away filming. His agent had gotten a letter from another of his stalkers, a psychologist, explaining they were uniquely psychologically suited for each other. Therefore, if she couldn't have Rise, she'd have to hurt him. A young man had stopped his mother in the grocery store and introduced himself as Rise's fiancé. Someone had followed and confronted his mom. His mom!

Rise hated being on guard all the time. Which was why he was sorry to leave the solitude of the cabin to rejoin the world in the morning. It was rented under his manager's brother's secretary's son's name. No one knew he was here.

The actor stood and stretched, then went back inside, and locked the door. He headed into the bedroom where he pulled on pajama pants and a t-shirt. He scrubbed his face in the master bath and popped two melatonin gummies.

The queen-sized bed had a quilt with an Adirondack design featuring bears dancing around a campfire. Rise picked up a script from the bedside table at random, put on his glasses, and began to read. Within ten minutes, he couldn't keep his eyes open.

It was all he could do to turn off the light before falling into a dreamless sleep.

His phone rang at seven the next morning.

"The car's on its way. It'll be outside in twenty," said Isobel, his agent. "See you at the hotel for breakfast."

"Roger. Wilco," said Rise.

He wiped sleep from his eyes and went to shower and dress. He was already packed. It wasn't long before the crunch of tires arrived outside the cabin. A glance out the bathroom window showed it to be a Range Rover driven by Castor, Isobel's favorite driver. Rise was grateful she hadn't sent the stretch.

Castor knocked on the door and Rise came through the room, pulling his suitcase. The shorter, stockier man gave Rise a friendly nod and took the bag. Rise walked around the living room, doing one last visual check. The puzzle. Should he rebox?

He stood in front of the table. And stared.

Castor was saying something, but Rise didn't hear him.

The puzzle was complete. All the pieces were locked in. None missing.

The paper towel next to the puzzle, which had a small rim of Malbec from Rise's glass the night before on it, now also had a tiny heart, drawn by pen. Filled in with lipstick.

Castor came and stood next to him, looking at the puzzle and the paper towel. A knowing smile crossed his face. "Fun night?" he asked. "Come on, we've got to go, or Isobel will have our heads."

Rise grabbed the paper towel and stuffed it into the pocket of his jeans.

It was only when he got into the car that he began to tremble.

1

EVENING'S END

TRANQUILITY, NEW YORK, held a new spark of energy. I felt it as I walked the nearly-empty sidewalks at 11:30 p.m. on that clear September Tuesday evening. A brisk chill seasoned the air around old-fashioned streetlights whose bulbs flickered merrily as if the lamplighter had recently come by. The shops of Main Street also spoke of an earlier day. They were brick or clapboard, one story or two, although the Adirondack Adventure Hotel had dared climb to four floors, the village's version of a skyscraper.

The Tranquility Film Festival was opening that weekend and I was looking forward to it. First, because I had friends whose documentary was certain to create a stir. Second, with the first festival screening on Thursday, actors, directors, publicists, and journalists were beginning to descend in their limos and fancy rental cars. Their imminent arrival excited the locals, even those who claimed disinterest, and the crowd at the pub I manage and bartend was buzzing with anticipation. Food, drinks, and high spirits flowed freely all evening.

MacTavish's, the Scottish-style inn that housed that pub—formally named That Ship Has Sailed, but universally called the Battened Hatch—was on the south end of Main, while my cottage was nestled in a hidden glade called Mill Pond off the northern end. I'd decided to walk to work that afternoon, in the late-summer heat with the teasing hint of autumn leaves. Tonight, the mountains that rimmed town loomed as a backdrop, purple and protective. We'd closed the bar at 11. My barback, Marta, and I took some extra time swapping out the next day's drink specials in the holders on each table. Marta then hurried off on her bike, and I headed home, savoring the pre-festival calm by strolling the walkways of my adopted home.

Most businesses, including restaurants, were closed, their nighttime illumination offering a soft glow over wares displayed in shop windows. There was one notable exception: the Orpheum Theater, where the festival was soon to begin. Outdoor lights shone and the marquee was aglow.

I paused to study the listing of films with the dates and times of their screenings. *Salty Sally and Pepper: Truth Be Told*, the documentary featuring as yet unknown stories about two screen idols of Hollywood's Golden Age who'd lived in Tranquility, would show on Saturday afternoon, a prime slot.

Glancing inside the hall that led to the lobby, I saw posters for the festival's other films lining the walls. It was kind of odd that the lobby doors were still open. Surely the night's final screenings of regular movies were done by now? As I entered to study a poster for an independent feature, Kyle, the lanky teenager who ran concessions during the week and usually closed up, walked into the lobby. He saw me and waved. I waved back.

"Just perusing," I said, signaling my willingness to leave.

He joined me in the outer hall. "You work around here, right?"

"Yes, I'm Avalon. Nash. I bartend at the Battened Hatch. In MacTavish's."

"Could you help me for a minute?" He looked nervous.

"What is it?"

"The last movie's over. I need to close up. But some girl fell asleep in the theater."

"You can't wake her up?"

"I tried saying, 'wake up,' but it didn't work."

"If she slept through an action movie, I'm not surprised. Did you try shaking her shoulder?"

Kyle looked uncomfortable. "I don't want to touch her or anything. We've had harassment training."

"Okay." How could I not help such a well-meaning kid?

The Orpheum was a grand movie palace back in the day. Now it was carved into three theaters, the largest of which was downstairs, in the footprint of the original. The once-commanding balcony was split in half to create two smaller screening spaces, but each remained large and raked with the original stairs going down each outside wall.

The sleeper was in theater three, upstairs. I trotted up the carpeted steps behind Kyle, who was obviously eager to get on with things.

All the theater lights were on, including the harsh work lights, which took away any golden veneer of the magic of storytelling. I headed down to where the young woman was seated, fifth row center, and walked across row four to be squarely in front of her.

The movie-goer was petite, perhaps in her mid-twenties, with the carefree good looks of youth, wearing a form-fitting white cashmere sweater that showed off her flawless tan skin, and jeggings. Her small popcorn was settled into the seat beside her. She hadn't enjoyed much of it before dozing off.

"Excuse me," I said. No reply.

"Miss?" I put my knee onto the folded seat bottom in front of me and leaned forward, reaching out and shaking the young woman's leg. I shook harder. Her naturally curly brown hair jostled, but she didn't move. "Hello?"

I glanced up at Kyle, who shrugged, *see what I mean?*

Willing myself not to think the worst, or even the second-worst, I walked back a row and across it. I put a hand firmly on the girl's shoulder and shook her. "The movie's over."

She fell forward.

Her popcorn spilled over her seat and onto the floor.

That's when I thought the worst.

Local police arrived first, followed quickly by EMTs, who were led to the young woman. Neither Kyle nor I wanted to stay close as they laid her down to see if any ministrations would make a difference. She'd been stiff to the touch; I guessed she hadn't seen much of the film.

Kyle waited back in the upstairs hall. He had a long face, peach-white skin and dark hair with a slight natural curl and a normal smattering of acne that would clear in years not far ahead. He looked like he wanted to throw up.

"Have you called Mr. Donovan?" I asked. Kyle looked momentarily surprised at the idea that calling his boss was a thing he might do. "If I ran a movie theater that held a corpse, I'd want to know."

Kyle nodded and began to text with trembling fingers.

The night had just gotten longer for both of us. I sat down and indicated a place next to me on the tufted hall bench.

Perhaps to keep from dwelling on the recent discovery myself, I found myself feeling protective of Kyle, who would remember this night all his life.

"Is someone waiting for you at home?" I asked the usher. "Do you want to call someone to come get you?"

"Maybe," he said. He stood up as he dialed and wandered down the carpeted hall. It was a good, thick carpeting with fleur-de-lis, a motif that would have played well in decades gone by. I thought about carpet for as long as possible to keep from remembering that girl the had friends, family and people who loved her who would be getting the phone call or visit no one wants to get.

"We have to stop meeting like this."

The speaker was State Police Investigator Mike Spaulding, and he had a point.

To be fair, I'd only found one other body since moving to Tranquility—which was how I met Investigator Spaulding in the first place. We'd worked together well to solve that murder, at least in my mind. The most recent death about which I'd been questioned had been under the auspices of Investigator Gerald Mason. I was not a fan.

Investigator Spaulding dropped next to me on the bench.

"I was passing by the theater on my way home," I said. "The doors were open, so I came in to look at the posters in the hallway. Kyle asked me to help wake the young woman up. She didn't wake up. That's the entirety of my story. There are witnesses who can place me at the Battened Hatch all evening."

He expelled a breath. "That matches what Kyle told us. Don't worry. I didn't think you'd try something this soon."

I looked at him with surprise. "Kidding," he said, raising his hands in a defensive position.

Mike was Black, his skin the dark mahogany of the wind chimes in my kitchen. Since he was an investigator, he wore civilian clothes, jacket and shirt starched and pressed, not unlike what he usually wore to the Battened Hatch.

Mike had dismissed Kyle before joining me. A man I assumed to be Kyle's father put a hand on the young man's shoulder and led him downstairs.

Marcus Donovan, the third generation Donovan to own the Orpheum, had arrived as the State Police did. Crime scene investigators took the girl's popcorn and soda for testing. They also shut down the concession stand, pending the results. That seemed to shake Mr. Donovan most of all.

"That's how we meet our overhead," he pleaded.

"Any chance you recognized the victim?" Investigator Spaulding asked me.

"No," I said. "I haven't seen her around town. I was wondering if she might have something to do with the film festival. She was an ectomorph—tiny bones, very skinny, and her facial features were unusually symmetrical, meaning she is classically beautiful, in the Hollywood sense of the word."

"I keep forgetting you're from L.A."

"I keep trying to forget, as well."

We both smiled.

Investigator Spaulding stood and stretched. "You can go. If you think of anything that might be meaningful, give me a call." He would have offered me his business card, but his number was in my phone from last time.

I glanced at my watch. 1:10. An hour and a half after I'd entered the theater. I headed downstairs, scuffing against the fleur-de-lis pattern, and passed the concession stand, now decorated with bright yellow crime tape.

The front doors were closed, and the outside lights were off. It was mighty dark out there. I was glad to be nearly home.

Streetlights threw enough illumination into the entrance hall that I could still read the posters for the festival films that had lured me in the first place. One on the wall opposite those I'd perused earlier caught my eye. I did a double take and took a step back to stand squarely in front of the poster for the independent feature film.

It was my second shock of the night. "Holy shit," I said.

It was 1:30 a.m. when I reached Cherry Lane, the pathway that led over the creek into the private glade where my cottage stood. I wasn't surprised to find lights aglow in the lodge where my landlord lived. Sally was a night owl who had undoubtedly just awakened.

I passed, a silent figure in the night, wanting but not wanting company, wanting but not wanting to be alone with my thoughts.

I crossed the footbridge past the small waterfall to my own achingly charming cottage. Inside, I turned on the small light above the stove, and made a cup of herbal peach tea, planning to sit on the terrace. I doubted sleep would come this night.

The terrace was chilly. Hands wrapped around the mug for warmth, I came back inside and went to sit in the dark on the couch in front of the picture window in the living room. I set the mug down on the coffee table and studied the lights from Sally's large log home across the waterfall, under the starry canopy of night. I meant to contemplate everything that had happened that evening, that had happened this year. It was a lot.

Much to my own surprise, as I began to contemplate, I fell fast asleep.

EVENING'S END

Mama's Medicine

Ingredients

Fresh whole orange (peeled and pulled apart, save peel)
1/4 teaspoon ground turmeric
2 oz honey (preferably local)
2 cups of water
1 1/2 oz Bourbon/Whiskey of your choice

Method

In medium saucepan add water, turmeric, one large piece of orange peel and honey. Let simmer for about 10 minutes and stir occasionally. In large mug add Bourbon or Whiskey and then add a ladle or two of hot toddy mixture.
Relax, sip and enjoy going into dreamland.

2

THE HISTORY OF STARS

THE THUMP OF a bass, the beat of a snare beneath it, and Willy Nelson's voice reverberated from the other room inviting me to join him on the road again as I pried one eye open. It took me a moment to comprehend that it was my phone, and that Hannah Bricksford was calling me.

I kicked blue square sofa cushions away and sat up, then put my feet on the floor and lurched toward my bedroom where my phone sat, now fully charged, on the bedside table, Willy still wailing away. I'd assigned Hannah a new ringtone when we went on a girls' trip after my grandmother's funeral. I had to stop being clever.

"Hello?"

"Are you coming?"

"Where are you? What time is it?"

"It's ten-thirty. I'm at the Cardamom Café. Where we're meeting for brunch."

"Sorry. So sorry. I got in late. Unexpectedly. You wouldn't believe my night."

"Knowing you, I probably couldn't guess, but I would believe. If you're running late, should I order takeout and bring it up to your place?"

"That would be great."

"Your usual, or do you want to branch out?"

"Surprise me."

I trod into the kitchen to put on the kettle, then hurried back to shower, willing myself not to think about anything besides shampoo and conditioner. I then dressed in one of my better bartender outfits, with nice fitting pants and a button-up white shirt and black vest.

Back in the kitchen, I prepared Lady Grey tea for myself and Paris tea—a blend of currant and citrus—for Hannah. Then I moved out back to the small terrace tucked behind the house and hidden from the world. White wicker furniture with cushions decorated with lilacs and hydrangeas were placed around, with several armless chairs pulled up at a white wicker table. I put down plates and napkins and sighed into a chair, grateful for a moment to reflect. I sipped and considered why my heart hurt.

It had been a rough and wonderful year. Last night tilted my insides towards the rough.

In the recent past, not only had I helped a traumatized usher find a dead girl, back in Los Angeles my close friend had died of an overdose. A few months after I settled in Tranquility, my beloved Mormor, my grandmother, died at our family home in Brooklyn. And, not that it mattered, I finally began to trust someone I could maybe be in love with. He'd put my heart in a blender and served it back to me as pâté on a cracker.

At least, that's how it felt.

On the other hand…I'd made good friends in my newly adopted home of Tranquility.

As if to underscore the point, Hannah turned the corner onto the patio carrying a familiar bag from one of our favorite local establishments. I was used to seeing her nicely dressed, even when she was casual. She admitted that, as a female clergy person, she felt she needed to present herself as respectable. I did know there were local folks who would jump on any chance to criticize her appearance or actions. Her actions, she said, she'd stand by. She didn't want a non-professional appearance to be distracting. But today she wore jeans that weren't crazy tight but fit nicely, and a black hoodie with a silver wolf head. Interesting.

"Morning," she said. "I've got the goods. And you've got tea for me. Thank heavens. You were up late. I was up early."

"On purpose?"

"Happy reason, actually. One of my parishioners went into labor. The midwife was finishing up another delivery, without a car available. I promised to make sure she got to Teresa's and Matt's, who live twenty minutes outside town."

"First child?"

"Fourth. Hopefully, her body has got the drill down. First girl after three boys. They're ecstatic."

Hannah's thick black hair hung just below her shoulders and bounced as she purposefully made her way to a chair. Her eyes were a deep brown with an amber ring, and they nearly glowed. She was the offspring of a Black father and a white mother, her father so dark-skinned that it was surprising she was so light she could pass for white—not that she ever wanted to. Now, seeing her sparkle, I was glad to join into her happiness, instead of immediately throwing a shroud over the day. "New hoodie?" I asked. "Is there a story behind the wolf?"

"Yes. I met a silver wolf once when I was out walking a trail. Magnificent. We stopped and stared at each other. For quite a while. Loved her. Felt a real connection. So I took the silver wolf as my animal. Strength. Awe. Beauty. All that.

"So, what's up with you? Why were you out so late?"

I told her about the theater, about the girl and about Kyle. It was a sad story, but, thankfully, pithy. I wanted to deal with it, but not dwell on it. And, frankly, in the light of day, it seemed surreal, as if it had been a dream or the beginning of one of the festival films.

"I don't know if this makes sense," I said, "but it somehow helps that she was already dead, not nearly dead. We didn't have to panic and try to save her, then wonder what we could have done differently." I sat back. "That sounds terrible."

"No," said Hannah. "I understand. Her death, while tragic, isn't on you. Does Mike think she was murdered?"

"He doesn't officially know what to think yet."

We sat a minute in respectful silence.

"Then, there was something else interesting as I was leaving the theater."

"Tell me." Hannah had brought savory crepes: ham, gruyere, and asparagus, with maple syrup for dipping. They were fabulous. I was starting to wake up.

"There was a poster for one of the festival films called *Triple Jeopardy*. It apparently stars an old friend of mine named Crispin O'Connor."

"Yeah?" asked Hannah. "How do you know him?"

"We've known each other since third grade at St. Alban's, the fancy-schmancy school Mom plunked me in when we moved to Los Angeles from Brooklyn on account of her career.

"We found each other pretty quick, the two kids on the side of the playground, not because we wouldn't be accepted by the other kids, but because we didn't see the point. Even then, the hierarchy of conferred popularity ruled, and what made you popular made no sense to either of us, even at eight years old. So instead, we played games of pretend and imagination. We were secret agents, dragon-slayers, knights, outer-space freedom fighters."

"Did it work? Did the other kids bother you?"

"Since the popular kids couldn't recruit, control or effectively shame us, they pretty much left us alone."

I smiled at the memories of that cobblestone courtyard, Franciscan-style school buildings surrounding it, in mid-Los Angeles. I told Hannah how, by middle school, Crispin and my friends had grown to a group of six compadres who began doing homework and hanging out together at Salty Sally's, a hamburger and shake joint on Salty Sally Alley, named after "Salty" Sally Allison, a golden era movie star who made her way through the studio system, using her own salty language. The joint served a sweet and salty ice cream flavor which featured chocolate and caramel. It was heaven.

Sally was now my landlord—a story in itself, although one with which Hannah was familiar.

Hannah was interested as I told the story of Crispin and me. I pride myself on being an intent listener, any good bartender's super-power. Hannah is the first person I've ever met who might have me beat. Listening was instinctual with her. She was gifted at shutting the world out and being laser-focused on whoever was talking to her.

In any case, I told her how Crispin was the first of our group to be discovered by Hollywood.

"So he's attractive?" She asked the obvious question.

I shrugged. "Sure, but I wouldn't say more so than any of the rest of the guys in the group. I mean, he was, but to me, it came from his personality. He had a kindness, and a charisma, that was effort-less. Who wouldn't want to be around him? Physically, when we were kids, he had thick brown hair kept close cropped, and sparkling green eyes, with a twinkle that always shone through his glasses. If you were parsing his looks, you might say his nose was a little larger than it needed to be. On a woman, Hollywood would demand a nose job. On a man, it was 'strong.' The one thing that perhaps set him apart was his set of deep dimples.

"At some point in sixth grade, he began arriving late to Salty Sally's, slipping onto the red vinyl of our corner booth next to me or Winsome, with a chipper, 'Hi, guys! What's the story so far?' Little by little, his appearance changed. His hair got longer and blonder. His glasses disappeared, replaced by contacts.

"One day, as we walked home, he sheepishly asked me to help him figure out a new name. He was named after the St. Crispin's Day speech in Shakespeare's *Henry V*, which I personally thought that was plenty dramatic. But in Hollywood, actors seldom go by the usual diminutives of their actual names. Who calls Christopher, Topher? So 'Cris' was out, and who wanted Spin or Pin? Together we landed on Ris, adding an 'e' to make the pronunciation obvious. It took some cajoling, but I agreed to start calling him that, and after subjecting him to a fair amount of ribbing, the Salty gang joined in."

"Wait a minute—Rise? Not Rise O'Connor?"

I nodded.

"Seriously. Your Crispin turned into Rise O'Connor."

"Yep. Shall I go on?"

"You'd better!"

"Rise made these changes under the tutelage of a manager, and soon an agent. It took a year, but he snagged a Disney sitcom, playing the annoying younger brother of the starring girl. We saw less and less of him, but it still wasn't unusual for him to slide into the booth with a 'Hi, guys! What's the story so far?'

"After three seasons of the sitcom, it got axed because the young female star got a tattoo, an attitude, and a venereal disease. No one outside Disney knew that last part. Well, except for us in the Salty Gang.

"After the sitcom's demise, Rise was called in for a meeting with the Disney casting folks. That summer, he went away for six weeks, 'on location,' and came back with the perfect nose. Afterwards, he was kicked upstairs by Disney, playing one of a group of five teen superheroes in training in a feature film—"

"*Owning It*," added Hannah.

"And then a continuing series. That's when we really lost him. If he wasn't filming, he was working out. Rise eventually walked away from the series—and Disney—the recognized breakout star.

"Not that I've kept up with him through *Variety*, but after that he starred in a film as a trained assassin raised by a survivalist dad. Then he allegedly found the transition to adult parts difficult, but eventually became a regular on *Sunrise Bluff*, that show about small-town lawyers. Again, he was the breakout. Unfortunately, his contract was ironclad and he couldn't break out. He had to stay while the network, and the show runners, ran the show into the ground."

"Have you kept in touch?"

"No. I haven't heard anything about him after that. Till now, that is. Apparently," I concluded to Hannah, "he's doing edgy independent features."

"Interesting, and kind of cool," she said. "If his film is opening here, do you think he's coming to the film festival? To Tranquility?"

"I don't know," I admitted. "I haven't been paying attention to the buzz around any films except Sally's."

"Would it be good to see someone from your old life?" she asked.

Hannah had an annoying habit of asking straightforward, personal questions like it's the normal thing to do.

I shrugged. "I haven't seen him for years. Really since we were high school sophomores. Once he became a superhero, he went to school on set."

How would I feel about seeing Rise? I guess it would depend on what had happened to him. Who he'd become.

Hannah's phone vibrated, and she looked at the text. She made a quick response, and it vibrated again. I saw tension seep into her shoulders.

"It's Matt," she said. "Something isn't right with the baby's delivery." She replied to him and stood. "Gotta go." We hugged briefly.

"I hope it works out," I said.

"I'll let you know." She was already heading around the house. She paused and smiled in my direction. "Try to have a slightly less interesting day."

I cleared the remains of our breakfast and pulled my stuff together. I wanted to get to the Battened Hatch early, as excitement was growing in town and people were beginning to arrive. Not to mention I apparently needed to stop by the Orpheum on the way to purchase a ticket for *Triple Jeopardy*.

As I was about to leave, the phone rang.

The ghost phone.

It was a phone from the olden days, and it was connected to one place: my landlord's lodge. It was white and heavy with a wide cord that ran into the wall.

Sally had only called me once, shortly after I'd moved in, when she'd invited me over to politely ream me out for letting my guest and Hollywood uber-publicist Jerry Raker run up to take a gander at her house. At the time, I was horrified. Now he was producing the film *Salty Sally and Pepper*.

What did Sally want now?

I picked up the phone.

"Hello, dear, when are you heading out?" she asked.

"In two minutes."

"Could you stop in as you pass?" she asked.

"Absolutely."

I don't carry a purse or a wallet; I stuffed my drivers license and debit card into my pocket.

I decided this week wasn't one to try to be driving up and down Tranquility's only Main Street, as the influx of out-of-towners makes the traffic flow, well, not flow. So I grabbed my trusty blue bike and walked it across the bridge that separates my cottage from the rest of the glade. I was, admittedly, curious about Sally's summons.

Sally's lodge is striking any time of year, made from whole logs, with a screened porch the length of the house and twenty feet wide. The outside ledge of the porch was now lined with mums, in orange, yellow and light purple. Pumpkins and corn stalks festooned the steps. The place was originally created by a Hollywood set designer and it looked now like the set dresser had returned for a guest appearance. I climbed the outside steps and swung through the door, where I was promptly greeted by Whistle, an adorable Pomeranian, who had stayed with me when her master, Sally's grandson Philip Young, was in the hospital. Philip had been away in Paris for two months now, painting, during which time Whistle had bunked at Sally's.

Whistle pawed at my leg till I picked her up. It's nice being adored.

"There you are, darling," said Sally, opening the front door and beckoning me in.

"Sally, the place looks great," I said. I mean, it always looked great, but now there were huge bouquets of fuchsia, dahlias and dianthus with bright pink cosmos and deep blue cornflowers for emphasis. New framed family photos sat on the bookshelves and the bar cart, and it struck me that she no longer had to hide who she was, or who her family was. That must be an adjustment, after all these years.

New paintings adorned the walls—four that I could see. One was a huge canvas, at the top of the wooden stairs to the second floor, that I recognized as having been painted by Philip. The boldness of the colors, paired with the intricacy of the strokes, and the overall sense of motion, caused a swell of emotion in me, as Philip's paintings always did. Damn him.

The others were equally intriguing, done by a different artist. If they had a theme, it was revealing what is behind. There were new lands behind a curtain, behind a window, behind a woman's eyes. I was pulled to the one of the woman with the translucent eyes as if to a magnet. I could spend the afternoon studying these new pieces. Each had an Indian vibe to it, and it occurred to me they were likely by Sally's husband, Saif Chander, a noted Indian painter.

Sally herself was paying attention to me, but she was uncharacteristically distracted. She paced her great room with an aura of excitement. I couldn't even imagine what it must feel like for her to know that soon the unsuspecting public would find out that a beloved movie star whom they assumed had been dead for fifty years was, in fact, alive and pouring whisky. The good stuff.

She wore her usual outfit, slinky silk pants and a camisole, this time in mint green, with a sheer white floral duster on top. Her face was long and oval. There were wrinkles, but I never noticed them— in fact, I seldom got past the fire in her green eyes. Her hair was blonde-white and silky at shoulder-length. I solemnly swear that if I met her on the street, I'd think she was fit for 72. She was 94.

"I wanted to check in with you before things get crazy," she said. "The movie premieres on Saturday, and there will be a champagne brunch after—to which you're invited, of course."

I did know about the brunch, as they'd rented out Pepper's, the new restaurant at MacTavish's, that shared a kitchen with the Battened Hatch.

"Thanks," I said.

"My family is all coming in, between now and then. I hope you can meet them."

"Me, too."

She smiled and put a hand on my wrist, as if for emphasis. "It's going to be important not to let people know where I live. Some locals do, of course, but the Tranquility community is good at looking out for our own. A couple of days before the screening, I'm going to move into a suite at MacTavish's, so hopefully, as far as the press knows, I've come in for the premiere."

"You know I'd never say anything."

"I do know. If word gets out, I'm worried about your privacy, as well as mine. To that end, we've hired security to live in the guardhouse for the time being—that is, Fenton's old house at the entrance to our glade here. They're under strict instructions not to be obvious to passersby, or anyone else, but they will keep anyone uninvited from coming up."

I hadn't thought about that. I'd always felt safe in our glade, but that was because we were 'out of sight, out of mind' and no one thought to venture up. By the same token, since we were secreted away up here, no one outside our hidden dell could hear or see if we were beset by tourists. Or something worse.

"In any case, they're professionals. I call them Stan and Ollie, so I don't have to remember their names. They know you live here, of course, and will let you pass. But they'll also ask for a list of folks you give permission to come back here—please be choosy and wise. They might even want photos of coming guests, just to be safe."

"Sure. I'll make a list. And I'll keep it short."

"I thought you would," she said.

"Shortly after the film's screening, after we've done enough press—or, more likely, when I've had enough of the press—we're heading for our Paris apartment."

"How long will you stay?"

"We're not sure. Till the hoo-ha blows over."

"Morning, dear," came a male voice, and a man several inches shorter than Sally emerged from the downstairs master bedroom suite. "Has the hoo-ha begun?" He was also fit, dressed in an open-collared blue shirt and white pants. His dark eyes smiled. His hair was full on top of his head, and his trimmed beard and mustache was woven with white. He spoke with a lilt of an Indian accent.

"Not yet, thank God. Avalon, meet my husband, Saif."

"Very nice to meet you," I said. Had she married a younger man? Was he this kicking in his eighties? Or was he cheating old age in his nineties like Sally? He was prominent enough in the art world that I could easily find out. "Are these your paintings?" With his nod, I added, "They're captivating."

He gave a small bow. "Thank you so much." Then he turned, gesturing to the stairs. "Did you see the piece by my grandson, Philip Young?"

"Yes," I said. "Indeed I did."

"Quite stunning," he said.

"Quite." I stood a moment, joining in his appreciation for the painting. "Well, I'm off to work. Again, nice to meet you," I said, and I meant it. I'd heard so much about him that he'd seemed legend rather than flesh-and-blood. "The times, they are a-changin'," I said to Sally with a smile.

"At long last," she replied.

I went out to grab my bike and walked it down the lane.

"Quite stunning," the prominent painter had said about Philip's piece.

Damn Philip. Anyway.

As I rounded the final bend, I found a middle-aged, brown-haired European-American man in jeans and a polo shirt on a garden kneeler, the fancy kind with side rails. He was spreading cedar mulch on the neglected flower bed in front of the guardhouse which sat squarely at the juncture of our lane and the main drag's sidewalk.

"Hello," I said, not knowing if he was Stan or Ollie. Or if he knew he was Stan or Ollie.

"Hello." He stood, took off a gardening glove, and offered me his hand. I shook it. He looked laid back and like some guy who was gardening, but his handshake was a whole other thing.

"Chet," he said. "In fact, all of us who live here are named Chet. You're Avalon."

"Yes," I said.

"Great. Anyone who comes in with you is welcome. If you have guests arriving on their own, we ask you alert us. May I have your phone? If someone comes and says they have permission to visit you, but we don't have their photo, we'll ask you to come down and get them.

"If, by any chance, someone is coercing you to walk them into the compound, simply say the word *chrysanthemum*. We'll take care of it."

"Will do." It seemed a bit overwhelming to have this many protocols to continue life as I knew it. I tried to seem cooperative. "Looks like we'll have a nice garden going."

"Yep," he said, in a chipper voice. "Need anything, just call Chet."

I nodded in a friendly manner and hopped on my bike, thinking, *The times, they are a-changin'.*

THE HISTORY OF STARS

Ingredients

1/2 oz Goldschlager
1 oz chocolate vodka
1 oz caramel vodka
1 tiny pinch of edible gold glitter
1/2 activated charcoal capsule
1 cup of whipped cream
1 teaspoon of chopped English toffee

Method

In cocktail shaker add ice, Goldschlager, chocolate vodka, caramel vodka, edible glitter, and half of activated charcoal capsule. Shake all ingredients together and strain into martini glass.
Whip heavy cream, then add a to small bowl and delicately fold in English toffee, making sure that whipped cream stays nice and fluffy.
Gently float whipped cream mixture on top of cocktail. Sprinkle a dash of edible glitter on top of whipped cream.

3

BATTEN THOSE HATCHES

I NVESTIGATOR SPAULDING WAS waiting in the lobby of Mac-Tavish's when I arrived, and he followed me into the Battened Hatch as I began to set up for the day. I locked the interior door behind me since we weren't open yet and only turned on the lights behind the bar.

I'd loved the Battened Hatch from the moment I'd first stopped in for a drink. It was a dream of a Scottish pub—large, light, with dark wood paneling and a hand-carved bar with matching back bar, both of which went on for days. The lighting design in the room—and on the back bar—was exquisite. The place could be cheerful and welcoming, it could be womblike and safe, or dark and mysterious after sundown if you lowered the lights. It could be anything. Since I am a professional story-collector, I consider it my private lair. I let other people in with the unspoken agreement they'll lend me their story.

Mike took a seat across from me. He wore pressed khakis, a shirt and a sports jacket. He looked fresh and rested, not like he'd been working all night. Someday I'll have to ask how he pulls that off. He leaned forward as I began wiping down the bar.

"Marissa Marisol," he said. "The young woman you found last night. You called it—she's an actress. Not sure why she was here, her IMDB account doesn't list her as being in any of the festival films. She has a part in an upcoming series, don't know if she's filmed it yet or not."

"So we have no idea why she was in a theater in Tranquility, New York, on a Tuesday night."

"None."

"I assume you're waiting on toxicology for cause of death."

"You know too much about murder investigations," he said. "However, I just heard from the coroner ten minutes ago, and one thing she could tell us was Marissa had no soda or popcorn in her system."

"Marcus Donovan will be happy to hear that."

He nodded. "It's how they meet their overhead."

"So I've heard."

"I'm assuming you haven't thought of anything you forgot to tell me last night?"

"Nope."

"That was my guess. Just thought I'd start my day with a friendly conversation."

"Can I get you a burger?" I asked and swallowed a grin.

Glenn had hired Chef Angelica Dormer to run Pepper's, the new iteration of the hotel's upscale restaurant. I had been looking forward to her arrival after Chef Paul and his moods and violent outbursts. Ironically, Chef Angelica had apparently been trained in the same French method. I had yet to see her happy, or even laid back. Fixing burgers or a "tavern menu" for the Battened Hatch was not something that tickled her fancy. Which is why I loved ordering them.

"No, thanks. I only recently had breakfast. I'm going to push off."

"Let me know if there are any developments you can share."

He gave me a thumbs up over his head as he walked out the door.

My barback, Marta, came in as he left. She had recently changed her hair color from teal to sapphire and I loved it. She was dressed up, as was I. For her, that meant the addition of dangly purple earrings. "Got some folks waiting outside already," she said.

I checked my watch. Twenty minutes till open. "Do you know who?"

"It's Mr. Davis from the paper and that crew."

"Of course they can come in."

I handed Marta the cloth—though we'd cleaned thoroughly before we'd left the night before—and went to open the door.

There, I found waiting Brent Davis, Jerry Raker, and Addie Moon. The three of them had produced the documentary about Pepper Porter, "Salty" Sally Allison's Hollywood nemesis, who had lived at the hotel. Well, it turned out Pepper had done a lot of things at the hotel. I unlocked the door and they followed me in.

"Hi, Avalon," said Brent.

"Great to see you," I said, and to Jerry and Addie, "great to have you back. Are you ready for this? Are you excited?"

"Yes, and yes," said Addie. Besides producing the documentary, she was Jerry's top publicist, one of the best in Los Angeles. Today she wore a form-fitting black and yellow sheath dress with a yellow blazer over it. It looked great against her gingerbread skin. Her full black hair was straightened, and her make-up was minimal but effective. She was definitely ready for prime time.

They took table 11, a four-top in the middle of the floor, so obvious as to be private.

"Do you have time to pull up a chair?" Brent asked. He ran the local daily paper, and also did work for the nearest PBS affiliate.

They'd given up finding any new angles until it turned out that Sally was still alive, and there were a lot of interesting goings-on that no one had heard about, including a faked death, an illegal marriage, an out-of-wedlock child and a friend-turned-attempted-murderer.

The world was about to hear it all when *Salty Sally and Pepper: Truth Be Told* debuted.

The Tranquility Film Festival was originally set for August, but with new developments in their own film entry as well as Jerry Raker's new book, it was had been pushed back to September. Two original film entries had to pull out, but two more quickly took their slots.

"Here we go. I can't believe the festival is actually upon us," I said. But, looking at Brent and remembering the newspaper, I added, "You heard about the dead girl at the Orpheum?"

"Yeah, has she been identified?" asked Brent.

"A young actress. Marissa Marisol. Don't know much more than that."

"I'll let Zelda handle this one," he said.

Zelda was his managing editor.

Wow, you knew big happenings were afoot when a local murder didn't wrest the attention of the newspaper editor.

"This is it, people," Jerry said, not even hearing the murder part. "It's all finally happening."

Jerry was an Asian man, the best-dressed Hollywood publicist I'd ever seen. Never mind that, he was likely the best-dressed man I'd ever seen, period. At some point, he'd fallen in love with Tranquility, possibly because of the extraordinary local topography: mountains, lakes, forests. possibly because Pepper Porter and Sally Allison had lived here and he had been writing a book about Pepper that became a documentary.

I'd known about Jerry Raker when I lived in L.A. My mom is in "the business," and everyone in the business knows about Jerry. If you're lucky enough to get him as your publicist, it's because you're already a big enough name that you don't really need him. But if you get him, your brand recognition is about to skyrocket.

Which is what he decided to do for the Tranquility Film Festival. It wasn't until Raker and Associates started promoting it that filmmakers in Los Angeles and New York began paying serious attention. He snagged debut films by several important new indie filmmakers, and some from television directors wanting to leap into features. There were also some documentaries, including *Seeing Color* by S.M. Hunt, *Stitch by Stitch: Saving the Little Blue Penguins of Australia* by B.K. Sherer and *Knowing Lisa* by R.O. Scott. Of course, filmmakers only come because potential distributors come, as do media outlets. Jerry had lined those up, too.

Which meant the films' actors would come to meet and greet and press the flesh. Would Rise be one of them?

Not surprisingly, Jerry's main focus was on his own film about

Sally and Pepper. With Brent's help, they were able to keep much of what went down with Sally and her former co-star out of the press, using her married name of Lee Chander in local write-ups. The hope was that the reveals in the documentary would be national news.

Seemed likely to me.

As I sat down next to Addie, she got a text, and breathed an *"oh, no."*

"What?" Jerry asked. "What's wrong?"

"We've lost one of the caterers," she said. "The one who was supposed to supply waiters for the cocktails at the Orpheum before the brunch—and the Fran's Famous Cookies they were serving. Crap."

She sighed and put her phone on the table.

"Get someone else," said Jerry, as if that wouldn't occur to her.

"Everyone in town, and in the surrounding towns, is booked," she said.

"This is for the brunch on Saturday, after the screening?" I asked.

"Yes. The actual brunch is here, at Pepper's, but we're going to start plying the press with alcohol and sugar back at the theater as they're waiting for the buses to bring them over."

Addie grabbed her phone and headed for the lobby to make calls.

"I saw Sally this morning," I said to Jerry and Brent. "She's excited. She knows her life is about to change."

"Yes," Jerry agreed. "In some major ways. But I'd expect the same for several other folks."

"Like Glenn," said Brent.

There would be revelations about my boss and his true parentage, as well as other things. Many ripples through this town.

I looked up to see diners arriving, being greeted and seated by Davros and Sandy, servers on for the lunch crowd. I recognized maybe half of the patrons. On a normal day, I'd recognize most. I knew the hotel was full up, as were the other hotels in Tranquility and the surrounding towns. I assumed some heavy-hitter Hollywood types would be staying at Chateau Tranquility just outside of town, which was crazy expensive and yet all the rooms and suites looked pretty much the same. Here at MacTavish's, each room was different, and wings of the hotel wandered off across the hills. My preference, for sure.

"If you're going to eat, best put in your order pretty quickly. Looks like a busy day," I suggested to Brent and Jerry.

I went back to the bar, where Marta was filling the first drink order to come in. "Someone ordered the Hollywood Sign?" I asked.

"Two already."

It was one of the drinks we'd created for the occasion. The Hollywood Sign was light and fizzy, with champagne, elderflower liqueur and vodka, as well as a secret ingredient.

Another drink order pinged on the POS from the floor, and when I looked, Davros gave me a signal that he'd put in a food order. I opened the door to the kitchen and said, "Ready? We're starting."

"Off to the races," said a sous-chef.

"Camptown Races," sniffed Chef Angelica, "do-dah, do-dah."

The kitchen door swung closed. Sandy was at Jerry and Brent's table, taking their orders. I noticed Addie hadn't returned.

Well, darn.

I motioned to Marta that I was ducking out for a minute, and I went toward the lobby, which was two stories tall, light and airy, and also bustling with activity. Clusters of adults whom I assumed to be journalists stood chatting urgently on phones next to the statue of downhill skiers under a large skylight. I walked behind it, and there, against a back wall, was Addie on her phone. She hung up on a call, with a look of consternation.

"I think I might know someone," I said, and Addie looked up, surprised.

"I mean, a caterer. She's good. Her name is Rachel Hunt. She used to live here, then moved to Saratoga a couple of months ago for greater opportunities. But she knows everyone in the area. She could get you super-special cookies, or whatever you need."

Part of me couldn't believe I was recommending Rachel, who

used to be Philip's girlfriend. Which I'd thought I was for a hot minute. Both "hot" and "minute" being accurate.

"Yeah?" asked Addie. "Can you text me her info?"

Addie told me her number and I Googled the name of Rachel's business. I surmised having on Rachel's resume that she'd served some of Hollywood's hot tickets could only help her new business, right?

But...if Sally's family was assembling from around the world, did that mean Philip, as her grandson, would be returning from Paris? How stupid did I have to be to bring Rachel back for the occasion?

"Also, if you need servers at the theater pre-brunch, I can lend you my crew from the Battened Hatch. It's before business hours. Marta could bartend and oversee." I was pretty sure my gang would get a kick out of that.

I sent the link to Addie, who nodded her thanks. She stood up and hit "call," and headed toward the lobby to have the conversation.

"Look who's here," Marta whispered as I walked back behind the bar.

"Who?" I whispered back.

"Whoa!" she said, and I looked to the door in time to see a young female actor from a CW show enter the bar with a non-famous person of the same age. She went straight for another actor, the one Marta was referencing, at a booth by the wall.

I had to smile. Living in L.A., first of all, I went to school with a raft of these people, and second, you just got used to seeing them jogging or walking their dogs. But in Tranquility, well, celebrity was still a discussion starter.

And then she walked in.

"Holy crap," I said.

Marta shot me a puzzled look.

"It's ThunderGlove," I said.

"Who?"

"Isobel Lester. One of Hollywood's top agents."

"What do they call her?"

"ThunderGlove. Because she never raises her voice, but there's so much power behind her whisper that everyone agrees to everything she says."

I'd seen her at parties and across rooms, but never close up. She was a white woman of a certain age, slim, brown hair with blonde highlights falling above her shoulders, perfectly coiffed. She wore fitted jeans with a shirt tucked in and a sweater around her neck, like she was going yachting after she grabbed a drink. As if she was here, at this festival in the middle of nowhere, but she was slumming, and not fully committed to being here in person. Instead, she'd sent casual Isobel.

I was only slightly surprised when she made a beeline for Brent and Jerry's table and took a seat. I immediately sent Sandy over to take their order.

As she did, Addie came back from the lobby, smiling triumphantly, and giving me a short nod. She headed back towards their table, then saw Isobel. Her eyes enlarged in precisely the same way mine must have, moments before.

Addie pasted on a wide smile and took the chair next to Isobel, since Isobel had taken Addie's chair without noticing someone else had obviously been drinking the water and using the napkin. As Isobel leaned back and the others leaned in, craning their necks to hear her, I cursed myself for not being able to think of a reason to mosey over to hear what was going on.

You've left Hollywood, Avalon, I said sternly. *You run the world's coolest Scottish pub. Pay attention and run it.*

And that's what I did. Until the order came up for Table 11. Sandy grabbed the two salads—the Call My Agent and the Trophy Wife (Chef Angelica thought she was clever that way)—and I grabbed the Volare for Addie and the Asian Avocado Wrap for Isobel.

"All right," Isobel was saying, with a soft smile. "I so appreciate your help. The press conference starts in—"

"Two hours," said Addie. "In the large ballroom. The one-on-ones are tomorrow just after the film."

"Two hours," said Isobel. "And, as his crack publicity team, I appreciate your help in putting a bug in his ear. Sign the contract. Ditch the manager."

"What if he doesn't feel comfortable without a manager?" Addie asked. I noticed she was the only one talking back to ThunderGlove.

"Darling, them thar Hollywood Hills are full of managers. We'll shake a few out and give him his pick. I've put up with this one for years. So has he. Enough is enough."

Isobel looked at her lunch as I put it down. "Delightful."

"You make a wrap out of it. With the lettuce leaves," I said and smiled, then immediately felt the idiot. Of course you did.

"So clever," said Isobel.

"Can I get anyone another drink?" I asked.

"What mixed drinks do you have that are non-alcoholic?" asked Isobel.

"Ah," I said. "Our specialty." I was on a kick of using mixers that had layered tastes without the alcohol. I turned the drink card around so those were facing her. Isobel smiled, then her eyes squinted to read the fine print.

As I stood, waiting to take any drink questions, a person with short, jet black hair and slightly tanned white skin walked into the bar, spotted table 11, and made a beeline. It was the first time I met Con Allred, whom I later would find uses they/them pronouns.

"Look who's here," they said, waving their phone.

Jerry looked up for only an instant. "I take it this isn't good news."

They were still out of breath as they handed their phone to Isobel, who looked at the photo. The newcomer took the phone back, changed the screen, and handed it back.

"Perhaps it will give us a chance to deal with them once and for all."

"Or perhaps one of them will succeed in getting to him." The newcomer looked concerned but not flustered. They were attractive but not Hollywood skinny-fake attractive, and wore jeans and a button-up black shirt. Street clothes. They kind of reminded me of Stevie from *Schitt's Creek*.

"Where is he? Where's our boy?" Isobel asked, still not rattled in the least, sliding the photos on the phone over to Jerry and Addie.

"We've moved him out of his suite and into a small bedroom behind the security office. He wasn't thrilled."

"I think Rise would rather be alive than thrilled," said Isobel. "I'll have the Batten Those Hatches," she said, dismissing me in no uncertain terms.

"Sit," she said to the newcomer, who pulled up a chair from an adjacent table. "Let's discuss options."

My heart started pounding.

Rise was here.

And the hatches, apparently, needed to be battened.

BATTEN THOSE HATCHES

Lilac Lemonade (non-alcoholic)

Ingredients

1 1/2 oz homemade Lilac Simple Syrup (recipe below)
1 1/2 oz fresh squeezed lemon juice
4 oz plain water
Fresh lilac florets for garnish
Fresh lemon wedge for garnish
Lilac Simple Syrup (refrigerate for up to two weeks)
Ingredients for simple syrup
4 cups fresh lilac floats (preferably purple)
2 cups sugar
2 cups water

Method

Find a nice full bloom lilac tree and cut 4 or 5 flower
bunches from different spots of the tree.
Remove florets from flower bunch, remembering to only
use the purple florets. Try not to get any green stems as
this will make your syrup bitter,
Put the florets in a fine mesh strainer and rinse with
cold water.
In a medium saucepan add lilac florets, sugar and water.
Stir gently, cover and let simmer for about 5 to 10 minutes.
Take off heat and let mixture cool and let your mixture sit
in the water from 3-7 hours depending on how strong of a
lilac flavor you want.

Strain syrup into a fine mesh strainer to clean all the florets out of the syrup.
Continue to make your lemonade.

Cocktail

Method

In cocktail shaker add ice, fresh lemon juice, lilac simple syrup and water.
Shake until ingredients are combined and shaker is cold.
Pour into a tall glass. Add fresh lemon wedge and lilac florets for garnish.

4

THE HOLLYWOOD SIGN

Glenn MacTavish, the owner of MacTavish's Seaside Cottages, was sitting at the bar as I returned. He wore his signature kilt with red and blue tartan, and Bonnie Prince Charlie jacket, with a shirt with frilly cuffs. He also wore the wary, semi-excited look of a Scotsman the night before battle.

"Ready?" I asked. The film would reveal some of his family's secrets.

"Aye. It'll be fine. It'll all settle down within the month."

I nodded.

Of course it wouldn't.

I had to admit the idea of a film festival to bolster the local economy was paying off. All our tables were full and there was a line in the hallway leading into the bar. On a Wednesday. For lunch. Pepper's, the upscale restaurant on the other side of the commercial kitchen, also seemed to have a bourgeoning crowd. It would host several of the festival's private events.

I joined Marta in making the mixed drinks, then put in a call to Manuela, usually a suppertime waiter, and asked if she'd like to come in early. She gave eager assent.

Addie slid into the last remaining seat at the bar. "Did you say you could lend us some servers before and after the screening on Saturday morning?"

"Marta," I called, and she came over. I was proud of her. When I first arrived, being slammed by orders like this would have flustered her. Now she was simply taking things one drink at a time. "Would you be interested in running a crew to keep Hollywood journalists and other assorted bigwigs happy at the Orpheum on Saturday morning?" I asked.

"It pays well," said Addie.

Marta's face brightened at the request. "Sure, I could do that," she said.

A tall white man with greying hair, wearing an expensive suit and vest, pushed past the folks in line and headed back to table 11. Without invitation, he took Addie's seat.

"Who's that?"

Addie saw him and sighed. "Dirk Fortney. Rise O'Connor's manager. Rise and the director of *Triple Jeopardy* are having a press conference here in the large ballroom in..." she checked her watch, "forty-five minutes."

As Addie spoke, Isobel stood and left the table and the restaurant. "Isobel and Dirk don't get along. Anyway—" she turned to Marta, "we'd need you there on Saturday by 9 a.m."

"Okay. How many servers do you need? And should we wear tuxes?"

All the regular waiters and bartenders at the Battened Hatch had tuxedos, ready for special events.

"Sure. That would be great. And you know what? I hadn't considered this, but tomorrow, after the *Triple Jeopardy* screening, Rise and the director are doing one-on-ones with the press. We'll also be shuttling the journalists here from the theater. Could we serve some sort of simple drink as the journalists are gathering afterwards? Especially for those who will need to wait for the second bus."

"What time would that be?" I asked.

"The movie lets out at 4:30."

Marta looked at me.

"That's slow time. Sure, if you want to."

"Any idea about a simple, festive drink?"

"How about Blumond? It's a French sparkling wine with notes of peaches. It's also blue, so it looks great in a champagne glass. I've got some bottles."

"That would be perfect," Addie said.

I left Addie and Marta discussing details for both gigs.

The rest of table 11 left shortly thereafter. Addie joined them as they headed out.

So, Rise was here, and having a press conference. I wondered if I could peek in. Would he even remember me after all this time? Likely he would. But would he care about reconnecting? Or was he part of a different world now, one to which I did not belong?

One thing about Chef Angelica: she runs a tight kitchen. Meals were flying out, and tables were turning over. As it approached 1:30, things started to slow down, and many patrons left. My guess was they were journalists or others "in the business," headed for the press conference.

As the place emptied out, a woman came in and took a seat at the bar. She wore a flowered tunic and navy-blue leggings, her face round and open, skin peach-colored with red highlights, sporting no make-up at all, except a line of bright green shadow above each eye. She was normal weight. I wondered if she was a journalist or a character actor. Mid-40s? When she spoke, it was with an Eastern European accent. "What do you have that would be quick to serve?"

I listed several choices, ending with, "Of course, soup is always fast. Today, it's an herbed chicken or gazpacho. Are you trying to get to the press conference?"

"Yes," she said. "Well, I don't have to be there right at the beginning. I'll let Rise start this one on his own."

"Oh. Do you know him?"

She smiled shyly. "You might say that. Hmm. I'll have the gazpacho." She ordered, then took a magazine-sized book of crossword puzzles out of her purse. I'd seen Rise's agent, manager and publicist. Who was left?

I put her order into the POS and sent it to the kitchen. "How do you know Rise?"

Her gaze fell to her hands. "We're friends," she said. Then, quietly, "We're dating."

"Yeah?"

"Yeah."

"How did you meet?"

Now, she looked up with a rosy glow. "I was a teacher," she said. "He came to our school as part of an assembly about possible careers. You know, to give the students some ideas of what they can do. I asked him to talk to my class after the assembly, because I knew they'd have questions. I was sure he would say no. But he didn't!"

I set an iced tea down in front of her. "Did they have questions?"

"A lot. He stayed until the end of the period. It was the last class of the day. He's really nice." She blushed. "I don't know where I got the courage, but I asked if he wanted to get a cup of coffee, and he said yes."

"Where are you from, I mean, originally? Your accent is charming." I asked.

Have I mentioned I like to collect people's stories? This woman was fascinating.

"Romania," she said. "I'm Betina."

"Avalon." I reached over the bar and we shook hands. "Nice to meet you."

"When did you come from Romania?"

"We emigrated twenty-five years ago when me, my brother and sister were teenagers," she said. "I'm the eldest. I try to help them remember where we came from."

"I bet," I said. "They're lucky to have you."

Betina rummaged around in her large, black, bag-sized purse and brought out a wallet. "Here, look," she said. "My nieces and nephews."

There were a lot of photos.

"Your brother's kids or your sister's?"

She laughed. "Some of each."

My mind was spinning. Yes, Rise was a nice guy. And he would never hesitate to date a teacher, I'm sure. But...Betina?

"Do they know you're dating Rise?"

"Who? My brother and sister? Well." She blushed again. "They know I'm dating someone famous. I'm waiting till there's news."

"News?"

She leaned forward. "I'm hoping...if this film is successful...we might become engaged."

"Wow," I said. "Wow. How long have you been together?"

"Since his second season of *Sunrise Bluff*. Oh, man," she said, remembering, "we were so glad when that show finally got cancelled. It was good, I mean, it was a quality show, but five seasons? He was ready to move on. We both were. His agent has been working to get him some great offers. His manager wants him to go a different direction. I think he should follow his heart, you know?"

I nodded again.

"What school in Los Angeles do you teach at?"

"Oh, not Los Angeles. It's in Ohio. West Boulevard Elementary. In Youngstown. I quit last year."

I served up her soup.

She picked up her purse again and rummaged around. "You don't have a pencil, do you?" she asked. "I'm not quite at the place where I feel comfortable doing the crosswords in pen. Oh, wait, here, I've got one. Never mind."

She plunked her bag down on the now-empty stool beside her.

It fell to the side, and a few of the contents spilled out. A small package of tissues, two extra pencils. And a knife. Like, a hunting knife in a leather sheath.

"Bon appetit," I said, and moved to the next patron.

Should I do something? Tell someone? Could it be that Rise was dating a hunter, who was planning to go from the bar to the countryside? Was Rise himself planning to decompress by stalking a deer? I didn't pay a lot of attention to such things, but I didn't think it was deer hunting season, and I didn't think you'd have much luck bringing down deer with a Bowie knife.

I also didn't want to alert my old school friend to my presence by turning his girlfriend in to the police.

I told Marta I was stepping away for a moment. I went out onto the smoker's deck which was, thankfully, empty. I pulled out my phone and found Addie's number in my text messages. I typed, *There's a woman here who says she's dating Rise. Is he dating a 40-something teacher? I only ask because she's got a knife.*

I wasn't sure Addie would even see my text, as they were undoubtedly in final boarding stages for the press conference. But my phone dinged within minutes. *Any of these look familiar?* she responded. And three photos of women came up in three different texts.

She needn't have sent the second two. The first was Betina. In a mug shot.

First one, I responded.

Give me a minute. Don't let her leave.

Hmm. I returned to my station. Betina was still sipping soup and doing crosswords.

I hadn't heard from Addie when Betina waved Marta over and asked for her check. I didn't get to Marta in time to advise her to slow down. Damn.

But as Marta handed Betina the bill, my phone rang. It was Addie's number. I moved away from the bar and picked up.

"Avalon?"

"Yes, it's me."

"Bring her to the press conference. Large ballroom. Don't come in through the main hall, come down the side hall. It's roped off right now, but it will be open when you get here. If not, come through anyway. It leads to the door where Rise and the director will be waiting to go on."

"Really?"

"Can you do that?"

"Yeah, I guess. I mean, I'll try."

"Good. See you in a bit."

I pocketed my phone. Okay, this was strange. And it would be a weird way to see Rise again after all these years.

Marta had processed Betina's credit card, and the woman was signing her receipt.

"Marta, I'm going to be gone for a minute. You're in charge," I said.

"Sure thing."

I headed for the door, then turned around as if a thought hit me.

"Are you going to the press conference?" I asked Betina. "I'm headed that way now."

"Do you know where the ballroom is?" she asked.

"Yeah, of course. I'll show you."

A broad smile crossed her face. She stuffed her crossword book, and everything else that had fallen out, back into her bag. We headed down the short hall to the lobby. She seemed calm, and normal.

"Your brother and sister have a bunch of kids," I said, trying to talk about something else. "Do you want to have any?"

"Oh, yeah. Rise does, too. A baseball team's worth."

"I could never handle that," I said.

We walked briskly through the lobby, turning down a long hall just past the reception desk. The press conference was about to start, and the hallway was pretty empty. Actually, oddly empty. Like, completely. There was a check-in table with badges. No one was at it.

Betina stopped in front of it and perused the remaining badges. She picked one and put it on.

I wanted to comment on this, but kept my mouth shut.

We turned a final corner. Ahead of us was the lobby outside the ballroom. The two double doors had already been closed.

As we approached, to one side was a small hallway that ran parallel to the venue, which housed the cloakroom and the restrooms. Down this hall, by a door that opened to the front of the ballroom, Addie stood, next to Rise and the director, as well as the tall person who looked like the actor from *Schitt's Creek*.

Addie saw me and gave a short nod.

"Let's go this way," I said.

"What? Why?" Betina asked. Then she saw Rise.

Something came over Betina. She was different. Quiet. Completely still, but not relaxed. Her whole body was like a reverberating harp string, ready to go off if it was plucked. Yet calm. Dead calm.

Holy smokes. Should I do something? If so, what was Addie expecting me to do?

Rise didn't see Betina, because as we turned down the hall and took several steps, applause erupted from inside the auditorium. Addie opened the door and pushed Rise and the director through.

Addie shut the door behind them, though she remained in the hall.

At which point, two local policemen stepped out of the cloakroom beside us.

They grabbed Betina and turned her around to face the wall.

"Betina Popescu, you're under arrest for violating the restraining order in force against you which states you cannot come within 100 feet of Rise O'Connor. We're taking you in. You'll be allowed to make a phone call or hire an attorney."

I recognized Officer Ackerman. As he slapped handcuffs on her, her bag fell to the floor.

He turned her around, while the other officer grabbed her bag. I knew they'd find the knife.

Betina looked at me, fury emanating from the depth of her being.

I must have looked shocked.

She also saw Addie at the end of the hall, watching the proceedings. Addie did not look shocked.

The officers pushed past me, Betina between them. They tromped into the main hall and left through an exit door to the parking lot.

Addie came to join me. "Thanks," she said. "That could have gotten scary."

Could have gotten scary?

"Want to come in and listen? The director, Xenia Adino is talented. We'll be seeing a lot more from her."

"Sure."

Addie and I went back to the main hall and slipped in through the far door. She took her position, leaning against the back wall. I did the same.

I was still shaking. I hadn't expected a local version of a SWAT team to come for Betina.

Richard Ruskin, a well-known film critic, was at a microphone, talking about the meaning and trajectory of Xenia Adino's career. Xenia and Rise sat at a table, a microphone in front of each of them. Xenia was tall, wearing all black. Rise was perhaps an inch shorter than she—though I knew he was at least six one—his hair long enough to display its natural curl. He looked like he'd gotten out of the shower and let his hair air-dry. I knew how much product it took to achieve that devil-may-care look.

Richard Ruskin asked Xenia a number of meaty questions about the issues she was exploring in the film, and she answered thoughtfully, with interesting sound bites. The only question Mr. Ruskin asked Rise was, "What attracted you to making this film?"

In some ways I am my mother's daughter. It pisses me off how dismissive folks can be of "the talent," i.e., the actors. Like they get the money and fame, so they don't deserve respect for their craft. Whatever was going on between my mom and me, she really did deserve more respect for how she worked at and used her craft, and she'd taught me to respect the art and craft of others.

Rise answered the question thoughtfully. Xenia added a secondary question, and the conversation between the two of them was substantive and unexpected, and made me eager to see the film. It was clear the director and actor shared mutual respect.

As the film critic blustered his way back into the conversation, the other person from the hall, the one who reminded me of Stevie, came in unobtrusively to whisper something to Rise. As they did, they put a light hand on his shoulder and he gave them a quick, intimate smile.

"Who's that?" I asked Addie.

"That's Con Allred," she said.

"Connie?"

"No, just Con. They're Rise's assistant and security."

"Are they dating?"

Addie shook her head. "But Con purposely acts as a sort of decoy."

After another ten minutes, the film critic opened the discussion to questions from the floor. This time, most were directed to Rise, who gave each questioner his full attention, as well as a thoughtful answer.

"One more," said Richard Ruskin, and he called on someone who queried Xenia.

As she began her response, Rise's eyes swept the room, taking in all the journalists, Addie beside me, and...me.

Our eyes locked. I saw a flicker of recognition. But instead of acknowledging me in any way, he simply looked away.

When Xenia finished her answer, I noted Addie had vanished.

Richard Ruskin thanked Xenia and Rise for their participation and said everyone was looking forward to seeing the movie the next day.

The two of them stood, accepted a final wave of applause, and before anyone could get to them, Con and Addie had entered stage left and swept them from the room.

I stood against the back wall as everyone gathered their belongings and the phones on which they'd recorded the proceedings. I waited until the room had emptied and headed out. Addie was still in the hallway, chatting to the journalists. Two assistants handed out press packets. They offered me one and I took it.

Addie saw me, finished up with the journalists, and came over.

"Hey, thanks for your help with Betina," she said.

"You might have told me what the plan was," I said.

"Con and the cops were pretty sure it would go better if you didn't know."

I didn't know what to say.

Addie continued, "And thanks for pointing me to Rachel Hunt for the catering. It seems she'll work out well."

"For that, no problem. You're welcome."

With that, Addie headed for the young women with the press packets and check-in lists.

I walked down the hall, not wanting to stay with the film people, but not ready to return to work. I pushed open the exit door through which the officers had taken Betina. It led to the rear parking lot.

Autumn air brought me fully awake.

What was Betina planning? Why was she carrying a large knife? She'd sounded so normal. Well, sort of. I couldn't begin to figure it out.

I walked slowly around the hotel to a bench I knew of that was stuck in the grass in the middle of nowhere but had a fantastic view of the mountains.

Out of everything that had happened, the thing that stuck with me, against my will, was that Rise had looked right at me and purposely moved on.

I had a complicated relationship with my past, but I didn't think I had a complicated relationship with him. We were friends.

Or so I thought.

He was one of those people I kept tucked in my back pocket, who I thought I could call on in case of emergency.

Apparently not. Oh, well. Life goes on.

THE HOLLYWOOD SIGN

Ingredients

1 oz fresh elderberry juice (store bought or home-
squeezed)
1 oz citrus vodka
4 oz dry champagne
Fresh lemon peel
Fresh elderflower or fresh elderberries
Fresh lemon wedge to squeeze into cocktail

Method

In champagne flute, squeeze one wedge of lemon, elderberry juice and citrus vodka.
Stir together gently and fill the remainder of glass with
dry champagne.
Add fresh lemon peel and elderberries.

5

ORCHESTRA AND BALCONY

THE NEXT MORNING, Thursday, I'd finished my first cup of coffee when Willie Nelson came wailing at me again. I was wearing basic black pants, a button-up shirt, and a red vest embroidered with black flourishes, a nod to the fact Hollywood had descended.

"Hey, Hannah," I said.

"Hey yourself," she answered. "I was going to return your waders, but there's a gentleman here at the little crooked house who says he doesn't have my picture and therefore can't let me up."

Criminy. "Can you put him on?"

She consulted briefly. "He says no."

"I'll be right down," I said.

The doorbell rang.

Nobody ever calls me or comes looking for me before noon, especially when Chet wasn't letting anyone back here. This was getting strange.

I went to the door. I would have looked through the peephole but my door doesn't have one, because, well, why? I opened it to find a tall, slim young man in a red sherwani, an Indian jacket with a tall collar, in green and brown with gold trim. He had light brown skin and large dark eyes in an oval face. He looked familiar and not familiar at the same time.

"Hello," I said.

Before he could speak, a small Pomeranian barked at me happily and ran between my legs into the cottage, where she began turning in circles.

"Well, hi, Whistle," I said.

The young man said, "Sorry to bother you, but my grandmother—and all of us—are moving into MacTavish's and my idiot brother isn't back yet to take his dog. Grandmama said you might be willing to watch her."

He paused a moment, waiting for me to speak.

What could I say? These would be a busy few days and the last thing I wanted to add was time to come home and see to the dog.

On the other hand, this particular dog *loooved* me, and who can resist that?

"Sure," I said, and he handed me a quilted bag with Whistle's accoutrements. "So you must be..."

"Jonathan Young." Deep dimples proved his family ties. "Philip's brother."

"I'm Avalon."

"Nice to meet you. I've heard the stories. Thanks for saving my brother's life. Well, and helping save Gran's."

"You're welcome," I said. "Have fun."

"It's weird being back here," he said.

"I bet." I'd nearly forgotten that Philip and Jonathan had grown up in this very cottage. "If you ever want to come in and look around, let me know."

"No, it's...it's okay. Well, we're off! Room service, here we come. I'll make sure Philip picks her up as soon as he gets in. It's not like we can take a dog to the hotel."

"Happy to help." I didn't say that Whistle became Philip's dog precisely because she stayed at—and was left behind by—her owner at MacTavish's after the owner skipped out on the bill for a summer's worth of hotel rooms. And that she was practically Philip's assistant when he was painting the rooms at the inn.

I looked down at the hopeful, happy creature. Then I sighed and called Hannah back. "Would you mind accompanying me on a walk? I suddenly have a dog who needs exercise."

We met up on the sidewalk. Chet was gardening, wearing jeans

and a forest green work shirt, only he'd morphed into a Latino 5'7"
hunk of muscle who could likely take down Jeremy Renner without
breaking a sweat.

"How do I get photos of my guests to you?" I asked. "I don't have
a lot of photos of my friends."

Chet took out his cellphone, and asked, "May I?"

When Hannah nodded, he snapped the photo. "Last name?"

"Bricksford."

"She's good," Chet said to me.

"Do you need a photo of Whistle?" I asked, displaying only a little attitude.

"Nope. Got her." And he showed me a cellphone snap of the
pooch apparently given him by Sally.

"Well. That's new," Hannah said as we turned and automatically
headed for the Cardamom Café on Main Street.

"Hopefully the guards will only be there for a few days, until the
festival is over and Sally and her family head to France."

"I guess it's kind of like having a doorman building."

"Where the doormen are all named Chet and are packing heat."

"You're right, that's odd," she said.

Once at the café, I waited outside with Whistle while Hannah
ran in for chai. In the window, prominently displayed was a sign
promoting Avantika Azni, owner of the Café, for mayor. She was
running against our current mayor, Arthur Bristow. Her signs
looked great, and I would have thought so even if they hadn't been
designed by Philip. He'd originally created the campaign for Joseph,
my predecessor at the Battened Hatch. Avantika was one of Joseph's
largest supporters. After Joseph's untimely death, Avantika was per-
suaded to step in and run for mayor, herself. She had an uncommon
head for business and an uncommon heart for people, as demon-
strated in how well she ran the café.

"Here you go," said Hannah, handing me a steaming cardboard
cup capped by the aroma of nutmeg and cardamom. "Do you mind

if we head back? I'd like to have time to work out before heading back to the hospital."

"Thanks." I took the cup and we turned back the way we'd come. As long as I lived here, I would never get used to the mountains that rimmed the town, and the glass-like Lake Serenity, sapphire-blue behind MacTavish's Seaside Cottage, although in no way a saltwater sea. Lake Tranquility was the next town over. Apparently, Tranquility and Serenity were the names of the founder's daughters. We assumed Fretful Pond, which ran parallel to Main Street and ended with a waterfall back by my cottage, was named after their brother's state of mind.

"The hospital? Oh! How is the baby? How is the mama?" I asked, remembering how Hannah had left to check on midwife and mama the day before. It seemed like it had been a week since then.

"There were complications, a tear in the uterus which caused excessive bleeding. Thankfully, we got her to the hospital in time and the baby was safely delivered. Teresa needs to stay in the hospital a couple of days, and the baby, little Sophia, will stay with her. Maybe."

"Maybe?"

"Teresa and Matt don't have insurance. They also don't have much in a savings account." Hannah gave a big sigh. "Did you know it costs $20,000 to have a simple, vaginal delivery in a hospital? They don't have $20,000 or anything near it. And this wasn't a simple delivery. Every day they're in the hospital, the meter is running. But it's complicated to take the baby home without the new mother."

"Sorry to hear that," I said, "I'm glad everyone is healthy."

"Me, too. Say a little prayer."

I left Hannah at the Golden Door, the gym we both frequented. I ran Whistle back up to the cottage before grabbing my bike and heading for work.

Main Street was bumper-to-bumper with cars arriving for the film festival. Festival-goers filled the sidewalk outside the Orpheum, people checking the available films and choosing their favorites.

At MacTavish's, the lobby was packed, with a tangible buzz in the air. There were long lines at check-in. Knots of guests chatted throughout the large space.

As I walked toward the Battened Hatch, there was a flurry of activity by the front entrance to the hotel. The door opened, and a man wearing an earpiece came through. "Move back, please, move back," he said. A white stretch limo had pulled up and the hotel's valet was opening the rear door.

If those in the lobby hadn't been curious before, they were now.

And then Sally Allison was there, Salty Sally, an icon of Old Hollywood come to life. She wore ecru trousers, a burnt orange sweater and an ecru jacket with a hand-painted scarf fluttering behind. Once inside, she removed her sunglasses, facilitating her ability to give a warm embrace of a smile to the room in general. Her hair was full and silky white, turned under near her shoulders. Her husband Saif was with her, and their daughter and grandson walked behind. The group followed the concierge through the lobby, cutting a path through the crowds like it was their own little Suez Canal.

Sally's name was batted throughout the lobby like a wiffleball birdie back and forth over a net. This was often accompanied by a "yoo-hoo!" kind of wave, by women hoping to catch her attention.

"Sally Allison! It's her!"

"No, that can't be. She's been dead for 50 years. A boating accident."

A nattily-dressed man next to me ventured, "She's staying here in the hotel!"

I couldn't resist. I leaned in and said, "I hear she's staying in the suite where Pepper Porter used to live."

Then I walked away. The decibel level of the conversation rose behind me as I entered the Battened Hatch.

Oh, this was going to be fun.

Lunch flew by. Marta was supposed to be at the Orpheum with Jason an hour before the screening of *Triple Jeopardy*. Since I had a ticket for the film, and I had the Blumond, I said I'd go along to help with the set-up. Things quieted down at the Battened Hatch after two p.m. I felt safe leaving Manuela in charge with Davros for back-up. They could text for help any time.

Thus, I ended up back at the scene of the crime.

Quite literally. We unloaded the bottles of the blue peach-infused sparkling wine at the rear receiving door of the movie the-ater, then made certain the glasses were clean and put onto serving trays for after the screening. The bottles themselves went into the theater's professional-grade refrigerators.

Marta was in charge of running this event, and I excused myself to let her do just that. The screening of *Triple Jeopardy* was in the downstairs, largest theater. It was the only film showing this after-noon which left the upstairs theaters vacant. It seemed the easiest place for me to get out of the way, so up I went.

Once in the upper lobby, I couldn't help myself. I returned to theater three. No lights were on, but the doors to the hall stood open. I leaned against the frame and looked at the seat where young Marissa Marisol sat last time I was here.

A shiver ran through me.

I heard a couple of the theater staff come out of an office back behind the upstairs lobby. They headed downstairs, chatting.

I wondered when Investigator Spaulding might have more news about how and why Marissa died. I make it a point not to be overtly religious, but I did say a little prayer for the spirit of the girl and the pain of her survivors. Then I remembered Hannah's request and said one for Teresa and new baby Sophia. I liked Hannah, I guess I'd even say she was my best friend, but if she thought she was going to turn me into a holy roller, she would be disappointed. Not that she was a holy roller. She was Episcopalian, and I believe one negates your chance of becoming the other.

The thick carpet prevented me from hearing anyone approach, but suddenly someone was standing behind my shoulder. I turned, startled.

It was Con, who Addie had identified as Rise's security. "Hi," I said. "You startled me."

"I didn't know anyone else was up here," said Con.

"Just me," I said. "Taking a look at the theater where I found the body on Tuesday."

That surprised them.

"That wasn't my first guess," they said.

"Right?" I asked. "It so seldom is. Thankfully."

As I said that, we both heard someone pound up the stairs back out in the lobby. Whoever it was paused at the top, breathless for a moment. Then the footsteps continued on. A heavy door squeaked open.

And...Con was gone.

I went back out myself, curious to see what was going on. Con crossed the lobby floor in four seconds flat and tore open the door to the men's room.

They disappeared inside.

Loud voices came from the men's bathroom, including a couple of what I might call high-pitched squeals. Should I call the police? Leave the area to show I wasn't trying to involve myself?

Finally, things seemed to calm down behind the swinging door. As it began to open, I panicked. Should I hurry down the stairs and out of the situation? Return to the empty theater where I was originally found?

With no information to help me compute an answer I turned quickly around and plunked onto the bench I'd shared with Kyle, and then Mike, earlier in the week, and attempted to look nonchalant.

Which was hard because Con marched out of the restroom pushing a stick-thin girl with hair in a blunt cut above her shoulders, the color and style of a haystack. She wore wire-rimmed glasses with round frames. Her arms were pulled behind her. As she and Con approached, I could see that her hands were anchored there with a white plastic zip tie.

To my surprise, Con plunked the girl down on the bench next to me.

"Stay," they commanded. Then, to me, "Watch her." They had their phone out, dialing the police.

If I expected the zip tied girl to be nonplussed, I was in for a surprise.

"Hi," she said, cheerfully. "I'm Olive. Like Oyl, Popeye's girl-friend."

"Hi," I returned. "Avalon. Like the island with Arthur's sword."

She nodded. "Do you live around here?"

"Yeah. You?"

"Nope. In from out of town."

"For the film festival?"

"Kind of. Not really."

Con had gone back to the restroom and opened the door. They put themself as a block between Olive and the young man coming out, who turned out to be Rise. He didn't look Olive's way, but followed Con to the business office, and disappeared inside.

"I'm here, following him. Rise O'Connor."

"Oh?" I said.

"Yes, I followed him across the country. It's like a quest."

"Why?"

"Eventually I'm going to marry him. He could do worse. I'm lots of fun. I'm also obsessive-compulsive, but I'm a very *high func-tioning* obsessive-compulsive. Like Adele H at the beginning of that movie. The Truffaut film. Did you see it?"

"Isabelle Adjani," I said. "Bruce Robinson."

"You did!" She seemed delighted.

"Does Rise know about this? About you?"

"I'd show you my phone but—" She moved her arms. "Do you have a phone?"

"Yeah."

"Go to my Insta. OliveZarkOConnor."

How could I not?

I went to her Instagram account, and there, as her account photo, was a picture of her and Rise. She was facing him, kind of tucked against his side. He had his arm around her. They were both smiling.

Her most recent post was a photo of the poster for *Triple Jeopardy*.

Having fun in Tranquility, waiting for my honey's film to premiere, she'd written.

"I have a very high I.Q.," she was continuing. "My mom died when I was little and my dad doesn't think I'll amount to much. That's why it's important to me to have really smart kids. That's partly why I chose Rise. He played an attorney. Oh, I know he isn't one, really, but you have to be smart, and have enough wherewithal to pull off pretending you do. I'm pretty sure Rise wants to have smart kids, too. And I'm available."

"What if he doesn't?" I asked.

"I can kill him as easily as I can marry him," she said with a shrug. "Maybe easier, because you don't need an officiant and license and everything."

"If you're high-functioning, you have to understand the fact that both these things are a possibility likely won't be a big draw for Rise."

She shrugged again.

"I've learned to pick locks," she said, "as part of my quest. I like watching him sleep."

Okay. That was creepy. Had she ever actually succeeded? It freaked me out simply to imagine it.

Con returned from their phone call, during which they'd kept a careful eye down the stairs, waiting for officers to arrive. Olive and I sat quietly on the bench.

I finally stood. I didn't really want to be associated with more police procedures than absolutely necessary. "Good luck," I said.

"Nice to meet you, *Avalon*," she said. The elevator door dinged, slid open and two local policemen came out, spied Con and headed over. I slipped back into Theater 3 and sat at the back. As I did, I wondered if I was imagining things, or if the "Avalon" spoken by Olive held a snarl.

What was going on in this town? It seemed a large coincidence that two incidents—involving Olive and Marissa—had happened right here. Could they be related? I was seldom upstairs at the Orpheum, and yet I'd been here twice this week, and both times necessitated police showing up.

One thing was certain. It wasn't a great time to claim to Con I was an old friend of Rise's. Who wasn't? Holy crap. I guess I could also claim to be pretty high-functioning. That might become a new category on dating apps.

As I checked my watch, I heard an announcement over a speaker system: "We are pleased to announce the kick-off of the Tranquility Film Festival. The theater is now open for the world premiere screening of *Triple Jeopardy*. Have your tickets out as you enter the theater."

I felt a shiver of excitement. I did, in fact, have a ticket to the film. I decided to stay where I was and let the crowds get settled before I went down.

Somehow I wasn't surprised when Con came and sat down beside me. For a couple of moments, neither of us spoke.

"So, is there a restraining order against Olive like the Oyl?" I asked.

"No. Not yet. They won't be able to hold her for long. Thanks for your help, though. The fact that both Betina and Olive are out of the way for a few hours will give Rise more freedom to interact with fans and press."

"No other stalkers around?"

"Yeah, there's a guy named William, but he hasn't become aggressive yet."

"Good to hear. Have you seen Olive's Insta account? There's a photo of her and Rise O'Connor by a lake."

"Photoshopped. Not the together part, the lake part. It was

taken at ComicCon back in his superhero days. She paid for a photo with him. As you saw in the picture, she was a grabber."

"Ah. She told me it would be just as easy to kill him if he doesn't marry her."

"Seriously? Do you know how hard it is to kill somebody? It takes a lot of effort, or a lot of precision. The human body doesn't shut down easily."

"You're not worried?"

"More about the Betinas, who have knives, than the Olives who go charging into men's bathrooms. But we keep an eye on both."

I liked Con. They seemed serious about Rise's safety but not overly aggrieved. Like it was a thing that happened, and you dealt with it.

They stood. "You coming to the film?"

"Yes."

"See you around. And thanks again."

And then I was alone in the upstairs theater, wondering what had happened to make Marissa's body shut down.

ORCHESTRA AND BALCONY

Lavender Lemon Drop Martini

Ingredients

1/2 oz homemade lavender simple syrup (recipe to follow below)
1/2 oz orange liquor (triple sec)
2 oz citrus vodka of your choice
Juice of a half of fresh lemon
Sugar (for garnish)
Lavender flower (for garnish)
Fresh lemon wedge
Lavender Simple Syrup
Yield 1 cup. If more is needed, double the recipe or triple
In medium saucepan, add about 2 tablespoons of dried whole French blue lavender flower to one cup water and one cup of sugar. After boil begins turn heat down to low and let sit for about 20 minutes until you mixture has a light purple hue to it.
Turn heat off and let sit until simple syrup comes down to room temperature and then strain through a fine mesh strainer to make sure all the lavender flower is out of the water.

Cocktail

Method

Take a small flat plate and pour sugar just enough to coat the plate add a sprinkle of dried lavender flower.
Take martini glass and use the fresh lemon wedge to rub

around the rim of the martini glass. Take glass and dip
into the sugar lavender mixture from plate.
Take cocktail shaker add ice, homemade lavender simple
syrup, orange liquor, lemon vodka, and fresh lemon juice.
Shake all ingredients together until cocktail shaker has a
nice cold feeling to it and stain into martini glass. Add
fresh slice of lemon to the edge for garnish
Sip slowly and enjoy

6

BUTTERED POPCORN

I SLID INTO the main theater downstairs after everyone was seated, just as the doors were closing.

Con and Addie stood at intervals against the back wall. I joined them there. Lights went out in the back of the house as Jerry Raker jaunted forward, followed by Xenia and Rise, who took their places in two seats off the aisle of the fifth row, in a make-a-run-for-it position. Jerry welcomed everyone to the Tranquility Film Festival and spoke of the fabulous slate of films. He called Tranquility his adopted East Coast home, a natural canvas for the arts, and said there'd be a very interesting announcement at the end of the festival. He talked with exuberance of the film we were about to see, of Xenia Adino, and of Rise O'Connor. Finally, Jerry gestured to the screen. "With no further ado, the world premiere of *Triple Jeopardy.*"

He was nearly flying with anticipation when he left the front of the house and the lights slowly went down. By mid-room, he was walking briskly. When he reached the back, he looked ready to punch someone. He shoved the theater door open, only enough to squeeze through.

Someone in the lobby grabbed the door from him as he passed and took the opportunity to inch into the theater before it closed and we were all enclosed in darkness. The screen burst to life with the names of all the various production companies, and Addie approached me.

"Now that the doors are closed, they won't let anyone else in," she said, and motioned to four empty seats which were blocked off at the end of the back row. "You're welcome to sit." She motioned to the newcomer as well. I went third seat in, newcomer went second seat in, Addie took the one on the aisle. A flame of excitement ignited inside me.

After logos from the producing partners, the screen went black until the words *A film by Xenia Adino* appeared. The screen began to lighten, and Xenia's name was replaced by Rise O'Connor, then, as his name faded, the name of the female star. It took a minute to realize we were watching a sunrise.

"Jelly Belly?" whispered a male voice from beside me.

Usually, I'd be annoyed if someone talked during a movie, but Jelly Bellies?

"What flavor?"

"Buttered popcorn."

Darn. Along with coconut and blueberry, one of my favorites.

"Yes, please." I partially turned to him, palm up. He shook some into my hand. "Thanks."

We both turned our attention to the screen, but my heart rate accelerated. I was sitting next to Landon Presser.

Fuuuudge.

Landon was the new hottest star on Earth, one of those overnight sensations who'd been working in the business for ten years. An ultra-talented actor, he'd recently starred in a limited series for Netflix that turned out to be the vehicle that launched him into the stratosphere.

What was Landon Presser doing in Tranquility, New York, offering me Jelly Bellies?

Rise's movie. I needed to settle in and watch Rise's movie.

I was sitting next to freaking Landon Presser.

Rise's movie.

And then it hit me. Landon and Rise had been Disney superheroes together in the movie and series *Owning It*, for four seasons, back in the day. Nice of Landon to come to see his friend's movie.

Thus I decided it was currently my job to sit next to Landon being Not A Stalker and watch Rise's stupid movie.

Only, of course, it wasn't stupid. It wasn't a thriller, exactly, but it held my attention like one. It was a relationship story about a scientist and the young man who has to convince her to let her child die to save all of humankind.

Rise was very good. In fact, he was so good I was captured by the story. Rise, and even Landon, left my mind.

Of course, Rise's character develops a relationship with the little girl, who does die at the end (spoiler alert, sorry). I don't believe there was a non-crier in the house.

I can't say for sure about Landon, because he was suddenly gone, as if he'd vaporized. Addie's seat was also empty. Lights came up, and the audience took a moment to gather their emotions. Then the applause started, hearty and deserved. Xenia stood, pulling Rise to his feet, and the clapping crescendoed. Then Addie stood next to them. She made an announcement telling those who were expected at the one-on-ones where to meet the bus before ushering Xenia and Rise up the aisle. Xenia smiled and looked straight ahead as she walked, but Rise took the time to make eye contact with, and share a smile with, as many moviegoers as he could.

As he passed the last row, he made eye contact with me.

He gave me the same mini-nod and smile he'd given everyone else.

There you have it.

Rise turned to the left into the large lobby, casually standing shoulder to shoulder with Con, as if Con were an old friend or even romantic interest, not someone ready to break your arm and have you hauled off. A crowd soon gathered. Rise signed things and talked and laughed, interacting with everyone he could.

I went in the other direction to make sure Marta was okay, though of course she was. Addie was corralling the journalists into a group in the outer lobby, where blue sparkling wine was already being dispensed. The carrier van pulled up and Addie read names off a list, and those selected bounced up and onto the transport, which took off up the street.

Addie used the time waiting for the van's return to chat up those remaining. She did an outstanding job of keeping everyone in good humor. As the rest of the moviegoers streamed out of the theater, I looked back to see that Rise and Con were gone.

The fancy van returned, and Addie loaded the rest of her crowd. She stepped on, leaned out, and said to me, "Hey, you want a ride? There's room."

I looked at my watch. The Battened Hatch would be gearing up for the supper crowd.

"Sure. Thanks."

The van was nice, the seats upholstered and comfortable. A smartly put-together young man from Jerry's agency met us on the other end, checking off names as the journalists descended. Addie said goodbye to each rider, addressing them personally. Once they were all accounted for, the greeter put a hand over his head and led them into MacTavish's like a tour guide in Venice.

Addie sat. I was still shaking off the plethora of unexpected events. I asked, "Do you need to rush to the event?"

It was being held in a two-bedroom mega-suite where Glenn had lived with his father after his mother died. The view of Lake Serenity was gorgeous, and it had a flow that allowed journalists to relax in a large living room while awaiting their turn. The bedrooms were undoubtedly set up with backdrops of *Triple Jeopardy* for interviews with Xenia and Rise.

"No, we have some eager assistants in training who've set it up. I'll give them a few minutes on their own to, well, own the event."

"In that case, could you use a free drink, alcoholic or non? I'm headed for the Battened Hatch, and I know someone who could comp you."

Addie smiled. She had large, expressive eyes that could laser-focus as well as dance with mischief. "I'd never say no...if you know someone."

We walked together through the lobby and into the hallway entrance to the pub, which was lined with stained glass in rich hues.

Inside, the place had only half a dozen patrons, as we were between rushes. I checked in with Manuela and sent her off for an hour to put her feet up before the supper crowd.

I needed to restock before supper, but I had some time, and I seldom got to check in with Addie.

"Do you miss Los Angeles, and being adjacent to the business?" she asked me.

"You mean adjacent through my mom? Can't say that I do."

Addie was one of the few people who knew who my mother was. She had been paying attention to Mom's life and career and had figured it out on her own, simply because she recognized my name. I don't announce the fact I'm Anna Nash's daughter, but I don't deny the relationship if asked.

"By the way, if your mom is ever looking for a new publicist, I'd really enjoy taking her career forward," Addie said.

"She'd be lucky to have you. But we're not exactly in touch."

"I know."

"What would you like to drink?"

"What do you recommend?"

"There's a drink I'd like to try. It came to me, somehow, magically, after the movie. It's kind of sweet, though."

"Does it have a name?"

"Buttered Popcorn. More along the lines of Buttered Popcorn Jelly Bellies. Fair warning, you'd be my guinea pig."

"Why not?"

"By the way, what was Jerry's deal after he introduced the movie?" I asked, grabbing the Buttershots.

"What do you mean?"

"He didn't seem happy as he left the theater."

"He wants the festival to go well. He has a lot riding on it. And he'll be relieved when all the Sally Allison reveals are done. Then, he's making a big announcement on the day after *Salty Sally and*

Pepper debuts. It's a lot of pressure. But he sails through the public part of it, he only lets his happy face slip when he thinks no one's watching."

"Do you like working with him?"

"Did I tell you how I ended up at Raker and Associates?"

"Nope. Did you grow up in L.A.?" I asked, my story-collector gene kicking in.

"Michigan. My friends mostly stayed put after high school or came back after college. But one of my friends went to the Fashion Institute of Technology in New York City, which made me think maybe I could move into a wider world, myself. I saw a movie around that time about some 'nobody' becoming a star because an agent saw talent in her. I didn't want to act, but I decided I'd like to have that power, to help the deserving get their chance. I thought I was pretty good at discovering people's talents. So I moved to Los Angeles, assuming I'd get a job as an agent in a week or two, or at least in the mail room. Ha!

"Applied everywhere. Nothing. Couldn't even get a waitressing job."

"What did you do?"

"Someone told me to sign up at a temp agency. Thank God I could type. It's the only reason I'm sitting here before you today."

"Yeah?"

"After about six months of working at poultry warehouse offices and the like, they sent me to fill in while Mel Evers looked for a new assistant. You know who Mel is?"

"Holy crap."

"Right?"

Mel was one of Hollywood's top agents. Was, in the past tense. His career got plowed under by the #MeToo movement.

"Anyway, Mel got bored of interviewing applicants and liked my looks—I think he wanted to brag that he'd hired a Black person—so he hired me away from the temp agency. Mel was unapologetically abusive to everyone. I had to work twelve-hour days or lose my job.

If anything went wrong with anything, he blamed me and was verbally abusive until I cried. If a client didn't get a job, Mel told them I'd screwed up communication somehow. One day when Jerry was in for a meeting, Mel was particularly evil to me. He also slapped my ass, hard, as I left the room. He then winked at Jerry.

"Jerry found me at my desk in tears. He told me to quit without giving two-weeks notice, simply quit, and come work for his publicity firm. I couldn't believe it. I unobtrusively packed things up, and when Mel went to lunch to drink with clients, I Ubered everything to my apartment, then came back and worked all afternoon. At seven, I called for another Uber, and when it arrived, I went in to Mel, who was meeting with a client. I said, 'I just want you to know you won't see me in the morning, or any other time, because you're abusive and I quit.'

"He told me I'd never work again in that town. He actually said the words. I started laughing and I couldn't stop. I laughed all the way out to the car."

"No."

"Yep. The next Monday, I started working at Raker and Associates as an assistant. In six months, I was a junior publicist with my own clients. The rest is history. All of us at the agency pitch in, of course, making sure all our clients are taken care of at an event like this."

"However it happened, I'm glad it did. You are a grounding presence for Jerry. I'm sure you made quite a difference on the documentary, too."

"Thanks. I like to think I did."

"Speaking of the documentary, what was the thinking behind letting Sally be seen today? Lots of people watched her parade through the lobby."

"Ah, but the key word is 'people.' Not reporters, not news outlets, not any of the entertainment channels. Ordinary people got snaps of her on their cellphones, and they are already posting them. Let's give *E! News* and *The Hollywood Reporter* and *TMZ* two days to get here. Sally won't be seen again until the screening on Saturday. Was it her? Maybe? Probably. Good enough chance, given that there's a documentary about her, to focus the attention of the entertainment community. How else do you get the major outlets to a small-town film festival in upstate New York?" She smiled. "Let's wait and see who rolls into town."

"Gee, it's like you and Jerry are crackerjack publicists or something. Say, by the way, did you have lunch?"

"Actually, no."

"Do you have time to eat now? I can rush something for you."

"How fast?"

"Give me five." Chef Angelica's lettuce wraps were tasty, and I had them in front of Addie in seven minutes, as the kitchen was empty except for my favorite sous chef, named Robert.

"So, does Rise usually have this intensity of stalkers?" I asked as I put down the plate. She wrapped the proffered ingredients with a designer's eye.

"Yes. He's got an unusual number. I think it's a combination of his looks, his charisma, and the fact they've watched him grow up on television. He doesn't usually have this many in one place at one time, though. My guess is they figure a small town means easy proximity."

"Are you talking about Rise O'Connor's stalkers?"

I looked up to find Investigator Spaulding standing behind Addie.

"Yes, in fact. Addie Moon, this is Mike Spaulding. Investigator Mike Spaulding with the State Police. Addie is Rise O'Connor's publicist."

"Ah. You'll be interested to know, we just heard from the local police. They were transferring Betina Popescu from the local police station, and she managed to escape."

Addie had started to relax, but I saw the effects of adrenaline jump through her system. "Okay. Got it. Rise is one of our clients. I've got to go. What do I owe for the wraps?"

"On me," I said. "If it's not one thing, it's something else."
"Ain't it the truth?" remarked Addie.
She waved as she headed out the door.

HOT BUTTERED POPCORN
(MAKES 4 CUPS)

Ingredients:

1 bag fresh popped butter popcorn (for garnish)
1 tablespoon of ground sugar cane (raw sugar)
2/3 cup dark brown sugar
1/2 cup unsalted butter (room temperature)
1/4 cup local honey
1 teaspoon ground cinnamon (1/2 for butter mixture, 1/2 for popcorn)
1/4 teaspoon ground nutmeg
1 dash of ground clove
4 oz of Sailor Jerrys Rum or your favorite spiced rum
4 oz of Buttershots liqueur
6 cups of hot water
Fresh whole cinnamon sticks for garnish

Method:

In a mixing bowl, add butter, brown sugar, honey, 1/2 teaspoon of ground cinnamon, nutmeg, and clove. Mix well by hand or with electric mixer on low for one minute.
Heat mugs with hot water and let sit for one minute.
Pour out water and add a dollop of butter mixture.
Add Sailor Jerrys or spiced rum of your choice.
Add Buttershots to each mug.
Slowly add hot water to each cocktail mug, stirring until hot butter mixture is melted and taste is perfect.

Take your freshly popped buttered popcorn and add 1 tablespoon of raw sugar and the remainder of the cinnamon, toss gently and add to the top of the cocktail with a fresh whole cinnamon stick.

7

INTO THE NIGHT

MIKE DIDN'T HAVE, or couldn't share, any more information about the death of Marissa Marisol. He was checking in partly because he heard there was another police call at the theater today, in the same location as the death and he wondered if I knew anything about it.

Can't put much past this guy.

"I'm thinking that Betina is heading out of town, and, if she's smart, out of state," he said. "They've issued a BOLO, but no one has the resources to track her down for a restraining order violation."

Mike couldn't drink since he was working, but I did comp him some wings. The simple act of being a Black investigator in an overwhelmingly white department deserved some support, as did the fact he took me seriously when I talked to him about his cases.

We promised to update each other on any developments, and he headed out.

I made a mental note to find out what I could about the late Marissa Marisol. I felt I owed her that much.

Dinner started and the place was packed, which I needed to take my mind off things. I enjoy the challenge of a rush and become more cheerful when handing out food and drink by the fistfuls, so to speak.

There were many locals, but there also many tables where the conversations centered around films the participants were bringing to the festival. It felt like the happy part of Los Angeles culture, without the nonsense of everyone constantly measuring their standing in comparison to others in the business.

Marta was back, and winded, but in a happy way. She had enjoyed serving the reporters after the movie, and she'd also enjoyed being in charge. She remained to help close long after the others had left to crash so we could do it all again the next day. No one was begging off shifts; in fact, the tips were so good that we would all likely take a nicer vacation than expected this year. All of us were therefore intent on powering through the festival weekend.

"See you tomorrow," said Marta, as she headed out.

"Good night, and thanks," I said as I went to fetch my bike from the storeroom.

On my return, I went to turn off the last remaining lights, those which illuminated the bar shelves. I stood a moment, proud of the display, and the blue and gold glow from beneath. It wasn't until I turned off those LED lights that I noticed the figure seated at the bar wearing a hoodie.

I stopped in my tracks.

"Hello?" I asked. "We're closed."

Obviously.

The person put down the hood. In the dim light from the circular kitchen window, it took a moment to figure out that it was Con.

"You scared me," I said. "What's up? What's going on?"

"I need your help."

Dread dropped into my stomach like a shot of Jägermeister—and who wants that? I knew, somehow, this was about Betina and her knife. Betina, who was now on the loose. Betina, who by the way, had sat in that very chair and spilled her life's story before I led her directly into a trap.

"Yeah? Help with what? What's up?"

"I need you to trust me. It won't take long."

"Look, it's late. I've done my bit."

"You've been very helpful. We appreciate it very much."

"I'm thinking I'm probably not Betina's favorite person at the moment."

Con looked thoughtful. "I can't argue with that." Silence enveloped us. "Please."

Here's the thing. Con Allred was one of those people who is inherently down-to-earth and emanates good-person vibes. I doubted they could or would purposefully lie unless someone's life was on the line, which led me to ask, "Will I be in danger?"

"Not in the least, if I can help it."

"And you're trained in martial arts?"

They laughed. "I work in security. I'm trained in lots of things."

It came down to one question: did I trust Con?

"Okay," I said. "If you promise it won't take long."

"You can leave whenever you want."

I put my bike back, silently arguing with myself the whole way.

"Is there a way out of here, besides the doors to the street and to the lobby?"

I nodded and pushed my way through the swinging door to the kitchen. A work light was on, but the place was squeaky clean and very empty. I led Con toward the exit sign.

Once outside, the fresh air was bracing. Con got their bearings quickly, walked us silently around the side of the building and through a parking lot to a side street. No one else was around. Con was hyper-aware, though seemingly nonchalant.

A white stretch limo, undoubtedly the one in which Sally had arrived earlier, sat dark and parked by the curb. As we approached, there was the clicking of a lock. Con opened the back door, herded me inside, and followed me in.

The door locked, and the motor started. The vehicle slid forward quietly, without any lights, into the empty streets. We went the opposite direction of Main Street and took a left turn, gliding out of sight of MacTavish's before the headlights came on, which also activated green passion lights in a rectangle around the top of the inside of the limousine.

"Thanks, Castor," said Con to the driver. "We're good. Privacy window, please."

"You're welcome."

The window between riders and driver closed.

"So," I said. "What's up?"

Con and I sat side-by-side on the back bench. I tried to focus on demanding an answer, but my attention kept being grabbed by all the amenities backlit in front of me. The limo had illuminated liquor shelves, thank you very much, as well as professionally-stocked snacks, including nuts, cookies and chips. I had no doubt there were fruit cups and acai bowls in the mini-fridge.

"You didn't tell me everything," said Con.

My mind raced. What hadn't I passed along? Something that turned out to be important?

"About Betina? She's from Romania. Came to the U.S. when she was a teenager. Her brother and sister both have kids and she's desperate to have some, too. A baseball team of kids, she said, though it seems she's getting a late start if that's the case. She made up some story about Rise coming to her school, about how they're dating and will get engaged if the movie is successful."

"Interesting," said Con.

I looked out the tinted windows, trying to figure out where we were headed. We had doubled back, still off main streets, and were headed toward the next town, which hosts Lake Tranquility, itself. This raised more questions than it answered.

Con didn't press me further about Betina.

"Wait...you mean about Olive? She's a high-functioning obsessive-compulsive. She thinks she's like Isabel Adjani's character, Adele Hugo, in *The Story of Adele H*, which, frankly, seemed to me more like a cautionary tale than something to aspire to. She wants to have intelligent kids, and that's why she picked Rise. She's good at picking locks. She likes to watch him sleep. When she said it might be easier to kill him than to marry him, I pointed out that wasn't usually a successful dating strategy."

"Good Lord," said Con, "Who are you? How did you learn all this stuff?"

"I love listening to people's stories." I had learned not to say I "collected" stories, as that could sound a little bit off-putting and perhaps put me into the camp of those who would benefit from therapy.

"She picks locks and watches him sleep?"

"That's what she said."

"Well, shit."

We'd finally swung around onto a major street and turned up a road with an inconspicuous sign that said we were headed for Chateau Tranquility.

Silence descended once again.

You'd think I'd have been to the Chateau, if for no other reason than to check out the competition. But life was full and busy, and I hadn't. Sneaking onto the grounds after dark in a stretch limo seemed a fitting way to arrive.

We emerged from the half-mile drive into what looked to be a magical land of the dwellings of happy rich people. As we passed, I saw the lobby of the main lodge was enormous, all wood, huge chandeliers, three story ceilings and two story fireplaces. If I recalled correctly, Rise was now stuffed into a small room in this edifice, behind security.

But we didn't head for the lodge. Instead, we drove past multiple swimming pools, illuminated, with waterfalls and fountains surrounding them. They must have had hot tubs, though we didn't go slowly enough for me to see, but warm vapors rose from the water.

Castor pulled into a side parking lot, far away from anything, and switched off the lights and the motor. He then opened the back door locks.

Con sent a text and reached for the door.

"Can I just ask...is there a chance we're going to run into someone with a large knife?"

Con looked at me, perplexed, before they got my reference.

"The police confiscated Betina's knife."

Okay. Comforting.

Con got out of the car, and as soon as I clambered out, they started walking down the hill.

Lake Tranquility shimmered at the bottom. Streetlights dotted a walkway around it. Down this way were a number of freestanding cabins and condos.

Con was a damn fast walker. It was all I could do to keep up. They chose one of the condos, walked up through a small front garden, knocked three times, paused, then knocked three more times.

Interior locks clicked. The thick wooden door slid open. Once again, Con pushed me through, as they'd "helped" me into the car. They then stepped back, closing the door with a thud. This was obviously a person who thought of open doors as a point of vulnerability.

The force with which Con pushed me had the unintended effect of thrusting me into the person who had opened the door. I fought to gain my balance and looked up into the face of Landon Presser.

Who laughed and caught me.

He then spun around, me still firmly in his arms, and set me on the path that led into the condo's living room.

"Hey," said a familiar voice from within. "What's the story so far?"

INTO THE NIGHT

Smoky Manhattan

Ingredients

Handheld torch
Hickory Smoked wood chips (small amount 1/2 oz)
Ceramic cutting board or wooden cutting board (something that can with stand heat) Please be very cautious with this step as you will be lighting a small amount of wood chips on fire to create smoke
2 1/2 oz bourbon or rye
1/4 oz sweet vermouth
2 dashes bitters of your choice
Luxardo cherries
Chilled martini or coupe glass, as the smoke will stick to a chilled glass better

Method

On your board take handheld torch and light small amount of hickory woods chips on fire or just enough for them to get smoking.
Take glass and put over the smoking chips for about 30 seconds up to a minute depending on how smoky you would like your cocktail.
Set smoked glass aside and make sure to extinguish the hickory chips right away.
In a cocktail mixing glass, add ice, bourbon or rye, bitters and sweet vermouth and gently stir for about 30 seconds.

Strain all ingredients into smoked glass and add Luxardo cherry for garnish.
Sip and enjoy.

8

SALTY GANG RIDES AGAIN

RISE HELD HIS arms open in welcome, and I walked into his embrace.

"God, it's good to see you," he said. "It's been way too long."

His words floated over my head, his warm breath as close as my hair. Then we parted, and he said, "This is my friend, Landon."

"Hi," I said, "thanks for the Jelly Bellies."

He laughed. "That was you? Any time." An upper class English accent encased his words.

Landon Presser, like my cousin Reggie, is tall, dark and handsome, but Landon is the movie-version of Reggie. While Reggie is hella handsome for a lawyer, Landon is so unnecessarily good-looking as to be distracting. His skin is a dark bronze, his eyes large and brown, a full lower lip with an upper lip like an invitation above it. His eyebrows are thick and expressive, his nose strong, nostrils ready to flare. Here's the thing: I don't read romances and I don't swoon over men, but Jeez Louise, what was God thinking when she made Landon? Who needs all that in one package? Seriously. I didn't even need to know about his package.

The irony was Rise O'Connor in the same room. It was hard to know where to look.

I held onto Rise's arms and took a step back. First off, he had grown. I'd known him when he was a handle-able four feet tall. Now he was six one and wearing black pants and a white t-shirt from which his arm muscles poured. His chin was also square—he and Landon could be in the chiseled chin club. Rise's skin was light tan with pink undertones, eyes blue. His nose, of course, was too perfect. I missed his old nose. His brown hair with golden blonde high-lights was casually hand-combed up away from his forehead, in a just-messy-enough way that it was begging you to run your own fingers through it. But none of that mattered when he grinned, and those dimples to the center of the Earth opened up.

More to the point, Rise's smile was so unaffected and truly happy that I couldn't do anything except grin back.

"Okay," said Landon, "what are you drinking?"

That's my line, of course, and it's been a long time since someone asked me. He showed me the array of possibilities in the condo's bar and I chose what they were having: hard seltzer, perfect for when you wanted a no-cal delivery system.

The three of us went into the condo's modern living room. The actors flopped down on the white sofa, obviously comfortable in each other's company.

"God, it's good to see you," Rise said again.

"The young man—Rise—has told me all about the Salty Gang he was a part of when he was growing up. I've been nothing but envious since I met him at fourteen. I must admit, by now I'd given up hope of meeting one of you in the wild. You've taken on mythic status."

I've taken on mythic status?

"It means a lot to have friends who stick with you, and later, remind you where you came from," said Rise.

"Yeah, we all knew you before you were Rise, back when you were Crispin with another nose." I stopped, immediately. Had I gone too far? I was tired and not thinking straight.

But Landon guffawed. "Yup, she's just as you described her."

"I'm sorry, it's been a long day," I said. "And, I'm supposing you've had a long day, too," I said, embarrassed again. After all, his film had premiered, he'd been accosted by a stalker in a restroom, and spent the entire afternoon doing one-on-ones with the press, and here I was, complaining.

"You can say that again," Rise said, and raised his glass to meet Landon's.

The room in which we sat had tall ceilings and felt airy. There was a kitchen, a wet bar, a large flatscreen tv and a dining table between the kitchen and living room. Tall windows were blocked from the outside by fir trees.

"How did things go with the interviews?" I asked Rise. "The film is really good."

"Aw, shucks. thanks. They seemed to go well."

"She's right, old man," said Landon. "You've got a modicum of talent." He winked at me. "We don't want him to get too big-headed."

"Now who's talking?" Rise asked. "Who is likely to be up for every acting award on Earth this season? Who suddenly has five million followers on Insta?"

"5.6 million."

"And just happens to be in town on his way to hosting *Saturday Night Live* next week?"

"That would be me," said Landon. "It's all a bit much. And it underscores why it's so important to have a group of friends you can count on. I think we all know that being successful in this business leads to misery more often than sustained happiness."

"True that."

"It helps when you've worked for a while and know who you are, and have learned to respect your craft, so you don't believe the bullshit," Landon said. He gave a deep sigh.

"Are you not happy with how things are going?" I asked. He wasn't currently on the A List, he was on the A+ List, and from what I'd seen, he deserved to be there, with both the looks and talent to back it up.

"I'm terrified," he said, quietly. "The air is too rare. The ledge is precarious. And both you"—he nodded at Rise— "and Kaylie need to keep reminding me it's about the work, and the stories we can tell."

"I thought you and Kaylie broke up?" asked Rise.

"Not yet. We're going to. Or we have. I'm not sure. It's tough after four years. Especially now, when the Fame Bat has smacked into me. She's said she'll stick close as long as I need her to. She's wise and grounded. But we both know we're moving on. I just don't need people to think I'm *available* right now."

"Not like me. Apparently, I'm engaged. To Olive. And Betina. And possibly, William."

"Don't you kind of hate to say their names?" asked Landon. "The fact you know who they are gives them a win."

"Or, conversely, have you thought about asking if they want to be sister wives? And husbands?" I asked.

"It irks me that I can't have any friends in public, except Con. You know how hard it was for me when I saw you, Av, and couldn't bat an eye? But anyone who is thought to be in my circle, be it family or friend, becomes fair game. And you, Goofball, are about to experience it times about a million. Sorry about the mega-fame," Rise addressed Landon. At first I thought he was being facetious, but he was dead serious, and Landon took it as such.

Landon sighed. "I'll put up with the fame because it brings me more opportunities. I just need to be smart about them. It's also nice to be a person of color riding this wave. And, you know what? I'm sure as hell going to enjoy the ride."

"You should," said Rise. "And thanks for coming. It's a schlep from NYC to Tranquility. Having both of you here is wonderful."

"Listen, when I told you before that your work in *Triple Jeopardy* is career-changing, I meant it," said Landon.

"Thanks. But could we not talk about it now? I'm kind of stuck between a rock and a hard place, and I don't want to get anxious tonight."

"You mean between ThunderGlove and Dirk, Incorporated? I feel you. We'll give them the night off."

There was a moment of silence as they kicked thoughts of Rise's agent and manager into the metaphorical dumpster.

I wanted to bring up something positive, not jump into a conversation about the mental states of Rise's two most recent stalkers, although it was a conversation in which I could, in fact, shine. I went another way.

"Since Jerry is your publicist, I'm sure you know all about his new documentary. Well, his and Addie's and Brent's."

"Nope."

"*Salty Sally and Pepper: Truth Be Told.* It screens on Saturday. Turns out Jerry is an expert on all things Pepper Porter. Pepper lived at MacTavish's, where you did your press junkets. But while Jerry and Addie were here, they discovered that Sally Allison is still alive."

"Salty Sally is *alive?*"

"Yup. Not only that, she's my landlord."

"Wait, wait, wait. What? Does the rest of the Salty Gang know this?"

"Actually, no. There's a whole story behind it. But I moved here last spring and haven't been in touch with anyone back home since. Actually, since Winsome died."

"Oh, God. We've got so much to talk about," Rise said.

"Yes, well, Sally lives here in Tranquility—oops, I'm not supposed to say that. She wants people to think she is coming into town for the documentary so they don't hunt down her house. But she's hired mega-security. At least four guys, two to accompany her and two to keep people off her property."

"Holy smokes."

"You might need more security," said Landon to Rise.

"I'll be out of here soon," said Rise. "Con is great."

"Con is great," agreed his friend. "But you're sleeping in a hovel behind the security office. Unless you give in and come crash here. I've got a bedroom and this lovely couch on which we're now sitting."

"Thanks. It's tempting."

"Or," I said, "if one or more of your stalkers know you're staying here at the Chateau, you could throw them off the scent by coming to stay at my place. I also have a bedroom and a couch. Not counting my bedroom. So I have two bedrooms and a couch, but I'm using one. Of the bedrooms."

Rise laughed. "You have had a long day."

"But think about this—staying at my place would mean you could take advantage of Sally's two security guys who won't let anyone onto the property."

"Yeah?"

"I live in a guest cottage above her meadow. Her security guys—I'm supposed to call them Chet—are stationed at the entrance, round-the-clock."

"Really?"

"Yep. Invitation available for either of you."

"I'm good for tonight, thanks," said Landon. "But it sounds like an offer too good for you to refuse, young man."

"You're serious?" asked Rise. "You're not just saying that because Goofball here said I was staying in a hovel?"

"I swear. Goofball? Young man?"

"When we first met, as young superheroes, Rise was two years younger than me. I've never let him forget it. And where did Goofball come from? I hardly even remember. You come up with some creative nicknames and curses when you're working for Disney and not allowed to swear," answer Landon.

"It's really weird how long the no-swearing thing follows you," agreed Rise, who was texting. "Not that we don't fucking swear, we just swear less than we probably would." He was texting as he spoke.

"I hate to say this, but I'm crashing. Still on London time," said Landon. "The offer holds that you can stay over. You both can. I'm sure the sofa folds out."

"I told Con I'm moving to Avalon's," said Rise. "How can I not stay near Salty Sally's with a member of the Salty Gang?"

"How often does life come full circle in such a...circle?" asked Landon. We were all getting punchy.

A series of knocks came at the door, this time four and four. Rise opened it to admit Con. "So, you're okay with this?" they asked me.

"Yes," I said.

Rise and I said good-night to Landon, who did indeed look like he was about to fall asleep on his feet.

We followed Con silently up a path that ended up by the limo. Castor, the driver, came down to meet us.

"Rise, do you want to wait here while I get your stuff, or do you want to come with?"

"I'll come," he said, then to me, "We'll be quick. I never unpacked after moving to the hovel. You haven't seen any lurkers, have you?"

"You never see the ones who count. But I think we're okay. If you're fast."

Castor used his key fob to unlock the car, then briefly climbed into the back to check that everything was shipshape. My guess was he'd counted on having till the next day to restock the chips. He climbed back out with an empty water bottle.

As Con and Rise left, walking quickly up the hill, I said, "Would it be okay if I sat up front with you while we're waiting? I'd feel a little bizarre back there by myself."

The request surprised him. He nodded.

We climbed in through our respective doors.

He was a compact man, tan skin, large ears that somehow anchored the rest of his facial features. He was nearly bald, the hair he had was white, and his forehead was wide and rounded. His nose was thin at the top and unusually wide at the bottom, his eyes small, I couldn't tell what color in the dark, and he had an air of intelligence about him.

"Where will we be going?" he asked.

"Did you pick up Sally Allison and her family at Sally's home this morning?"

"Yes."

"Same place."

He looked at me, surprised. "Are you related?"

"No. There's a cottage I rent from her."

"There are guards. They won't let us up."

"They will. Their name is Chet. I have privileges." I had to smile. This was a man who had to be on his guard against people who claimed to belong places they didn't actually belong. "There is a way to get there on back streets, to come up from outside town."

He nodded, as if he was familiar. "Are you in the business?" he asked. "An actress?"

"No, but thank you for thinking that was a possibility. I'm the bartender at That Ship Has Sailed—known as the Battened Hatch—at MacTavish's Seaside Cottage. If you're ever up there and have a few minutes break, come on in and I'll be happy to comp you."

"How do you know Rise?"

"Childhood buddies," I said.

He nodded, as if that was a new one.

We were sitting in the dark, without lights or motor. It would have been easy to spot movement if anyone was near or watching the car. So far, so good.

The front seat was impeccably clean. The only personal touch was a photograph of a woman and two young girls. "Is that your family?" I asked.

His initial reaction was almost a recoil.

"I'm sorry, I don't mean to pry."

"No, no, it's all right. Yes. My family, yes. Donata and my girls, Calista and Emilia."

"The girls look so spirited and full of life."

"Yes," he said.

I left it alone. We sat in the quiet night for five minutes until Con and Rise appeared from the side of the vehicle.

Before they reached for the door, Castor said, "Emilia died of cancer. It's hard for me to talk about. I appreciate your asking." Then he popped the switch to unlock the back.

Con held a carry-on bag, and Rise pulled a suitcase. I got the feeling that usually Castor would pop the trunk, but we were making an escape under cover of darkness, so they quietly stuffed the luggage inside the limo and climbed in.

Con got back out.

"Where's Avalon?"

"I'm here," I said, climbing out of the front seat. Con herded me into the back. I was getting used to being herded. This was the first time I was making an escape under cover of darkness, however, and I planned to enjoy it.

Castor turned on the motor and running lights but didn't turn on the lights in the back. He chose to leave through the back entrance to the property. It wasn't a shortcut, I'll say that. But nothing followed us. The drive to Cherry Lane was twice as long as it needed to be, but when we finally turned in, the street and environs were quiet.

Sure enough, Chet 2 was up, having a cup of cocoa and watching the stars.

"Hi, Chet," I said. "It's me. And I have a friend. I think you know the driver. He's just dropping me and Rise off."

"Send me Rise's photo."

I sent a photo of Rise and Con leaning together, and he waved us up. I imagined Castor shrugging at the discovery that I was telling the truth.

We pulled up to the hidden parking area and disembarked. Con went forward to confer with the driver. Rise leaned over to one of the consoles and opened a panel that blended in. A manila envelope was inside, and he pulled it out to find his name typed on a sticker on the front. He gave an unhappy sigh. Then he reached in and pulled out a small packet. He shoved both into his carry-on.

"What?" I asked.

"My agent often uses this as a private mailbox," he said, his tone far from enthusiastic. "Nothing that can't wait until tomorrow."

We clambered out.

Up ahead, one chandelier was lit in the main lodge, which gave the place a rustic glow.

"That's Sally's place?" asked Rise with a hint of awe in his voice.

"Yes, indeed. You should see inside. It's been set designed."

The two old-fashioned streetlamps flickered along the lane. It was enough to guide the procession of Rise, Con, and myself to roll his luggage across the wooden footbridge that curtsied over the waterfall and stream. Once we reached the other side, Rise stopped.

"This is your place?"

"I rent it."

"Wow, Av, well done."

"You can thank Whistle." In fact, it was while walking Whistle I'd stumbled upon the place. Being reminded of poor Whistle, languishing in the dark, I hurriedly led the way around the side of the cottage to the back door, where I'd left a back light shining, punched my code into the lock, and opened the door. The small dog, rather than sulking, started immediately into her Joy of All Joys dance. She hardly stopped to pee, only slowed down a bit.

Rise laughed. "Who's this?"

"This is Whistle. Sally's grandson's dog. I'm dog-sitting while they're at MacTavish's."

I turned on the lights and my guests followed me in. At least, I had assumed Con was also a guest. However, unlike normal company, Con went from room to room, checking any hiding places, making sure windows and doors were locked.

"Clear," they said. Then, to Rise, "You sure you're okay here till morning?"

"I think we made a clean getaway," he responded. Rise turned to me. "Con's going to stay in my original suite, in case there are any unexpected visitors."

"If anyone breaks in, I'll be waiting," said Con.

"Good thinking," I said. As if I knew what represented good thinking in these situations. It sounded like as good a reason as any to stay in an available suite.

Rise gave them a hug and said, "Thanks for everything."

"See you in the morning."

And they were gone, back to the limo where Castor waited.

And Rise and I were here, in my house.

My Rise. Actually, my Crispin. Which led me back to, "God, I'm sorry I said that about your nose. I don't know what I was thinking. You obviously have a great nose. I'm like, mortified. Please forgive me."

Rise looked at me, and I could see his total exhaustion. "You're forgiven." There was the ghost of a smile. "I cried. Not afterwards, though that was miserable, for a lot longer than they said it would be. But before. I liked the way I was. I didn't want the surgery. It took Dirk and Dad together to manhandle me into the car. They threatened me with all kinds of things. Said I'd never act again."

"Oh, God, I'm really sorry. I can't even imagine. I liked you the way you were, too. Still, truth be told, the way you are now is not nothing."

He laughed out loud. "Point me to the guest room."

I showed him his room and bathroom.

Then I gave Whistle a late supper, which she was used to, and went into my room to change. I guessed it was safer to turn the lights off in the house, so if anyone got past Chet, they couldn't see in? I did so, climbed under the covers to hide from the new autumn chill, plugged in my phone and turned it on. The screen came to life in Instagram, the last place I'd searched: OliveZarkOConnor.

There was a new post: Olive in front of the poster for *Triple Jeopardy*. "Academy Award? I think so! But I'm biased. Honey's best work yet. O&R."

I guess since there was no restraining order, the police couldn't hold her. And they apparently couldn't hold on to Betina.

Damn. The vitriol in the tone behind Olive's final word played back to me. And she picked locks. I didn't want to think the worst, but I also didn't want to go in to wake Rise tomorrow and find him dead.

Damn. Why did I even let that thought into my head?

At least I had Whistle on my bed and on alert.

As I reached to pet her, she leapt to her feet, snarling at my bedroom door.

I sat up, quickly, looking for some sort of weapon, ready to roll out of bed on the side by the wall while I dialed 911.

It took only a moment to see that it was Rise.

"Hey," he said, in a voice devoid of any swagger.

"Hey," I answered.

"I am so very tired, Av," he said. "But I can't sleep. I can't get my body to relax. Every time I think I'm safe, someone has figured out how to get to me."

"I'm sorry." And I was. This didn't seem like the time to show him Olive's post on Instagram.

"Could I...would you mind...could I sleep in here with you? I promise I won't try anything."

To my mind, if you look up the dictionary definition of good news/bad news, those are the exact sentences you'd find.

"Get over here," I said.

He padded across the rug and pulled back the covers on the other side of the bed. He fell onto the sheets and was out cold.

Whistle did her little circle dance and laid down between our two sets of feet.

And that was the last thing I knew until morning.

SALTY GANG RIDES AGAIN

Ingredients

    1 1/2 oz tequila of your choice
2 oz grapefruit juice
Soda water
Kosher salt
2 small pinches ground cayenne pepper
Fresh sliced grapefruit

Method

On a small plate, pour a thin layer of kosher salt and a small dash of cayenne pepper. Mix together.
Rub fresh sliced grapefruit wedge around the edge of a Collins glass, then dip into cayenne salt mixture.
Fill a cocktail shaker with ice. Add tequila, grapefruit juice, and pinch of ground cayenne.
Shake ingredients together and pour into the Collins glass.
Top with soda water.
Use a fresh grapefruit slice to garnish side of glass.

9

LIGHT THE LIGHTS

I AM NOT pleased to admit that my first thought upon waking up next to Rise, who was snoring gently, was, *if only Philip could see me now.*

Part of what got me about the ashes of my relationship with Philip Young was my total misreading of the situation, of his character, of how clearly he saw me.

I thought he saw me all the way down to the bone. I thought he recognized positive things inside me and called me to be that person. I thought I recognized a goodness and a burning talent inside him.

I don't know what hurt more: that I had cared so deeply about him, or that he hadn't cared deeply at all about me. But what frightened me was that I could be so completely wrong about someone.

When Philip and I parted that last morning, I thought we were bonded, more than friends, souls that recognized each other. At which point he'd gone straight back to his girlfriend, Rachel.

That was months ago. Shortly after Philip had uttered our two-word uncoupling, ("I'm sorry") Rachel had left for the greener pastures of Saratoga, and Philip had left for the artistic climes of Paris, where his family had a flat, and where he'd attended art school.

I told myself I could appreciate his paintings, and even like his grandmother, without having feelings about him one way or the other.

But how did he deserve such a great little dog?

I got up, pulled on pants, let Whistle out back and gave her breakfast.

Then I took my phone and went out to the terrace to look up Marissa Marisol, feeling only slightly guilty for being remiss up to this point. IMDB had already added a death date. She was twenty-six. Her bio was basic; she was known for *The Hardy Boys* and *Rachel and Zoe* (playing neither Rachel nor Zoe). When I Googled her photos, it was clear she started acting as a little kid, maybe seven or eight, with guest starring roles, but nothing solid. A career in the middle that would now never soar.

I decided to run and get some chai and breakfast before Rise awoke. I was able to grab a sweatshirt and shoes without him stirring, and I set off down Cherry Lane toward the road.

It was a magical autumn day, one of those you wish you could catch by the tail and hold onto before the beast of time plunges ahead into winter.

I'd missed the breakfast rush, so it was quick to order. While I waited, I saw a sign announcing a news conference about the new arts complex outside of town. The time and the date led me to believe it was the press conference Addie had told me Jerry Raker had set up the day after Sally's movie premiere. I was curious. I did remember, though, that our current mayor, Art Bristow, was against it. This poster fit well into Avantika's business with all the truly arresting works of art on the wall. We did have a clear choice in who to elect. It wasn't like they were so much the same you couldn't choose.

Back home, Rise was still asleep and I couldn't bear to disturb him. It was possibly the first full night's sleep he'd had in quite a while. I did have to open the Battened Hatch for lunch in a couple of hours, so I showered and dressed.

The bed was empty when I came back through. Shortly thereafter, I heard the shower in the guest bathroom turn on.

I reheated the crepes and the chai and went outside to enjoy the brisk air.

"Hey," said Rise as he came out to join me. He wore black pants and had on a button-up shirt open over a fresh t-shirt.

"Hey," I said. "Did you sleep okay?"

"Best I've slept for a long time."

"I got us breakfast. I hope you like crepes. I got the Vermonter, which involves ham, cheddar and maple or my personal favorite, which involves bananas, coconut and cardamom. There are also muffins."

"Dear God, I might weep. That's it. I'm taking the next couple days off from my eating regimen and being a normal person. Throw me either crepe. They both sound great, and I'm starving."

We ate and chatted about nothing deep, simply enjoying the kind of golden air that surrounds you when you're truly happy to be with someone. I didn't know what I'd expected, but he was still Rise, my Rise, and we were tickled to be together. For any fear I had about trusting my instincts, our old friendship was one thing I was reading right.

Once we were fed and relaxed, Rise asked about the death of our friend Winsome, one of the original Salty Gang. It's never easy to lose someone to addiction, especially when you try so hard to help.

"I loved him, for sure. I'm so sorry I was away for the funeral," said Rise. "It must have been hard for you, trying so hard, and then being the one to find him." He put his hand gently over mine. "How about everybody else? What do you know about them?"

I knew that Kelsey was in real estate and Jasmine went to med school but left to join Americorps. She now worked at a national animal shelter that pledged to make kill shelters obsolete. "I think Troy is acting."

"I think so, too," said Rise. "I feel like I should know more about him than I do. He's looked me up now and again."

I found his page on IMBD and found guest spots on several long-running series. "I guess he is also pursuing his passion. That leaves me, collecting stories in an Olympic town in upstate New York and paying the rent by bartending."

"You were always collecting stories," he said. "Or we were making them up. That's what I loved about you. Your curiosity and imagination."

"Thanks. It's what I loved about you, too. And your kindness."

"I try."

"Is this what you imagined you'd be doing?" I asked. "Or is it beyond your wildest dreams?"

"The career is fine, though the only thing my manager and agent agree on is that my next move is crucial. They just see that move completely differently. Is this what I imagined I'd be doing? Maybe. Is this what I thought my life would be like? Is this who I thought I'd be?" He paused and looked at his hands. "I don't know."

"I didn't know your dad and your manager were so heavy-handed with your career."

"Yeah," he said. "When I first said I wanted to act—and it was my idea, originally—my dad quit his job to shuttle me to auditions and Mom began working 12-hour days at her salon to meet the mortgage and my travel expenses and acting lessons and stuff. Finally, Dad had to go back to work. Thank god, you know? I was ready to throw in the towel. I was only a kid and the few gigs I got didn't seem worth all the rejection.

"But then Dad found Dirk and Dirk found an agent. Acting lessons and auditioning became my full-time job.

"Dad had a construction company, if you recall, and work wasn't exactly steady. I came downstairs once in the middle of the night, and found Dad several martinis in. He told me it was up to me, if I wanted my mom to be able to work less than ten hours a day, six days a week, I had to start bringing in the dough. Or I'd have to leave St. Albans, we'd lose the house and she'd lose her hair salon. The salon was hers. She'd worked so hard to make a name for herself.

"I remember going to back to bed and not being able to breathe."

"God, Rise, this was when we were still at St. Alban's? I wish you could have told me."

"I didn't feel like I could tell anyone. Mom was great, she checked in with me to make sure acting was still what I wanted to do. She never gave me any kind of ultimatums. Looking back, of course, if Dad's job plus Mom working decent hours wasn't enough, we should have gotten a smaller house. I could have gone to public school."

"It shouldn't have been on you, that's for certain."

"When I became a Disney kid, doing guest shots, and then being cast in *Jessica, For Sure*, I was relieved. Maybe now Dirk and Dad would let up. Maybe there would be enough coming in that we'd be okay. But it was only two years until Melanie—she was the star— blazed out. We all saw it coming. It was kind of a relief when it finally happened.

"Dirk knew I was in the running for *Owning It*, the superhero series. To this day, I don't know if Disney said or implied anything about my looks. I'm positive they'd deny it...but I did get cast quickly after we got back from the clinic and the aftercare facility with a new nose."

"Still, that must have been rough."

"Yeah. It was. I felt like they were taking away the one thing that made me different. Made me, me. But, as you said, I guess the result is not nothing."

I grinned. "You can hold onto that. On me. So, how are your parents?"

"Oh. Dad died, unexpectedly, of a heart attack. Two years ago."

"I hadn't heard. I'm sorry."

"Do you remember my mother?" His eyes went soft and his tone became gentle. "My parents were older when they had me. They'd given up on having kids, honestly. Mom was in her forties, and Dad in his fifties when I came along."

"I do remember your mom. When we were in elementary school, she came in to read to us on parent days. I remember her hair was so pretty. She always stooped down to our level to talk to us. Her eyes were shiny, somehow. Friendly."

"Yes. That was before Dad's drinking, and the troubles."

I laughed. "Sorry. You're the first one I've heard refer to starring in a Disney series as 'the troubles.'"

He laughed, too. "I meant troubles at home."

"Yeah, I figured. So, your mom. Is she..?"

"Alive? Yes. But she has been diagnosed with dementia. It's still in early stages, and hopefully won't progress, or won't progress too fast. But it's terrified both of us. Not that we've talked about it."

"When was the last time you saw her?"

He calculated. "Four months ago?"

This time, I covered his hand with my own.

"Do you remember *my* mom?" I asked.

Rise's laugh was unaffected. "How could anyone not remember your mom? It was like a party every time she came to class. She was so vibrant and fun. I always had the feeling Miss Hastings hushed her as much—or more—than she hushed us! And when she read stories to us!"

"All the voices," I said.

"All the voices. It was a production. It was grand."

"Grand," I repeated.

His phone buzzed silently with a text and he shielded his eyes from the sun to read it.

"Okay. Here we go."

"What's up?"

"Dirk found out where I am from Con. He wants to come over this afternoon. I'd better read the damn script."

"Do you have a photo of Dirk for me to show Chet? I can do it on my way to work."

"Yes, sure. What's your number?"

I told him, and he messaged me the photo. The simple act of him typing in my number and my phone receiving his text made me happy. Even if he left now, we were officially back in touch.

"When do you have to leave? Can you stay to see *Salty Sally and Pepper: Truth Be Told*?"

"I'd sure like to. I don't need to be anywhere for a few days. And, boy, I love hiding away here at your place. It would be great to never have to leave, to have disappeared. Poof!" He made a disappearing into smoke motion with his hands. "Sorry, I realize that sounds presumptuous. What do you have going on? I didn't mean to invite myself to stay! I can leave with Dirk later today."

"Don't you dare. Hideaways are us." I stood to get ready. "I'll put Dirk on the list."

"Thanks, Av."

We both grabbed our plates and cups and headed inside—he to get his script, me to get ready for work.

On my way out, I found him in the living room, settling in to read. I checked my phone, and in doing so found my last search.

"By the way, did you know her?" I asked, showing a photo of Marissa to Rise.

He saw the photo and looked at it. For the briefest moment, something flashed behind his eyes. "I don't think so. Who is she?"

"Her name is Marissa Marisol. She was found dead in the movie theater on Tuesday."

"Seriously? Wow. What happened? She looks young."

"Twenty-six," I said.

"Damn."

"And they don't know what happened yet," I said.

"Maybe everyone should hide out up here at your place," Rise offered.

Neither of us knew how prescient that remark truly was.

"Okay, I'm heading off. Make yourself at home. See you later."

"Will do. Thanks again, Avalon." Rise put on reading glasses and picked up the script.

One of the first patrons to sit at the bar once we opened was Castor the limo driver, taking me up on my offer. He wore a suit jacket and open-collared shirt.

"You do work here," he said.

"Yes, indeed. What can I get you to drink?" I asked.

"Can't drink," he said. "Occasions like this film festival, I can be called upon any time—like last night, for example. Already heading for bed, and the young man needs to go to your place. So, no drinking. No one can forget what happened to Diana."

I suppose if you are a professional driver, you'd think of the car crash that killed the British princess from a different perspective.

I showed him the current specials that were mixed drinks, therefore complex flavors, but non-alcoholic, and he selected Light the Lights. "Can I get you some wings?" I asked.

"I'd prefer a salad."

"Take your pick."

I put in the order, made the drink, and went to check our current stock of bottles. I put more champagne, sparkling and white wine in the fridge, and was surprised to find how low we were on chilled vodka, though given the crowds coming through, it made sense. What to do? You can always make cold vodka drinks with ice, but for vodka martinis, I am a purist: take ice cold vodka, a bow towards the vermouth (or, as Churchill counseled, toward France), and olives of choice. I knew better than to try to put anything in a refrigerator or freezer in the kitchen under the auspices of Chef Angelica, so I grabbed bottles of our three most requested vodkas, five bottles altogether, slid quietly through the kitchen, and carefully down the steps to the basement.

Once there, the automatic sensor cued overhead lights to flash on. I turned left toward the walk-in freezer, set down two of the bottles to free up my right hand, and pulled open the door. I made certain to leave the door open as I set the vodka bottles on a shelf inside it, then turned back for the other two bottles.

They were gone.

As I went to investigate, a voice said, "Thanks for getting me locked up. Let's see how you like it."

I had only the briefest sighting of Betina, her face contorted with fury, before the freezer door slammed shut. She was short, and must have stood on tip-toe to look through the circular window. She smiled. Then she was gone.

In one moment, my day had gone from ordinary to cold.
Very cold.
I pulled violently on the door. It was locked from outside.
Very locked.

LIGHT THE LIGHTS

Non-Alcoholic Cocktail

Ingredients

2 oz AMASS Non-Alcoholic Riverine
1 teaspoon of Small Town Cultures Lemon Curd (on
Amazon and elsewhere)
Sparkling Water
Blood Orange Slices (for garnish)
Fresh Sage (for garnish)

Method

In cocktail shaker add AMASS Riverine Non-Alcoholic
Spirit with ice and Small Town Cultures Lemon Curd,
shake ingredients together and pour into Collins glass.
Fill the rest of the glass with sparking water.
Add blood oranges and fresh sage as a garnish.

10

LEAVES ME COLD

I STOOD FOR a moment in shock.

Betina had obviously turned her focus to me. How long had she been lying in wait?

Had she been planning to hurt me, or was the freezer a happy surprise for her?

Most important, what should I do?

I dug my phone out of my pocket and prayed as hard as I'd ever prayed that there would be a bar, or even half a bar of service, that the metal walls of the freezer would not entrap me.

There were none. I tried calling Marta, anyway. No service. I tried texting, hoping against hope that a few words might slip through.

Fail.

Take a breath. Then take a minute to think things through. Calm down.

What were the chances I'd be found today? What were the chances someone else would come to get something out of the freezer?

Surely Chef Angelica had the supplies she needed for tonight's dinner already upstairs. There was a chance she might need to begin defrosting something, some pork belly or something, for later in the week. But there were two large freezers upstairs that likely held the things she was working with in the immediate future.

Don't panic. Assess the situation.

There were two things working against me: the cold, and the limited amount of oxygen.

What I remembered about being shut into a freezer (yes, I'd had this conversation, perhaps in jest, but I'd had it) was not to breathe deeply, as every breath replaced oxygen with carbon monoxide. Once the oxygen was gone, it was Game Over.

The other was, stay warm. Don't sit on the cold metal floor. Build a shelter. Find some kind of blanket. Put something over your head, if you have to tear off your own shirtsleeve to do it.

But first...do everything humanly possible to get out.

I exhaled and saw my breath as icy air. Even the inside of my nose was cold.

Getting out was such a priority, I'd give up a good bit of oxygen to give it a go.

I walked over to the door, where the small window sat at the height of a head a bit taller than mine. As I stood on my toes and peered out, the lights in the basement room flickered and went out. That meant Betina must have returned upstairs and there was no longer any movement to trip the sensors. Great.

I pulled on the door lock again. The handle didn't turn.

Next, I felt the sealing strips that hung down and kept the freezer closed tight. Sometimes they got stuck in the door and kept it from sealing, and therefore, from shutting completely.

Unfortunately, not the case.

Shit, shit, shit.

Last shot, but a good one: there should be a panic button. For times such as these. Times exactly as these.

As I wondered where one would place a panic button, the lights inside the freezer flickered once. Flickered twice. Went off. The freezer lights, apparently, were not on a motion sensor. They went on when the freezer door was opened, and off ten minutes later.

Fantastic.

My phone battery was at 60 percent. I turned on the flashlight feature and looked around the door. I had almost given up when I saw a round white button that glowed in the dark. Could it be?

I pushed it, I mean, really leaned on it, with my hand. It didn't move. I tried it again, with both hands. It was freezing, this button, which meant the shaft didn't press in at all. Even trying made my hands cold.

Seriously? A panic button that could freeze and not work? In a freezer?

I tried warming it with my hands and going after it again. Nothing.

I stood there in the cold, shivering.

Then I used some of my much-needed oxygen.

I screamed. And screamed again. Ending with, "Marta! Angelica! Help!"

I looked through the round porthole out into the dark basement, and I pictured scenes from countless movies in which a person screams through a porthole in space, under the sea, in the hospital, in a basement, and the camera pulls back from outside the door and you see them screaming, but you hear...nothing.

I screamed three times. Then I got a grip.

Okay. What materials were here to sit on, to make a shelter, to make a head covering? Thankfully, I was wearing long pants and long sleeves.

There was an apron on a peg. That was all I saw. I guessed I could roll up in it and conserve body heat. For the moment, I tied it around my head, not letting that 10% of body heat escape.

I wanted to sit down, but there weren't any good choices. Frozen metal floor, frozen metal shelves. Ah, in a corner, there was a cardboard box of something. It was from a restaurant food service, as it only had numbers printed on it.

I went and sat on the cardboard box.

Who knew I was here?

No one. I hadn't even told Marta. I thought I could grab the bottles, run them down, and be back in a matter of minutes.

How long would it take for Marta to wonder where I'd gone?

I shivered, hugging myself tight, and remembered the first time

I'd met Marta, when she had no idea where the Battened Hatch's bartender, Joseph, had gone.

He was found dead.

May I not suffer the same fate.

Certainly, if I was gone long enough, and my phone went straight to voicemail, someone would figure out something was up. Someone would come looking for me.

But how would they think to look in the walk-in freezer?

Freezing is not how I want to go. As a matter of fact, the route to freezing was becoming very unpleasant, already.

Betina, really?

She was free, and she was vindictive. It's not that I didn't understand how she might be angry at me. I had, after all, walked her into a trap. I hadn't known, exactly, that we'd get within 100 feet of Rise, and that the police would be waiting. But I knew that they knew she was coming, and they wouldn't let her get to him. Something was going to have to happen.

If Betina was vindictive and free, and capable of killing someone, the next obvious person could be Rise. Mike Spaulding thought she'd left town, possibly left the state.

Not so.

I wanted to cry. I hugged myself tighter. My teeth began to chatter.

I hadn't really talked to my mother, even when I saw her at Mormor's funeral. It seemed like she knew I wasn't ready and gave me space. Losing her mother and her only child within months of each other, that would be terrible for her.

Would my father even care?

Fuck it. I wasn't going to die.

Well, I mean, of course I'm going to die, everyone is going to die.

Just not now. Not like this.

I stood up, went to the door again, ran my hands around it. Looked again at the panic button. The frozen panic button. I wondered again about the point of having a panic button if it didn't work when you needed it to.

I needed it to.

I looked at it more closely. It looked less like a panic button that would set off an alarm than an inside release button.

Okay, you freaking inside release button.

I turned on my flashlight app again and went back to the shelves. There was a leg of lamb. Or leg of something. It was frozen solid, rock hard.

I picked it up.

I ran at the inside release button, holding it aloft. Then I battered that damn button with every fiber of my body. Again and again and again.

The last time, the white button budged. It slid in.

There was a hiss.

The door opened.

Just a little bit.

I pushed through that sucker and ran out into the hallway.

The lights, which I assumed were confused by this turn of events, blinked to life.

Fuck. Fuck. Fuck.

My heart was beating a million miles a minute.

I looked around for the other three bottles of vodka. They were nowhere to be seen.

Not only had freaking Betina tried to kill me, she had stolen my vodka.

I stood, panting, with tears running down my cheeks.

I'd really thought I was done for.

I knew I should close the freezer door behind me, but I couldn't do it. What if I got sucked back in somehow?

Still shaking, I walked heavily up the basement steps, sounding like Frankenstein's monster, even to myself.

I pushed through the door and walked out into the kitchen.

A sous chef saw me first.

Chef Angelica saw me next.

Everyone who saw me stopped what they were doing.

"Rise O'Connor's stalker locked me in the goddamn freezer," I said.

Angelica, despite my appearance, and the fact I was trembling violently, had only one question: "Why are you carrying my leg of lamb?"

LEAVES ME COLD

Ingredients

    1 1/2 oz coffee flavored rum (Ron Colón or other)
Matcha green tea powder
5 oz coconut milk
Raw granulated sugar (for rimming)
Crushed red peppercorns (rimming)
Fresh mint leaf
Coupe glass

Method

Mix the sugar and red peppercorns on a plate.
Pour a small portion of the coconut milk in a bowl wide
enough to fit the coupe glass.
Dip the coupe glass in the coconut milk to wet the rim,
then dip it into sugar and red peppercorn mixture.
In a cocktail shaker, add the coffee flavored rum, ice,
matcha green tea powder and coconut milk.
Shake all ingredients together and strain into coupe glass.
Finish with a fresh mint sprig for garnish.

11

PUZZLE PIECES

THEY ASKED IF they should call 911.

I said no. I didn't want just any old police officer to come demanding explanations.

I handed the leg of lamb to the sous chef. "The freezer door is still open," I said.

Then I headed for the Battened Hatch. On my way I took out my phone, which now had three bars of service. I stopped just before I swung through the door and found Rise's number. I texted, *Betina is still in town and she's dangerous.*

Thanks for the heads up, came the quick reply.

She locked me in the walk-in freezer at work.

WTF?????

I'm okay.

Should I come?

For God's sake, that's the last thing you should do.

I then dialed Investigator Mike Spaulding.

"Avalon. What's up?" he asked.

"Betina Popescu didn't leave town," I answered. And I filled him in on what had happened.

Like the kitchen workers, Marta stopped cold when she saw me. "What happened to you?" she asked. I checked the time on my phone. I'd been gone twenty-five minutes.

I nodded to Marta to follow me into the women's room. It's small, with three stalls and posters telling you which drinks to ask for if you want someone at the bar to help you make a getaway from the jerk you're drinking with.

"How terrible do I look?" I asked.

"Your skin...is white," she said. "I mean, like drained of blood."

I explained what happened.

"Holy shit," she said. "Did you call somebody?"

"Mike Spaulding. He should be here soon."

"Do you want to go home?"

"I'm basically all right. Let me talk to Mike and see how I'm feeling."

Mike Spaulding arrived within ten minutes, two crime scene investigators trailing behind. I took them down to the freezer, and we left the CSI women there, taking prints.

"Should we call EMS to check you out?" one of them asked.

"Naw, too late for that. I'm doing fine," I said. The first part was true.

"Can you talk to me up at the Battened Hatch?" I asked Mike. "We're getting busy."

"Yeah, okay."

We went back upstairs. He sat at the bar, on the stool recently occupied by Castor. I told Marta I'd cover the drink orders that spit out of the POS machine from the floor. Having drinks to make focused my mind and my hands and I began to warm up.

I told Mike exactly what had happened. He didn't ask me to wait to tell the story until the local police arrived. I wondered if that meant he suspected Marissa Marisol's death and Rise's stalkers were linked somehow, which would make the information pivotal to his own investigation.

"Are you putting Rise O'Connor's stalkers together with what happened to Marissa Marisol in the theater?" I asked.

"The pieces don't fit, exactly," he said. "But they do look like they come from the same puzzle."

"Is anyone on the lookout for Betina?" I asked. "She doesn't seem to be in a healthy state of mind."

"There's a BOLO," he said. "Do you feel safe here?"

"The place is hopping," I said. "I feel okay for now."

"We'll put extra security around," he said.

"Will you let the film festival's security, and Rise O'Connor's security, know that Betina is still out and about?"

"Yes," he said. I saw the thought occur to him. "Have you met Rise O'Connor? Are you in contact with him?"

"I've talked about Betina with his security, Con Allred," I sidestepped. "As you may know, I was unwittingly involved in the plot to get Betina picked up."

"I'm sure Mr. O'Connor is an upstanding person," Investigator Spaulding said. "But between you and me, if you run into him, don't trust him completely."

"What? Why?"

"Looking for a nexus," he said. "That's all."

For the first time since we'd met, I didn't tell Mike everything I knew.

Two members of our local police force did arrive then, and I led them back downstairs, noting how easily someone could slip in and out the kitchen's back door, which was now held open by a chair for ventilation. The stairs to the basement were only feet from the exit, designed to make deliveries easier.

Tranquility has a police force of nine, suitable for a town of our size. However, there's a large State Police barracks and training center ten miles outside of town, and if anything of consequence happens, the State Police help out. Or jump in. Or take over. Depends on who you're talking to.

The CSI folks had already fingerprinted the door handle and the metal railing by the stairs and left. It felt odd after talking to Mike, an investigator with the State Police who wore street clothes, to be talking to these two uniformed patrol officers. Something about holsters and guns as signs of locked and loaded masculinity put me on edge. But I did describe, yet again, how Betina's story intersected mine, with disturbing consequences.

"I didn't know the plan," I said, referencing the arrest. "But I can see how Betina thought I did."

Another call came in and the officers headed out.

I went back to work.

While talking to Mike and mixing drinks, I'd been too busy to keep an eye on the crowd. I returned to find Addie Moon, Jerry Raker, Brent Davis and Isobel Lester back at Table 11. I hardly remembered the time, only days earlier, when I'd been awed by the Hollywood power on display at that table.

Now I marched over, pulled up a fifth chair and leaned in.

"So," I said. "Rise O'Connor's stalker, Betina, whom I walked into a trap and got arrested, is free and mad as hell and just tried to kill me by locking me in the walk-in freezer."

Conversation stopped.

"Oh my God," said Isobel.

"She's mad. She thinks I did it on purpose."

"Avalon, holy shit! I'm sorry," said Addie. "Has anyone called the authorities?"

"Of course we've freaking called the authorities. I know you work for Rise, and not for the general population—like me—but did it ever occur to you there might be collateral damage? Like another human being?" I never imagined I could get this mad at Addie, but I was livid.

Addie stood up and looked meaningfully at Jerry and Isobel, in an "I'll handle this," kind of way.

"I didn't appreciate being an unwitting accomplice."

"Is there somewhere we can talk?" she asked me.

Where to go so we wouldn't be observed by the Betinas and Olives of the world?

I took Addie down the hall and unlocked the storeroom, relocking it behind us, and turning on the lights.

"Sorry," she said. "Tell me what happened."

I repeated the story.

"Good heavens, Avalon. I'm really sorry you got dragged into this."

"Look, I realize I got myself involved by texting you about

Betina. And I also know that if you'd told me the plan, I would have chosen to help. Probably acting more nervous. Still, please, let me know what's going on in the future. I don't want to take any more risks blindly. I mean, I'll take risks, especially if it will help Rise, but not blindly."

"You're right. I'm sorry. I knew Con would think of something, and we didn't have long to set it up."

"Let's hope the cops find Betina before anything more happens. At least now, I hope they can hold her for doing something more than violating parole."

"They should be able to."

"So, what's going on with the publicity for *Salty Sally and Pepper: Truth Be Told*? Did the photos of Sally in the lobby make much of a stir?"

"Yes. A big stir, as hoped. We now have most of the networks and entertainment shows attending both the screening and the news conference/brunch afterwards. Usually pulling off something like this has Jerry happy and in his sweet spot. I think because it's his documentary and book, he's more anxious."

"Why is Isobel still here?"

"She's not leaving without a signed contract from Rise. It's top secret, but it does involve the Marvel universe. She's got big plans for him, going forward."

"I hear his manager wants him to go another way?"

"I've heard that, too. Having too many great choices is actually a tough thing. This Isobel/Dirk feud has been simmering for years. Seems it's finally coming to a boil. Anyway, Isobel is flying out today from the local airport. She does have to see to other clients."

The local airport was small, servicing private planes and commuter flights.

Unexpectedly, my knees buckled. The adrenaline keeping me upright drained from my body. I put a hand on the wall to steady myself.

"I think you've got to go home," said Addie.

"Yeah, I think so too. I truly hope it all goes well for you guys tomorrow. See you then."

"It will. Sally deserves her happy Hollywood ending."

"So do you. This isn't only Jerry and Brent's film."

"True that. And thanks."

My phone buzzed with a text alert.

Sorry to bother you, but my manager needs to bring me a contract. With everything going on, I'm kind of afraid to leave your place. Is there any way Dirk can come up?

Damn! I'd promised Rise I'd leave a photo of Dirk and I'd totally forgotten.

The lunch rush was over. I had no more energy or chutzpah to get me through the afternoon. But how to get out of here without being seen or followed should random stalkers be peppered about?

After Addie went back to her table, I stayed in the empty hall. I took out my phone and called Hannah. Usually, I'm hesitant to ask for help. But when she answered, I blurted, "Whatever you're doing, can you get out of it? I need a ride home."

PUZZLE PIECES

Non-Alcoholic Cocktail
Ingredients
A few droplets of Amoretti Jamaican Rum Extract Water
Soluble
5 oz Passion Fruit Juice
Passion Fruit (cut fruit open and scoop out the seeds set
aside for garnish)
Fresh Ground Cinnamon
Fresh Ground Nutmeg
Fresh Ground Turmeric
Method
In cocktail shaker add ice, a few droplets of Amoretti
Rum Extract, passion fruit juice, a pinch each of cinna-
mon, nutmeg and turmeric.
Shake all ingredients together and pour into rocks glass or
Collins glass.
Add fresh passion fruit seeds as a floater.

12

THE GANG'S ALL HERE

HANNAH PICKED ME up at the back door by the hotel dumpsters. I didn't see anyone around. She barely needed to slow down for me to jump into the back seat of the car and lie down on the seat.

I had her drive out of town going the opposite direction of my cottage, then double back when we were sure the coast was clear. We drove through the next town over and approached my place from the small roads that led into Tranquility, not the main road through town. There was no way Betina—or anyone else—could keep up without us noticing. I gave her the story highlights as we went.

"It's never boring being your friend," she said.

An Aston Martin with an Enterprise rental sticker on it was idling by the turn in to Cherry Lane. I panicked momentarily, then remembered I said I'd meet Rise's manager, Dirk, here to let him in. I hopped out and we walked together to chat with Chet, then Dirk got in his car and went roaring up the lane ahead of me.

"Do you have many more people coming?" asked Chet. "We weren't expecting a whole crew."

"I wasn't expecting this many, either. This is the last, that I know of."

I got back into the car. Chet One waved me and Hannah through. We drove up the lane and out of sight into the glade, where she paused to let me out. Dirk was already parked and rushing up the hill to get to his client.

"Well, you've had a harrowing day," Hannah said.

"Can you come up to the house?"

"I need to pick up mama and baby from the hospital, but I can stop back after," she said. "I need to hear the whole, complete story of what's going on."

"Great. I'm feeling kind of funky, and took the night shift off, so stay for dinner if you can. There's someone I'd like you to meet."

"Sure. I can do that. Someone who's got business with that nervous guy you just vouched for?"

"Well, yeah."

Hannah did a double take as she started the car's engine again. "Wait, did you say you took the night off? Are you the real Avalon? You haven't been replaced by aliens?"

The truth was, Marta and Manuela together forbade me to come back. With all other hands on deck, they swore they had the night covered. Marta promised on a stack of coasters that she'd call me if she needed me.

Aw, was all I could think about my protégé. *They grow up so fast.*

I trudged up through the glade and across the footbridge. Through the living room window, I could see Rise involved in an intense conversation with the infamous Dirk, who was old enough to be his father. He had loosened his tie, but his muscles remained taut. The energy that piped through him forced him to pace around Rise, who stood solidly in one place. Both were talking, each intent on making his point.

Rise saw me and gave a short wave, which caused Dirk to look out to see who was coming. I gave him a nod, then left them to it and continued around to come in through the back door.

I came into the kitchen, said hello to Whistle, and put on the kettle. There was nothing like pretending to be British and having high tea to help you imagine circumstances other than the current ones.

"You know what I think." The man's voice was as taut as his muscles. "And it's come to the place we always knew it would. Me or Isobel. I can't work with that controlling harridan one more day. Ask yourself who got you here. Who has been with you for ten years.

Who is...who has been a father to you." Dirk let his voice crack, as if with emotion. Nice move. Expected, but well played. "I'll head out. You've got till tomorrow to decide. The choice is pretty clear."

"Thanks, Dirk. I appreciate it. You know I do."

"Then sign the damn contracts."

"You said I have till tomorrow."

"You're doing this to make me twist in the wind, aren't you? Just like you always did. You enjoy watching me suffer."

"Yes, I enjoy watching you suffer." This said with an ironic sigh.

"I wish you were still young enough..."

"I know you do. We'll talk tomorrow."

I turned around to politely say farewell to Dirk as he exited through the kitchen, but he threw the front door open and made his exit that way. Alrighty, then.

The kettle whistled as Rise joined me in the kitchen.

"Tea?" I asked.

"Green, please."

I chose mugs, added tea bags and poured the water. As I put them in to steep, Rise turned me around and pulled me to him. Then he gave me a giant bear hug.

"God, Av, I am so sorry about what happened," he said.

I melted into his embrace. I hadn't realized how much I needed the safety of someone's arms. I got the feeling he needed a safety net right about now, also. We stood together for a good minute.

"It was Betina?"

I nodded. "On the plus side, you don't have to worry about not finding a mate. I personally know of two people ready to marry you on the spot. And children! One wants smart kids, one wants a baseball team."

We took our tea outside to the back terrace and sat down. Whistle, happy for the company, curled in my lap.

"They aren't playing around, are they, your stalkers? She locked me into the restaurant freezer and left me there. I could have died."

Rise cupped his hand over mine. "I'm so sorry. Now you know

why I can't be seen in public with anyone. If anything had happened to you..."

"How do you cope?"

Rise sighed. "No one knows this except Con...I flew east from L.A. a few days early and rented a cabin, to clear my head. The last night I was there, someone broke in. Didn't take anything, didn't hurt me. Watched me sleep. Left a lipstick heart."

I got goosebumps. "Watched you sleep? No wonder you felt better in a room with someone else last night. Did I tell you I talked to Olive, while she was waiting to be taken in by the police? She told me she learned to pick locks. That she enjoys watching you sleep."

"Fuck. But I'm not surprised. It's so hard, Av. It's hard not to let the threat leak through the corners of your life, till the outer boundary melts away, and all you feel is threatened."

"I can't imagine."

"Hopefully, things are coming to a head here, and we can get some of the threat neutralized."

"I sure hope so. I know that I, for one, do not care to run into Betina again." We sat, sipping. "Oh! I forgot we were having a British tea. Would you like some cookies? Or a muffin?"

"No, thanks. I'm not allowed to eat sugar. Or carbs. I know I said I was taking a few days off, but depending on which project I commit to next, it would be more pain to work off what I enjoy eating than to simply not eat it."

"Do you always have to keep your abdomen in shape? Keep a six pack? I'd think that is actor abuse."

Rise laughed. "No, thank God. The regimen for a six pack is grueling and unsustainable. But I have to be six-pack ready."

"Can I ask what your choices are for the next project?"

"Will you sign an NDA?"

It took me a minute, until he laughed at my consternation, to realize he wasn't serious. His shoulders released some tension. "It's pretty much a decision between Green Screen Universe—I mean,

Marvel—and committing to untold seasons of a Netflix series as a romantic lead. Well, three seasons is standard for the Flix."

"So, Isobel wants you to choose Marvel and Dirk is angling for Netflix."

He nodded.

I sipped tea and sat back. "I would never, ever want to get caught between—what was it Landon called them? ThunderGlove and Dirk, Incorporated?"

Rise raised his mug as if for a toast.

"On the other hand...first world problems if I've ever heard them."

"Exactly. I'm going to lose either my agent or my manager. Lots of anxiety and nothing I dare complain about."

"You know, it makes me wonder about Troy. Salty Gang Troy. I didn't know he was still making a go of it as an actor. I wonder if he looks at you and is envious."

"I'd love to know what kind of stuff he's been doing. Troy is the man. He always seemed to have more common sense than the rest of us put together. This business is tough, really tough. It's nothing to be embarrassed about if you don't break out of the pack. Actually, the guest starring credits he has, says he's in the pack. You have to have an agent to get television work."

Rise and I knew that to be true. 98% of the people who try to make a living as an actor, don't. Growing up with my mom, as successful as she is, let me see first-hand the anxiety and the hustle involved even when you're in that two percent.

"Troy has come to see me a couple of times. Like when there was a premiere in San Francisco. Once when I was doing a charity gig in San Diego."

"Yeah? How was he?"

"It was one of those awkward few minutes of 'hello' time when there were lots of people around. I really have no idea how he is."

"You don't think he was hoping...you could help him somehow, do you? With his career?"

Rise looked surprised at the suggestion. "I hope not. He didn't say anything. It never entered my mind."

Rise's phone buzzed with a text.

He read it, looked up, and smiled. "How serious were you when you said Landon could stay here, too?"

"Sure," I said. "Any friend of yours..."

Rise texted.

"When will he be here?"

"He's down chatting with Chet One as we speak."

"I'll go get him." I hoped I sounded calm as I stood. I couldn't dart inside to brush my hair and refresh my lipstick for Landon, not in front of Rise.

Instead, I walked around the side of the house and crossed the bridge over the waterfall.

As I did, I got out my own phone, and texted Hannah.

"You've got to come for supper. Trust me on this."

THE GANG'S ALL HERE

(This drink is strong, please sip responsibly)

Ingredients

1/2 oz of tequila blanco
1/2 oz vodka
1/2 oz gin
1/2 oz white rum
1/2 oz Chambord
4 oz sour mix
Splash lemon lime soda
Fresh lemon slice (garnish)

Method

Fill a pint glass with ice. Add all ingredients and gently
stir with cocktail spoon.
Add lemon on glass or squeeze into cocktail.

13

HIDING OUT

LANDON PRESSER HAD a black carry-on bag and a matching medium suitcase, neither of which he let me take charge of as we went up the lane and into the private glen.

"This is the last person I'm clearing to come up," I said to Chet. "Promise."

"It would be good if that was true." Chet was unamused.

Landon had walked on ahead to duck out of sight around the corner in the glen. He was well put together in black jeans and a beige shirt with a tan quarter-zip sweater over it. If he was just a guy and you saw him in line for a bus, you'd want to make him a movie star. "Glad you could stay," I said.

"Me, too. I haven't gotten to spend time with Rise, really, since our Disney days. We did meet for an hour once when we were both shooting in Rome, but that doesn't count. And it's always great to add new friends who are actual people. In short, I'm grateful to you for letting me bunk in. I am trusting you, one hundred percent, to tell me politely when it's time to leave."

"No problem there," I said. *Like that would happen this side of fifty years from now.* "Although I thought you're doing *Saturday Night Live* next week?"

He nodded, as if it had momentarily slipped his mind. "True. I do have to be in New York for the writer's pitch meeting at 9 a.m. on Monday morning. But you can still throw me out at any time."

Landon stopped for a moment once we were completely inside the glade and perused Sally's beautiful lodge, then the footbridge over the waterfall that led to my cottage. The intensity with which he took in his surroundings was noteworthy.

"Okay," he said to me. "Well done."

"I'm glad you think so. Too late to change now."

Rise came around the front of the cottage and waved. Landon returned the gesture. Once we'd crossed the bridge, Landon and Rise grabbed each other in an embrace as if they hadn't seen each other for years, instead of since last night.

Rise grabbed Landon's carry on and led him in through the front door.

"This was really created by a set designer? I'm going to keep that in mind, should the time come I get to settle down," Landon said. "Where should these go?" He pointed to his luggage.

I honestly didn't know how the friends were going to handle who got the guest room and who got the living room couch.

"You can put your stuff in the guest room," said Rise, playing the host. He led his friend towards it.

"That doesn't mean you're stuck on the sofa?" asked Landon.

"Naw. Avalon has been kind enough to let me share her room. We're old friends. We've been camping together as nine-year-olds. Purely platonic."

Landon smiled at his friend. "Sure. And if I believe that one, you've got a great extended car warranty for me."

Rise shoved him forward.

"And the bathroom?"

Rise pointed it out.

Then Landon stopped and looked at me. "I don't want you to think I'm weird or anything, but I was wondering if you'd be kind enough to let me...take a nap?"

As he said that, I saw his eyes actually drooping.

Instead of teasing him, Rise turned to me, also, like napping was an idea he hadn't dared consider. In all honesty, Rise looked as if he didn't get some more rest soon, you'd need to check him into a hospital for exhaustion.

"Yes," I said. "You may both take naps. This is your safe space. For as long as you're here, you're off duty. Eat, sleep, sit, stare off into the distance."

"Where did you find this one?" Landon asked Rise happily.

I shooed him toward the guest room.

"You, too," I said to Rise. "You look like you haven't had eight hours of sleep total over the last week."

"You're a lifesaver," Rise said, as he headed into my—our—bedroom.

Ah, the exciting life of movie actors.

A text came in from Hannah: *Still want me to come over later?*

I took my phone and went outside, crossed the bridge and sat on the white bench. It was a great place to talk. Thanks to the waterfall, no one in either house can hear what you're saying.

I called Hannah. "Yes, please come by later, if you can."

"I have a few things to finish up. Maybe four o'clock?"

"Sure. In fact, I had another favor to ask you."

"Shoot."

"You know how I invited you for supper?"

"Yeah."

"Could you maybe...bring supper? I was planning to run out to get something, or have something delivered, but the whole town is crammed full of festival-goers, and there's this stalker thing happening."

She laughed. "What *The Music Man* would call an Iowa Welcome. 'You can eat your fill of all the food you bring yourself.'"

"I'll happily reimburse you."

"What do you want? Steak? Chicken? Barbeque? Crepes?"

"Actually, I was remembering this really good salad you made me once. My guests would likely appreciate salad and lean salmon."

"Whatever you say. I'll stop by the supermarket on my way over. If you think of anything else you need, text me."

"Thank you from the bottom of my heart."

I ended the call and continued to sit. This was a very good bench on which to ruminate. Also on which to have conversations.

Apparently, it was good for other things, too. Philip (why am I thinking of him *now*?) admitted that when he was naughty as a child, this was where his gran (Sally) would spank him. To this day, Philip referred to it as the spanking bench.

Enough about Philip.

The advent of Rise brought my thoughts back to the Salty Gang. I'd lost touch with Kelsey and Jasmine. That left Winsome, Rise and Troy. The only one I'd stayed close to was Winsome. He was a talented painter, as was Philip, but their work couldn't have been more different.

I didn't know how long it would take before the smallest thought of Winsome wasn't accompanied by vestiges of sorrow and guilt. I missed him. He didn't have to be gone. But he was, and the world somehow kept spinning. I know 'what if's' are moribund anchors to the past. It was hard to cast them off for good.

"Hey." Rise slid onto the bench beside me.

"Good nap?" It had been twenty minutes at most.

"Honestly, I'm still having a hard time turning off my brain."

"I don't blame you."

"I've got one of the best agents in the business, and I've got a manager who's been with me for ten years, and they've both given me ultimatums, refusing to work with each other any longer. Tomorrow, one of them will be gone. How do I possibly decide?"

"I guess you figure out what you want your future to look like and pick the person who sends you in that direction."

He flexed his hands. "Aye. There's the rub."

We sat, looking at the tall trees that ringed the glade, their leaves turning crimson and gold.

"Thank you again for letting us hang out here." He laughed. "I almost said 'hide out here.' That's what it feels like."

"That's what friends are for."

He was flexing his hands again, nervously.

"What's on your mind?" I asked.

His eyes stayed locked on the red maple tree straight ahead in our field of vision.

"I did know her," he said.

"What? Who?"

"Marissa. The girl who died. I knew her first of all from auditions. For a while, we were the two kids who almost got the parts. They'd have a blonde pair and a dark-haired pair, then they'd choose one. For the longest time, Marissa and I were the kids who almost got chosen. Then I got a Disney contract and quit the regular kid audition circuit. She was talented and got a bunch of guest-shots. When I became a teen superhero, she called to congratulate me. We went out a couple of times. Really nice kid. Then things got busy, and if someone wasn't on the lot, I didn't see them. I guess you know that.

"Anyway, Marissa texted recently, on an old phone number I keep around. She said she finally got a series and was heading for Toronto to start filming, when she saw I was going to be here for *Triple Jeopardy*."

"You were going to meet up?"

"I was going to try. As you've seen, meeting up with me isn't the easiest thing in the world."

"So, why then? When I asked, why did you say you didn't know her?"

Now he looked truly nervous. "Because something is happening, Avalon, and I don't understand what it is and I don't know how to stop it."

"You mean, with the stalkers and all?"

"Maybe. Maybe they're part of it? But..."

Hot tears carved a path down each of his cheeks. "Marissa wasn't the only one," he said.

"What?"

"There was another girl. LeAnn Astor. She and I did a play together at the Pasadena Playhouse. We were the only teenagers in the cast. Of course we had crushes on each other, and we dated, as much as 13-year-olds can. Moved on pretty quickly. It's hard to date in L.A. if you don't drive. But she reached out to me a couple of years ago. We were going to have a drink and catch up. As a matter of fact, Troy had just come back to L.A., also. So the three of us were going to meet. LeAnn never showed. Troy was late, but he came. He and I had a drink and reminisced. Two days later, I saw on the news that she'd been found dead."

"Holy crap," I said. "Have you told anyone? The police? Con? Dirk?"

"Dirk knew about LeAnn. I mean, Dirk is always around, how could he not? But he told me not to say a thing. He said if it got into the news that someone I dated—or was even just going to meet for one drink—ended up dead, my career would become about that."

"Oh my god, Crispin," I said, reverting to his old name without meaning to.

"What is going on, Av?" he asked. "I'm scared."

"I don't blame you," I said. "And wait—Troy was there?"

"Yeah. Seems he's somehow around when things go wrong. But LeAnn and Marissa—this is happening to friends of mine," he said. "I'm sad. And really scared."

Another first: I wasn't sure he should call Investigator Spaulding, either. Mike Spaulding had told me not to trust Rise. He was already suspicious of him. Being treated as a suspect, or even just a 'person of interest' couldn't be good for one's career. Or mental or spiritual health.

Dirk was right. Rise O'Connor being linked to a series of deaths would be more interesting to the large news outlets even than the possibility that Sally Allison was still alive. It would be everywhere. It would become what he was known for.

And yet, for better or worse, Mike Spaulding was also right.

Rise O'Connor was the nexus.

HIDING OUT

Ingredients

  2 oz Screwball peanut butter whisky
  2 1/2 oz Godiva chocolate liquor
  Chocolate syrup (garnish)

Method

  Design inside of martini glass with chocolate syrup.
  In a cocktail shaker add ice, Screwball and Godiva liquor.
  Shake ingredients together and strain into martini glass.

14
THE NEXUS

WE WERE STILL sitting, clueless about next steps, when late afternoon birdsong was interrupted by a car motor. Hannah's Prius glided into view. Since no one was at the lodge, I waved her up to park near Sally's.

"This is my friend, Hannah," I said to Rise. "She's bringing in supplies from the local supermarket."

"Ah," he said, standing up and heading for the car. "What bags might I carry?"

"There are a few in the back." Hannah popped her trunk and stepped out of the vehicle before realizing who was making the offer. Rise stopped beside her, offered his hand, and as she shook it, said, "Hi, I'm Rise."

"Hannah."

Hannah looked over at me, her eyes purposefully widening and gave me one of those "you *go*, girl" looks.

If only it was as simple as going.

We wrangled the bags across the bridge and around back. Hannah said, "Let's put them here while we figure out what to do."

"What to do?" I asked.

"It seems to me you have a grill," she said. "Should we grill the salmon?"

"Did someone say 'grill the salmon'?"

The kitchen door opened and Landon stepped out. Hannah turned around, saw him, but smoothly turned back to me, her eyes conveying simply, *wtf?*

"Why wouldn't we grill the salmon?" asked Rise.

"I volunteer," added Landon. "In fact, I beg. Please, please, *please* let me grill the salmon."

Hannah turned and held out her hand, which he shook. "Hannah Bricksford," she said.

"Landon Presser," he replied. "Bricksford? As in the Reverend Almighty Samuel Bricksford?"

Hannah laughed out loud. "I just call him Dad Almighty."

Landon looked at me. "You knew this?"

"I knew her dad was Samuel Bricksford. I didn't know the Almighty part."

"It's his nickname in parts of the Black community." Then, to Hannah, "Wait—"

"Yeah," she said, "I know. My mom is high yellow. Even so, it took generations of intermarriage to come up with me. Frankly, it would be easier to be a Bricksford if my skin was darker. I'm often mistaken for white—but it gives me an area of service."

"You're a local pastor?"

"Yes. St. Barnabas Episcopal church. What are you doing here, Mr. Presser?"

"Landon. I'm visiting with Rise, meeting Avalon, and hoping for some RWT."

"RWT?"

"Real world time. Time to be a normal person doing normal things."

"Well, if you want to help marinate the salmon, I won't stop you."

"Can I grill it?"

She laughed. "Okay by me." Hannah looked at me suspiciously. "You got anyone else hiding in there?" She nodded to the house. "Who's bringing dessert? Anna Taylor-Joy?"

"Nope."

"Well, I overbought ingredients so you'd have leftovers. It should be enough, even if more guests show up."

"God forbid," I said.

And thus began as enjoyable a meal prep as I'd been a part of, well, ever.

Hannah mixed her ingredients and put the salmon in to marinate. Then she oversaw the washing, peeling, and slicing of the salad by herself and Landon. Rise came in and leaned against the far counter, holding a glass of iced tea.

"I should admit that my mother is an Episcopal priest," Landon said.

"Holy smokes," said Rise. "I'm surrounded by p.k.s." He looked at me, as I gave him the side-eye version of *Shut. Up.* There was a lot of eye-talking going on.

"I know, I know, you prefer m.d.—minister's daughter—to p.k., preacher's kid."

Like that explained the dangerous ground he'd stumbled onto.

They finished the *mise en place* for the salad, and we went out to sit while the fish marinated.

I jumped in to change the subject. "How are mama and baby?"

Hannah smiled. "Teresa and Sophie are well and healthy. We'll try to concentrate on that."

"What else would you concentrate on?" asked Landon.

"There were complications during the birth. They had to be hospitalized. Their family has no insurance."

"Oh. I'm sorry."

"Yeah. Not sure yet how it will all play out."

"Health care is broken here, that's for sure," agreed Landon.

"You have no idea how many people die from lack of proper care," sighed Hannah.

"Or even lack of good care." This time it was Rise. "You've met Castor, Isobel's driver."

I nodded. "I talked to him while waiting for you and Con to get your stuff the other night. Saw the photo of his wife and daughters."

"He told you one of his daughters had cancer?"

"Yes. He said she died."

Rise ran his hand through his hair. "Castor used to work for one of the big production companies. Was number two for Frank Gatwick, a guy known as a real jerk. Made okay money, again, no health insurance. He and Donata had two daughters, Calista and Emilia. In a very strange turn of fate, Castor's daughter Emmie and Gatwick's daughter both got a rare form of lymphoma at the same time. Gatwick had insurance and money out the wazoo and flew her all over and got her into consults with top doctors and experimental treatments. She recovered.

"Whereas Castor and Donata did everything they could, took out multiple mortgages on their house, got Emmie the best treatment they could. Still, Emmie died. They lost their house, had to declare bankruptcy, and the marriage didn't survive.

"Castor had been putting in his time with Gatwick to get the experience and contacts to start his own production company, but he lost the heart for it. Started driving for Isobel. Hasn't seen his older daughter, Callie, in years. He told me once he's saving every penny for her."

"I'm sorry I asked him about his girls," I said. "It took him a while to answer."

"You shouldn't be," said Hannah. "Just because someone's dead, doesn't mean their loved ones want to pretend they never existed. Even though it hurts, you want other people to know of, and remember them. It's important."

We were all quiet for a moment.

"Hey," I said to Hannah, "will you be around in mid-October? I keep forgetting to tell you you've been invited to Brooklyn by my family—for our annual harvest meal."

"Wow. Sounds like fun. Let's talk when I'm by my calendar. I'm being pressured by my dad to come to some rallies and speak, along with him."

"Yeah? Are you going to?" I asked. "You'd be great."

"I...large crowds are not really my thing. It's planned for the same time an ultra-conservative anti-immigrant coalition is meeting that weekend. Their head honcho, Reverend Walker Weatherstone, is having a series of rallies in support of it."

Rise shot a look at me. I shook my head.

"You speak to crowds every weekend," I said. "It's called giving a sermon. I don't know why you'd not feel comfortable."

"I just...I just feel called to parish ministry."

"Or it could not be the right time," Landon said, smiling at her. "You'll know when it is."

"What do you think?" Hannah asked, taking her own turn to change the subject. "Is it time to fire up the barbecue?"

"Sure," Landon and I said at the same time, then laughed.

Rise's phone buzzed and he looked at his text. "It's from Con. They're down at the guardhouse with Chet."

"Great. You said we had extra salmon?" I asked Hannah. Then, "But Chet has already okayed Con. What's the problem?"

"They say someone else is there who says he knows you. Con sent a photo."

"What is this? Old home week?" What I was really thinking was, Betina? Olive? Who has found us?

Rise turned his phone around so I could see the picture.

"Holy shit," I said.

It was Troy.

"Old home week, indeed," Rise said.

THE NEXUS

Non-Alcoholic Cocktail

Ingredients

> 1 1/2 oz Seedlip Garden 108 Herbal Non-Alcoholic
> Liquor
> Purple shiso leaves (about 10-15 leaves)
> Sparkling water
> Fresh cucumber (thin slices)

Method

> Purple Shiso Tea
> Pour 3 cups of boiling water into a container and add
> about 10 purple shiso leaves. Let steep for about 20 min-
> utes or until water has turned a light purple color.
> Remove leaves from water and bring water down to room
> temperature or put in cooler to chill.

Cocktail

Method

> In a cocktail shaker add ice, Seedlip Garden 108 Herbal
> Non-Alcoholic Liquor, and purple shiso tea. Shake
> together.
> Pour into a Collins glass.
> Add sparkling water and stir gently.
> Add a sprig of fresh Purple Shiso leaf and thinly sliced
> cucumbers for garnish.

15

OLD HOME WEEK

Con drove onto the property as I headed for the guard-house. I waited for them to get out of the car. "Hey," I said. "Good to see you. I hope you're hungry. Landon and my friend Hannah are grilling salmon. There's plenty."

"Thanks," they said with a friendly tone. "If it's okay, I'll head on up."

I watched Con climb the hill. How did they do it? How did they remain so cool and collected when they were security to someone who had dangerous stalkers? I certainly wasn't cut out for that.

I continued down to get Troy Minturn. Salty Gang Troy. I loved Troy. I tried not to be spooked by the fact that Rise said Troy tended to turn up at places where unfortunate events happened.

Should I even let him up?

Troy, it was Troy.

Con could incapacitate him—or anyone—in thirty seconds flat.

How did Troy know where Rise was? How did he know where I was?

I didn't even glance at the evil eye Chet One was sending in my direction. For there, in front of me, was my old friend. He was grinning and I was grinning, and we gave each other giant hugs.

"Come on up," I said.

Troy climbed into his rental car. He nodded to the passenger's side and I climbed in. I instructed him where to drive and where to park, around the corner and well out of sight of the road. As far as anyone walking past was concerned, this glen was empty. Unoccupied. He got out and locked his vehicle.

"I hope you're hungry, we're about to eat."

"When have I ever not been hungry? You know me better than that."

We walked together up the hill. "How did you find me?" I asked, trying to sound casual. It was *me* he found, right? Not Rise? Please God, don't let Troy be a Rise-stalker.

"I'm here talking to Jerry Raker about a project. When he found out I knew you, he told me you helped him find Sally, that you lived up near her place."

"And he told you how to get here?"

"I had to swear on a stack of Screen Art Deco histories not to divulge the location."

I was a little surprised Jerry hadn't at least texted me to make sure it was okay to tell someone where I lived. On the other hand, he was so entrenched in the next day's activities, I wasn't surprised at all.

Troy was taller than I, but a head shorter than my other two actor-guests. Five foot eight? His skin was as dark as a stately oak tree, his eyes smaller than Rise's, but still searching and sparkling. His hair was curlier and longer than Landon's. He was in good shape, didn't lose breath at all, climbing the hill toward my place. He wore pressed grey slacks, a grey shirt and a leather jacket. Perfect for autumnal meetings with Hollywood-types like Jerry Raker.

We were almost to the bridge when Rise came around the corner of the house, waited for Troy to see him, and gave a friendly wave.

"You're shitting me," said Troy.

"Did Jerry not mention that Rise was here?" Although, I wasn't sure how much Jerry and/or Addie knew about the fact that Rise and I were friends. As far as Addie knew, I simply had my uses as a stalker magnet. They had no way of knowing Rise and I were close enough that he would stay with me.

It was a happy dinner.

We all put our anxieties away, even Con, somewhat content that the Chets could keep stalkers at bay, at least for the evening.

Con and Rise were happy and comfortable in each other's company. Rise had told me Con was his assistant, as well as security, that they'd been working together for three years now. Nothing romantic, Rise assured me (did I ask?) Con was currently with a guy, and they seemed very happy together. Con had a wicked sense of humor and a refined sense of irony, which tickled me, partly because that meant Rise valued those qualities and those who had them.

Troy relaxed immediately and joined the conversation wholeheartedly. It turned out he'd been married for six years to a high-powered woman who coordinated saving refugee families around the world, getting them out of camps and resettled. They had two daughters, who were three and five years old.

This information hit me like a steel girder. Someone who was my age—Rise's age, and the age Winsome would have been—was somehow all grown up. He was married, he had been since he was 22. He wasn't a child groom; he'd gone to college and met his wife and married her after graduation and had children. Like a normal person.

I wondered what effect that information had on Rise, or if he was already aware, having met up with Troy several times in the past.

Usually, when I talk to people who are married with children, I regard them kindly, but as a separate species of human being.

Not Troy. Troy was our same species. How could we be so different? Was there something wrong with his choices, or my choices?

I didn't dig too deeply to find the answers. There'd be plenty of time for that after the film festival when everyone had left, and I was on my own to ruminate to my heart's content. Or ruminate my way into depression. Could go either way.

Still, I didn't have too much time to start ruminating. I was at a table with Rise.

Rise O'Connor, my old friend who had matured into a fine human being. Usually, when I 'collect' people by deep-diving into their stories, I purposefully lead them on, asking questions, filing their answers in the 'hunh, how about that?' section of my mind. But with Rise, I didn't need to ask questions. In fact, I didn't talk much at all. I could sit there and simply soak him in. I did my best not to stare—at how he listened, how he laughed, how he ran the fingers of his right hand through the bangs portion of his hair.

So, how are my thoughts different than Olive's? Or Betina's? How can I enjoy watching him this much and not be slipped comfortably into the stalker camp? If they somehow actually knew him, would it be one of them sitting here with him?

Every once in a while, his eyes flicked over toward mine, and he smiled. Then we both looked away.

There was a chill in the air for an hour before anyone of us gave in and noticed it. It was almost ten o'clock; Troy needed to get back to his hotel room and Zoom with his family. He and Hannah headed together to the cars.

There weren't many dishes since we'd grilled the meat, but the four of us remaining went inside and cleaned up. As we did, Con said, "So you know, I'm going to sleep in my car tonight. I'm grateful for the security by the lane, but it's on me if someone gets past Chet One or Chet Two and up here."

"That sounds completely uncomfortable," said Landon.

"Let me check something," I said, and walked back outside and around the cabin. I dialed my landlord, a little nervously, knowing she had a lot going on. To put it mildly. But she was polite, as almost always, listened to and granted my request.

I went back inside and said to Con, "If you want to be here in the glade but out of sight, Sally has invited you to sleep up on her porch. It's a huge, screened room, with many a sofa wider than most beds. It also has a commanding view of the entire property, and it's dark, so no one can see you, but you can see them."

"Really? That would be great."

"All yours. Assuming you don't mind antlers in the chandeliers. Don't worry—deer shed them every year, you don't have to kill a stupid yet magnificent beast to make a lighting fixture."

"Thanks for the info."

They bid their farewells and headed down to get set up and settle in.

That left Landon, me and Rise.

"I'm going to excuse myself again to get to bed," Landon said.

"There's a television in your bedroom," I offered.

"I'm enjoying being unplugged for a few days," he said, and I couldn't blame him.

"Good night," Rise said. "You'll be around tomorrow, right? We should have a real chance to catch up then."

"I will be. Good night, you two. Have fun 'camping.'" He gave us a wicked grin and headed off to his side of the cottage.

Which left me and Rise standing in the kitchen.

"What do you think?" I asked. "Are you still exhausted? Would you like to go straight to bed? Or should we sit outside for another minute?"

"Sure," he said. "Let's sit outside."

We each grabbed sweaters and went out back. I sat in the free-standing swing, and he sat beside me.

We didn't talk.

Rise sank back into the cushions. It was as if his muscles gave a sigh of relief.

It was a clear night, the moon only beginning to rise, so the stars were bright and mysterious and getting their due. The stream and waterfall provided soothing ambient sound, the kind you'd pay for in an app.

Rise took my hand.

"Of all my problems, here's the one that's plaguing me now," he said.

"I'm listening."

"You're one of my oldest, best friends. Someone I can be myself with. Tell anything to."

"I feel the same way. Why is that a problem, exactly?"

"I'm...dying to kiss you. But I don't want to muck anything up. Lovers are a dime a dozen, but true friends are priceless."

Lovers—high quality lovers—are a dime a dozen? Really? I guess we're shopping at different stores.

"You can't kiss a friend? I think, ideally, relationships that last are both."

"It's okay?"

"Oh, for…"

I didn't finish the sentence. He kissed me.

And when Rise O'Connor kisses you, *holy pilgrim's kiss*.

I felt it to my toes.

Maybe I'd always wanted to kiss him. Back when he was Crispin. Back when we were best friends. This longing felt familiar, my body recognized the taste and smell of him at once. We melted into each other.

"Should we go inside?" he murmured.

"Camping, you mean?"

He laughed. "Camping."

We held hands and walked in together. I locked the kitchen door behind us. I also closed and locked the bedroom door, leaving poor Whistle to sleep on the couch.

As I started to remove my sweater, Crispin said, "Let me."

So I did. I let him take off my sweater, my shirt, my pants. I then stood him solemnly before me and discarded those same items of his.

He was gorgeous. I wouldn't have cared if he wasn't, because he was my Crispin. But as long as he was fit and toned, I took full advantage.

We moved across the room together as he unclasped my bra and stared at my breasts in wonder. I knew he was a gifted actor, but I took the naked appreciation as authentic. I ran both hands across his sculpted chest.

And soon we were on the bed, and all I could say, all I could fathom was, "Crispin."

"Avalon. My Av."

He stood up and went to his suitcase and came back. "Open your mouth," he said, softly.

"What?"

"Trust me."

I did. He slipped something under my tongue, and under his own, and as he kissed me, the tablets dissolved.

WTF? He said, "Trust me," but did I? Should I? I didn't want to give over control of my body to something without knowing clearly what it was and what the ramifications might be.

I lay there, not knowing whether to be annoyed or excited or horrified, not knowing what to expect.

There was no grand effect, but a slow cascade of tingling, like Christmas tree lights that ran down each strand, flashing as they went.

Where he touched me, my skin turned golden, not the color, the feeling. He was murmuring and kissing every inch of my skin and I didn't know where I was or who I was if I wasn't part of *us*.

I'm pretty sure it was an extraordinary night.

I'm also pretty sure, since I lost track of any inhibitions that warned me to be quiet, Landon knew we were camping. Repeatedly.

I'm also pretty sure there were some kind of amphetamines involved, because although both of us were tired, neither of us slept till nearly dawn.

Which was when my phone rang, and Investigator Mike Spaulding answered my drowsy "Hello?" with a very much awake, "Where are you?"

"At home. In bed. Like any sane person," I said. "Why?"

"There's been another murder," he said. "Can I come up?

OLD HOME WEEK

Ingredients

Cabernet poached pears (keep a little extra cooking liquid on the side)
2 oz vodka
2 oz Ramazzotti aperitivo rosato
Cocktail skewer (garnish)

Method

Fill cocktail shaker with vodka, Ramazzotti aperitivo rosato and about 1/2 oz of Cabernet poached pear cooking liquid. Shake all ingredients together and strain into Coupe glass.
Add Cabernet poached pears to cocktail skewer and place in cocktail.

CABERNET POACHED PEARS (MAKE A DAY AHEAD)

Ingredients

3 pears, peeled and cut into small cubes
3 cups Cabernet
1 cup water
1/2 cup of orange juice
1/2 cup ground sugar
1 tbsp ground cinnamon
1 tbsp honey
2 whole clove pieces
Small dash of allspice

Method

In medium saucepan add all ingredients and turn on medium to low heat. Let simmer on low for an hour, until pears have turned a deep dark Cabernet, but still have a little crunch to them.
Take off heat and let sit until room temperature.
Transfer into a container and place in refrigerator, making sure to keep the cooking liquid, which will be used in the cocktail.

16
EARLY MORN

"WHAT? No. Of course not. It's the middle of the night."
I was panicking because I wasn't completely lucid. Thoughts drifted by me but I couldn't fasten them to anything.

"Well, it's 7:30, but I catch your drift."

I took a breath. Someone who was coherent—what would they say?

"Who is it?" Yes, that way he would know I didn't know who was murdered so I couldn't be the murderer.

"Your friend Betina."

"Seriously?"

"Yes. Well, don't tell anyone I said it's a murder. Right now it's an attempted murder. She isn't dead yet."

I got out of bed, grabbed a t-shirt and undies and pajama bottoms.

"What do you mean?"

"I mean, she's holding on. She's in the hospital in critical condition."

"What happened?" I put the phone down on the bed quickly and pulled the shirt over my head. Pulled on the bottoms and headed out of my bedroom. Whistle, abandoned outside the door, was suddenly up and dancing. No middle ground with that puppy.

"Don't know yet. Eerily the same as Ms. Marisol. No signs of violence on her person."

"Where was she?"

His voice got quiet. "That's all I can say at the moment. Are you awake now? Can you meet me in town?" He cleared his throat.

"Wait. Before you answer that: can you trace your movements yesterday? And is there someone who can verify where you were most of the day?"

Yesterday. Think.

What was that freaking stuff Rise gave me?

"Yeah. I was at work, and then I came home. Sally has guards here 24/7 to stop anyone from coming up. They can tell you I came home and didn't leave."

But don't ask them, because I don't necessarily want you to know there was a party up here and who all is around. I don't want you to know about Rise.

Or Troy.

Dear God, what is going on?

I opened the door to the terrace. Cold air smacked me in the face, which was what I needed. Whistle happily joined me outside.

"That's good to hear. Are you doing all right, by the way? You did have a dramatic confrontation yesterday."

"I'm coping. I didn't try to kill her, Betina, though, Mike, just to be clear."

"Always good to know."

"And I do hope she gets better. Is there a chance she will?"

"It would take a miracle. I'm sorry to wake you if you needed the sleep."

"Well, today is the big movie premiere. Are you going?"

"Afraid not. I'm working a case."

"Of course. But you had a hand in ending the attack on Sally, which I believe is part of the documentary's narrative."

His tone changed. "Have you seen it?"

"No, not yet."

"Well, when you do, let me know."

I was a little worried about how much screen time I would get in the darn thing, myself.

"Also, let me know when you're out and about."

"I will. This is not an official interview request though, right? I'm not currently a suspect?"

"Of course not. Although, you did have motive."

"Honestly? Which one? 'Of course not'? Or, I 'did have motive'?"

"Thankfully you've got someone to vouch for your whereabouts. And professional security types tend to be reliable."

"Good to know."

"The truth is, I find it helpful to talk to you. You have a good mind for putting things together."

"Especially if I alibi out."

"Never hurts."

"I'll let you know when I head into town."

"Thanks."

I disconnected and settled back.

Coffee. I needed coffee.

I went inside, fed the dog, jumped straight past tea to coffee and added half and half. Then I went back out and inhaled the air above my mug. The steam and the scent wafted. I found great solace in the wafting.

My mind was churning.

Betina. Someone tried to kill Betina.

Rise. I had slept with Rise. Well, not slept, exactly. Had mighty good sex.

Rise had drugged me, without asking. Well, he'd asked me to trust him, but I hadn't been expecting...whatever that was. He hadn't asked if I'd like to do drugs with him.

This was all so freaking complicated.

I sipped the coffee, which had caffeine, also a drug.

I worked as a bartender, serving beverages containing alcohol. Also a drug.

Winsome died of an overdose of opioids. Also drugs.

The thing is, addiction is an awful, terrible thing, whether it's opioids or alcohol or sex or hoarding cats or hoarding money. A terrible thing. I was trained and TIPS certified in my job how not to let people overdrink, and I did my darndest to talk to people about what was going on with them, and why they felt they needed to over-drink before I cut them off, if I needed to, and called them a ride.

The fact that Rise had drugged me with something that took away much of my agency and sense of control made me crazy. I was still struggling to center my thoughts. What made it confusing was the fact I'd had sex—fantastic sex—with someone I loved.

The kitchen door banged open and Landon came out, wearing pajama bottoms and a t-shirt with a robe over it for warmth. "Good morning," he said.

"Good morning. Why are you up so early?"

"I set an alarm. Trying my best to get on Eastern Standard Time before Monday."

"Good thinking. How are you getting back to New York City from here?"

"I've got a plane chartered from Adirondack Regional tomorrow afternoon."

"Oh. Good plan. Did you truly sleep well?"

"Out like a light." Awareness dawned. "Ah. The answer you seek is, I'm chipping away at my exhaustion, but it's still there. I passed out and was not even marginally aware enough to be impressed by the activities of yourself and Mr. O'Connor. Should there have been any."

I chose to neither confirm nor deny.

"What are *you* doing up this early?"

"Got a call a little while ago from the State Police. Betina Popescu, the woman who locked me in the freezer yesterday, was the victim of an attempted murder."

"What? Really? Will she be all right?"

"It isn't looking good."

"I'm so sorry. I'm sorry she attacked you, of course, and that she's been stalking Rise, but no one should..."

"I agree. Wholeheartedly." We sat, respectful of Betina, who'd terrorized both Rise and me, for a moment. "Meanwhile, I'm going to get dressed and head into town. Going to check things out at my place of business before the big premiere and brunch. Are you going to see *Salty Sally and Pepper: Truth Be Told*? Perhaps standing in the back?"

"It was great that I could see *Triple Jeopardy* that way. But with all the press pouring into town, the risk is too great." He sighed. "I can't tell you how brilliant it is to disappear for a few days. I'm truly grateful."

Landon had a five o'clock shadow—well, by now it was more like an eight o'clock shadow. He looked good with a beard. I did wonder, if your signature look is a five-o'clock shadow, how do you keep it at exactly that length?

I know nothing about men's beard maintenance.

"Shoot. My cupboard is bare. Before I go I'll run down and get you guys something for breakfast."

"Hannah brought fruit and yogurt yesterday, along with the salad and salmon. She said it might come in handy."

I laughed, and texted Hannah, *thanks for the yogurt.*

I knew she was probably working out at the Golden Ticket Gym. In fact, her answer came quickly in response. *No problem. If there are still stalker issues going on and you're busy, have them text me and I'll drop off lunch.*

"Hannah says rather than risk stalkers, you and Rise should text her and she'll bring you lunch."

"That's very kind."

"Do you want her number?"

"Sure."

So Landon Presser put Hannah Bricksford's cell number into his phone.

I smiled. Then I went inside to get changed. I was able to shower and dress without waking Rise. He was out cold, as I would have been had Mike Spaulding not called, bandying about the word 'murder.' I wore my bartender's blacks and my celebratory red vest as a nod to the day's festivities.

I headed across the bridge and toward the street.

"Morning," said Con as I passed Sally's.

"Morning! There's coffee and yogurt up at the house," I answered, like a regular host who would provide such things.

"Thanks."

"Oh, hey…" I went up to Sally's porch so Con and I could speak quietly. I told them what had happened with Betina.

"One less stalker to worry about, but that's not the way you want it to happen," they said.

Con looked remarkably refreshed and put together for someone who probably got little sleep. We bid farewell, and I headed back down the hill.

I couldn't help but think, were things normal, this day would be all about the documentary. There was cell phone footage of an attack on Sally, and I had been there. Like Mike, I was dying to know if I was in the documentary. I had signed a waiver when they started, but at that point they didn't know what footage they'd use.

The Chet with the eye patch was outside, sitting, enjoying some water from a coffee cup. I was getting the numbers I'd assigned them mixed up. "Hi," I said. "Do you want any breakfast?"

I assumed he was taken care of, so the offer should be easy points with nothing actually ventured.

"I'm good, thanks."

"Say, if someone from the State Police came by and asked if I was here yesterday, you wouldn't need to tell them who all was here with me, would you?"

"Do I look like a gossip rag?" he asked. "I wouldn't even tell them about you, without specific instructions."

"Oh. Can I instruct? I mean, I know I haven't hired you, but if anyone asks you if I was here, could you tell them I was? I mean tell the truth?"

"Yeah, can do."

"Without mentioning anyone else."

"I don't 'mention.'"

"Got it. Thank you."

I crossed the street quickly, to distance myself from the entrance to my residence. As I reached the intersection where Main Street headed into town, a familiar white stretch limo pulled up at the stop sign. The front passenger's side window slid down and Castor said, "I'm heading to MacTavish's to be at Sally Allison's disposal for the day. If you're going that way, I can give you a lift."

"Sure. If I can sit up front."

He popped the lock and I climbed in. He was fully dressed in his limo driver uniform, black suit well pressed, hat squarely on head. I thought I even caught a whiff of cologne. Not much, subtle. Nicely done.

I kind of expected him to take the local road that ran parallel to Main Street and park in a back lot, but today he wasn't slinking people around, he was showing off Sally Allison in grand style. White stretch limos say, 'look at me!' and that was today's goal.

As we drove onto Main Street, I remembered Hannah's words and said, "Rise told me more about Ellie. I'm so sorry. I'd like to hear about her someday."

"Thanks," he mumbled. "She was a good daughter." It was clear 'someday' wasn't going to be today. "And thanks again for the salad."

"Stop in whenever you can. We'll take care of you."

He nodded. "You're different than the girls Rise usually..."

Then he realized discussing a client's love life wasn't the best thing.

"Whatever," I said, then laughed. "But thanks."

Was I different? Did Rise and I have something unique in his life? In mine?

"What did you mean, I'm different? In what way?"

I knew Castor wouldn't gab about specific girls. Had Rise had long-term relationships? He and I had some things to discuss.

"I only meant, you're down-to-earth. Not...entitled."

"I'll take it." I bet people climbing into limos often acted obnoxiously entitled.

"Some actresses think the world owes them."

Yes. Yes, they do. They likely treat those in service professions as below them. I know those people, also. Not only actresses.

"I'll bet you could write a book."

"Or a screenplay."

The town of Tranquility was in the throes of awakening on a September Saturday morning. Folks chatted outside the Cardamom Café, and the line wound down the block leading to the tiny Belle's Bakery. There was already activity at the Orpheum Theater. A couple of press vans from local affiliates of national stations were parked on the street, and press photographers chatted with each other while paparazzi prowled. Ten-foot-tall posters for *Sally Allison and Pepper Porter: Truth Be Told* flanked the doors.

We continued on. I'd be back. I couldn't wait.

I texted Investigator Spaulding. *Heading for the Battened Hatch. There shortly.*

Usually, Mike doesn't text me back, he shows up.

But what would I say? I had to know before Mike came.

It was clear Rise was at the center of what was happening.

I didn't want to lose Mike's trust.

I didn't want to be the one to ruin Rise's life.

I didn't want a killer to be roaming free; I didn't want there to be danger to anyone else simply because I withheld information.

What I decided was this: I wouldn't lie to Mike. Which didn't mean I'd tell him everything I knew.

Given that Rise was freaked out about what was going on, I'd try to persuade him to talk to the State Police.

I hoped I could persuade Mike Spaulding to trust Rise was telling the truth.

I hoped I could convince him to trust Rise, period.

Castor expertly pulled up in front of MacTavish's. I jumped out of the passenger's seat, and he pulled forward to a predetermined spot to wait for his celebrity guests.

I went through the lobby, where the air crackled with excitement. I was happy for Glenn and Sally, and nervous for them, too.

Marta had left the Battened Hatch in great shape when she'd closed the night before. There wasn't much to do besides restock the low liquor bottles. I thought about trying to get out of working the dinner rush tonight, since my guests would not be in residence for long. I hadn't mentioned to Marta that I had two well-known actors staying at my place. I wished I could: she'd get a kick out of it.

Also, if I found out Rise O'Connor and Landon Presser were staying at Marta's and she hadn't told me, I'd be miffed.

The Battened Hatch was ready to open when Investigator Spaulding walked in. I was always glad to see him. This is the first time I felt a bit apprehensive.

"Hey, Avalon."

"Hey, Investigator."

Usually, he sat at the bar and I stood behind it. Now, I stood leaning against the wall next to the door to the smoker's porch. He came and leaned next to me. We both looked straight ahead.

"I'm kind of scared to ask, but what happened to Betina? Where was she found?"

"She was found in the woods outside Chateau Tranquility. We're not publicizing how we found her. But, as I said, there were no marks on her, no visible trauma."

"I have goosebumps. Yesterday, she was very alive. And very angry at me. Are you certain she didn't commit suicide? I mean, she could have come to the end of the fantasy and realized there was nowhere to go, and she didn't want to go to jail. She was a wanted woman."

"No, we're not certain she didn't attempt to take her own life, but the parallels to thae last case are harrowing. We have to—"

"Wait for toxicology," we finished in unison.

"You're a little too good at this," said Mike. "Have you ever considered joining the force?"

"Yeah, that's something you'd really want," I said, and we both laughed. "I'm about done setting up. I'm going to head to the theater to beat the rush. Sorry you can't see the film."

"I'm sure I will eventually."

"You came dashing in at the end to save the day, so if you're in it at all, I'm sure it's...dashing." We both managed wonky grins. "So, this is when the world finds out Sally isn't dead, but we've known for a while. I never thought to ask, but I'm sure law enforcement checked into it. It isn't illegal to fake your own death?"

"It's called pseudocide, and no, it's not technically illegal. What's illegal is what happens in the wake of pseudocide. It's fraud if someone cashes in your life insurance policy. It's illegal to get a fake social security number so you can work, or to work without one. Etcetera. However, Sally is a very smart woman. She already had her money in France, the property here is owned by a corporation with her daughter, she owned the boat that sank, no one collected life insurance or boat insurance, she no longer had to work so didn't defraud social security, etcetera. Then she got married, so her legal name really is Mrs. Chander. We did check into it. She didn't get greedy, nor did her heirs, so nothing prosecutable. Well done, Sally." Mike stood straight and stretched. "People disappear every day. Speaking of which, it seems Rise O'Connor has more than his share of stalkers. Apparently, he's disappeared, at least, left Tranquility, which should remove some of the threat to him, to our town, and to the stalkers themselves."

I had no answer for that. So I said nothing.

EARLY MORN

Knocking at Death's Door

Ingredients

1 oz vodka
3 dashes of Angostura bitters
2 oz ginger ale
1 oz fresh grapefruit juice
1 oz fresh orange juice
2 oz sea salt
Slice of fresh cut grapefruit (garnish)
Slice of fresh orange (garnish)
Luxardo cherry (garnish)

Method

Take slice of either fresh citrus and rub around the edges of glass. Pour sea salt onto a small plate.
Dip the glass into sea salt to rim.
In a cocktail shaker, add ice, fresh juices, vodka and bitters. Shake together until shaker itself is cold. Pour into salt-rimmed glass, top off with ginger ale, then add fresh citrus and Luxardo cherry.

17

TRUTH BE TOLD

I LOCKED UP and headed for the theater. I had my ticket, a head-ful of curiosity, and excitement borne of either adrenaline or the remains of amphetamines.

Crazy times.

Tranquility was used to camera vans during the Olympics and other sports competitions, but it felt unusual to see so many reporters and photographers framed by fall foliage.

When I arrived at the theater, I had to grin as I studied the two long vertical banners out front. One was of Pepper Porter in her prime, gossamer dancing dress twirling around her, ginger hair flying, happy smile. The other was of Sally Allison, laughing, also in a flowing, form-fitting dress. At the bottom of each banner was the name of the film and of the filmmakers.

My now-friend Kyle was at the front door, and he waved me in. "How are you doing?" I asked.

He shrugged.

"I hear you."

The film was being projected into all three theaters. The stars and the VIPs would be downstairs in the largest.

Addie came running down the stairs and gave a brief wave. I walked back and found lovely tables set for journalists awaiting transport to the fancy brunch. The tables were empty yet, but servers in tuxes were going back and forth to the back storeroom. A young woman in a form-fitting red dress came out, her thick black hair pulled back in a ponytail, a headband with small pearls keeping her hair down in front. Even though she was working, she looked stunning.

Rachel Hunt. Philip's old girlfriend.

She saw me. There was a moment of startled recognition, the sheerest moment of armor rising, then she remembered, and her shoulders relaxed.

She came over to me. "Thanks for recommending me," she said. "I really appreciate it."

"Sure."

We smiled at each other. There was a day, literally 20 hours of one, when she and I both considered ourselves Philip's girlfriend. Now neither of us did. And, you know what? Even if they got back together—fine with me.

It even generated a kind of symmetry for her to be catering Sally's movie. Rachel and Philip hung out with Sally. Especially with Rachel moving away, this was a nice tribute to her time with Sally's family. Huzzah.

I checked my watch. Only an hour now until the screening started. I considered staying away from the hullabaloo and watching upstairs in one of the smaller screenings.

Hell, no. If Jerry Raker had come all this way with the intention of bringing a screen icon back from the dead, I sure as hell wanted to see it happen.

The people milling outside were starting to become a crowd. I peeked inside the downstairs theater to find Addie there, hard at work. I stepped inside and let the door close behind me. "What can I help you with?" I asked.

"Putting these press packets onto each seat?" she asked.

I took a stack, glad to have a purpose, and started balancing one on each seat. "Things under control?" I asked.

"From your mouth to God's ears."

The back row was roped off. There were also seats roped off on the fifth row. I decided to claim places for Marta and myself on the far aisle, second row from back. Unobtrusive, able to see everything, but still escape in time to make it back before the brunch at Pepper's, the restaurant with which we shared the kitchen. We would not open the Battened Hatch until mid-afternoon, to keep the lobby traffic and orders handleable. We were providing strawberry champagne punch (as well as strawberry ginger ale punch). Other drink orders would be taken inside Pepper's and sent by the magic of POS into the Battened Hatch, where they'd be filled. Marta would oversee this with Davros to serve and assist. If things got out of control, I was already dressed for work. However, if there was a chance I would be in the freaking movie, I wanted to observe the press conference afterwards.

There was a photo of Pepper and Sally, young and vibrant, on the cover of each press packet. I wished I'd known Sally back then. Speaking of symmetry: half of the Salty Gang who hung out at Salty Sally's in Hollywood was now gathered at Sally's own property.

So much coming together.

Addie checked her watch and went to the auditorium door to let members of the press enter, especially those with cameras large enough to set up in the back of the room. I stood against the far wall, watching them work.

It wasn't long before the doors were officially opened and patrons poured in. Most folks with regular tickets were being steered towards the upper screens. Addie was at the doorway. She saw Marta and waved her in, pointing me out to her. Marta was a key part of the night Sally fought off an unexpected attacker, also. The night Philip almost died.

Unexpectedly, the fear and horror of discovering Philip shot and bleeding out washed over me. Not a part of the movie. Not a part of my current life. Pull it together, Avalon.

"Are you excited?" whispered Marta.

"Yup. Are you?"

"Yup."

I had to laugh. Both Marta and I knew Sally. Marta also had interacted with Pepper Porter, although in ghostly form. It hadn't scared her, in fact, it was something that happened to her pretty often.

"Is Pepper here?" I whispered.

Marta shook her head. "I think she's moved on. In the best sense of the word."

The seats filled up. Addie directed Brent Davis and his wife Susan to claim seats in the roped off back row. And then it was time.

Doors were closed. The crowd rustled expectantly.

Then the door opened again, and Jerry Raker strode down the aisle, followed by Sally's children and grandchildren. Jerry was in one of his uber-trendy suits. Sally's children and grandchildren were in traditional Indian garb. Philip walked beside his brother, Jonathan. He was wearing a red sherwani in deep scarlet with gold and black trim. His hair was longer than I remembered it and he wore a beard and mustache, professionally styled and trimmed. He looked more handsome than I'd ever seen him. He looked like he'd just arrived from India.

He looked like the freaking man who held my heart.

Damn, damn, damn.

Damn, damn.

Damn.

Neither Sally nor Saif were anywhere to be seen.

The family was seated, and Jerry, Brent and Addie went to the front of the auditorium.

Jerry made some remarks that were touching and charming and funny. He introduced Brent and Addie.

The crowd applauded.

Jerry, Brent and Addie returned to sit in the back row.

The lights went down. Music came up, the wonderfully evocative, fully orchestrated music of another era of film. Jerry being Jerry had gotten every studio at which either star had worked to open their vaults. The filmmakers also had unprecedented access to the stars' families along with private photo collections and memorabilia. Not to mention the tell-all Pepper had penned that had been discovered only months before and was finally in print, as of today. And the whole crazy truth recently revealed by Sally herself.

The stories of both women were fascinating, behind the scenes stuff you never hear in these Hollywood tribute films. It would have been a riveting documentary even before the last third of the picture. That's when the "truth be told" part came into play. Sally's disastrous engagement and fake marriage that she was forced into by the studio. Pepper, notorious goody-two-shoes, falling in love with a married man and bearing an illegitimate child.

Sally faking her own death.

Sally falling in love with, and marrying, Saif. Their children and grandchildren.

Sally nearly being murdered by her one-time 'fixer' when he became disillusioned.

Yeah, I was there for that part. Brent had had the presence of mind to film the whole encounter on his cell phone. It was raw and dramatic. I was in the middle of it.

"Holy shit," whispered Marta, as I sat on Sally's assailant, and Sally flung me off to free him, not fully believing what we were telling her.

Then Sally herself kneeing him in the balls. Yup. That was a thing that happened.

"Holy shit," whispered Marta again. "I mean, I knew you guys were up there fighting him, but..."

Philip hadn't exactly known what had happened at Sally's place, either, how close his grandmother had come to death. How I was sort of in the middle of it.

I wondered if he was thinking "holy shit." I wondered if he was thinking about me.

As the audience sat, transfixed, the door opened just enough for two people to slip through.

I really didn't want any reporters to notice I was the person in the film doing that stuff and want to talk to me. I didn't want someone deciding to 'go after a different angle' and making me the centerpiece of a story or even putting together that I was Anna Nash's daughter, and I lived here now.

The filmmakers had done a masterful job of not letting anyone know where that final confrontation had taken place.

I whispered to Marta, "I'm going to make a break for it."

She stood to come with me.

Then the movie was over with a dramatic finish.

Lights came up.

Sally Allison herself, along with her husband Saif, strode down the aisle with Jerry, to the front of the auditorium. The crowd, in shock and awe, leapt to their feet, applauding wildly.

I scurried behind as many reporters as I could and ducked out the door. Marta was right behind me.

"Let's get out of here," I said, and we both headed, walking quickly, towards MacTavish's, where Pepper Porter's illegitimate son was pacing nervously in his red and blue kilt and Bonnie Prince Charlie jacket.

"Good luck," I said to Glenn, and headed, along with Marta, to hide out at the Battened Hatch.

TRUTH BE TOLD

Ingredients

  1 1/2 oz Rutte dry gin
  1/2 oz triple sec
  1/2 oz fresh lemon juice
  Dash of simple syrup
  1/2 oz pasteurized egg whites (optional)
  Fresh lemon peel (for garnish)

Method

Fill cocktail shaker with ice. Add all ingredients and shake
lightly a few times. Strain into coupe glass.
Twist fresh lemon peel over glass to open up the oils of
citrus, then add peel to drink.

18

THE BOYS ARE BACK IN TOWN

From what I could see of the brunch/press conference, it was a smashing success. The food was a win for Chef Angelica; she served Eggs Florentine, Pepper's favorite brunch item, and salmon with Hollandaise, which was Sally's, with some gastro pub stuff of her own. The strawberry champagne punch was also popular.

As they finished the meal portion of the event, Mike Spaulding and Lisa Shelton, his second-in-command, came in and stood unobtrusively against the wall near the door. Both were in street clothes, and no one took any notice. Mike and I sighted each other, for sure, but neither of us gave an overt sign of recognition.

There was a table on a dais at the front of the room, reminiscent of the bride and groom's table at a wedding. As soon as everyone was served, Jerry Raker, Addie Moon and Brent Davis slid into the waiting chairs and bantered cheerfully about the making of the movie. Then Addie and Brent left, and Jerry said, "Before we bring on the person you're all dying to meet and ask questions of, I have a wonderful and important announcement to make. My associate Addie Moon is currently passing by your tables, distributing information on the brand new Pepper Porter/Sally Allison Theater and Arts Complex right here in Tranquility."

This was enough to elicit a murmur through the crowd and certainly to pique my attention. I walked from the bar at Pepper's to grab one from Addie.

And, by the way, not a single person recognized me as a participant in the final fight. The young woman in bartender's clothing elicited no interest from anyone. Drivers, maids, waiters, bartenders, no one even notices we're here. Terrific way to hide in plain sight.

Thus, I was able to stand by the bar and peruse the materials without interruption. The theater itself looked great. Jerry was explaining that, since Tranquility had newly-built Olympic housing for the athletes, they would convert the original Olympic village into housing for artists of all disciplines to be in residence.

He then said, "Important guests, and members of the press, I'd like to introduce you to the first Resident Director of the Sally Allison/Pepper Porter Theater, the much-respected director whom we were able to steal from the San Diego Globe, Troy Minturn."

And our Troy, my Troy, went bounding to the front of the room.

He smiled and waved and said he was very much looking forward to speaking to all of them, with more details about the upcoming project, and the first season which would take place even before the new theater was built.

I thumbed through the packet and found the page about Troy. Was I an IMDB snob, or what? He might only have had a few movie and television credits, but his theater experience, as both actor and director, and artistic director, was extensive.

Holy smokes. How had I not known what Troy had been up to, all these years?

And he was moving to Tranquility? Really?

I saw members of the press thumbing through the pages and taking notes. Jerry sent them to the new website for more details.

I wondered how the citizens of the town of Tranquility felt about this. There was a divide between those who found art and artists intriguing, and those who thought the arts brought trouble and undesirable kinds of people.

In fact, it was very likely to play into the upcoming mayoral race. Our current mayor was quick to equate artistic people with drug addiction and moral depravity, while challenger Avantika had great respect for the arts and undoubtedly supported the center.

Let the games begin.

Jerry took questions about the theater and the center, both of which would honor the two actresses and house a collection of their memorabilia. He invited them to an informal question and answer session by the fireplace in MacTavish's lobby at 7 p.m., where cocktails and appetizers would be served. He also said there would be tours of the site the next day, involving him and the architects, and Troy, who would be available to fill in any other information they would like.

Then it was time for the main event. Jerry introduced Sally Allison's family, including her grandchildren, children, and husband, who came in and were seated in chairs in front of the dais. Philip didn't look at me. Or maybe he did. How would I know? I didn't look at him.

Finally, Jerry announced, "Esteemed guests, members of the press, I am pleased to present to you the one, the only, Sally Allison!"

With that, the crowd went wild.

Sally swept in, looking gorgeous and welcoming and like she was your best friend. Not everyone's best friend, but yours, each person's separately. After seeing her films and hearing her story, the fact she was here, still alive, still wonderful…it was almost too much.

Even for me, who ate her blueberry pancakes on a semi-regular basis.

"Hello and welcome," she said. "So. I never married Cliff, who already had three wives, I didn't die in a boating accident, I married a famous Indian painter, and I have kids and grandkids and was nearly killed by another golden era movie actor. Any questions?"

Yep. That was Sally, all right.

After fifteen or twenty minutes, the discussion was just getting started. I was leaning against the bar (it had no bar stools; at Pepper's you had to have a table and drink orders are prepared by us at the Battened Hatch) when I realized Troy had come to stand next to me. "This is fascinating," he said, "but I think I'm going to take a break."

"Want to come to my place? I'll walk you there. I'm going to take a break before we open for dinner, myself."

By this time, I was chomping at the bit to talk to Rise. About Marissa and Betina. About talking to the State Police.

About not drugging me, going forward.

Troy and I disappeared into the kitchen, then exited into and out from the Battened Hatch onto the sidewalk.

"You're really moving to Tranquility? This is great news. I had no idea!"

"And I knew you'd left L.A., but I had no idea where you'd ended up."

"Your wife is moving here, too? And your children?"

"Well, Janeen—my wife—is the high-powered one. She was offered her dream job in Boston. It put us into a quandary since I was at the Globe. But then, Jerry heard I might be looking, and asked if I'd be interested in starting the new Allison/Porter StarLight Theater. What theater director isn't interested in starting a completely new, but nearly funded theater? He wants it to showcase talent of all ethnicities."

"But...Tranquility isn't Boston."

"Yeah. Got that. But there is a commuter flight between Logan and Adirondack Regional. The plan is, I'll get a house here, she'll get an apartment in Boston. Her employers have signed off on her working in the office four days a week, so she can be here three days. We're hoping to eventually flip it and have her working Boston three days a week and remotely four. It's a risk, especially since the kids are nearly old enough for kindergarten."

"Have you checked out the local schools?"

"The teachers seem friendly and great. But the schools, and the town, is not exactly multi-cultural."

"Maybe you can help along those lines."

"I've spent my entire career doing what I can to help along those lines. But it's different when you're offering up your children."

"I imagine." And, being white and without offspring, imagining was truly all I could do.

"We'll see."

We'd been walking at a good clip, and as we passed the theater, I said, "Rise's film was great."

"Rise is truly talented," said Troy. "I think he started a little early for his journey to have a healthy beginning."

The original version of Chet waved to us as we turned onto Cherry Lane. The day, which had been sunny when we began our walk, was clouding over.

Landon was sitting on the white bench on the lawn below the waterfall. He stood and waved at us. "Looks like it might rain," I said.

"Yep. The radar on my weather app shows showers approaching," Landon agreed. "But Hannah will arrive momentarily with lunch. I'll take the risk to wait here to help her carry."

"Thanks," I said.

I wondered if Hannah would do her sometimes-trick of overbuying because she knew more people might show up. Fingers crossed. Neither Troy nor I had eaten at the brunch.

The two of us headed up to the house. Inside, Rise was on a phone call, walking around the living room with an earpiece. He saw us and smiled, giving a 'just a minute' sign.

The call ended, and he strode over to Troy. They did the handshake-with-one-hand-clap-the-back-with-the-other man hug maneuver.

"How did it go?" asked Rise.

Before Troy could answer, the front door opened, and Landon and Hannah came tumbling through, holding cardboard trays of food in front of them, a gust of wind and a smattering of rain at their backs.

I lurched over to push the door closed behind them.

"Lunch," said Hannah. She looked over and caught sight of Troy and me. "Fortunately, I brought extra!"

We went into the kitchen to set out the dishes on the table. I got out plates, which were white and blue wind-in-the-willows and had been art directed into the house and suggested we fill our plates and go eat in the living room, in comfy chairs around the coffee table.

"So," said Troy, when everyone was seated, "did everyone know that our friend Avalon here is a real-life superhero? As highlighted in the documentary, she took on a murderer and emerged triumphant. Not to mention, it looks amazing on film. The women from Themyscira will be looking to recruit her."

"Hardly," I said, deflecting, but also a little pleased. It could have looked worse. "Did you also know that Troy has been lured away from being Assistant Artistic Director at the San Diego Globe to open the new Allison/Porter Starlight Theater and Arts complex here in Tranquility, where the original Olympic Village was?"

"Whoa, sir, congrats!" said Rise. "They're lucky to have you."

"I've had a lot of great opportunities," said Troy.

"You prefer theater to film?" I asked.

Troy laughed. "I went to Howard University—where I met Janeen—they have a fabulous theater department. One professor, who had a reputation for being a little too truthful, told me I had a 'theater face.' That might have made some actors angry, but I love theater. I love digging into meaty rolls and classics and doing the same show multiple times, all the scenes in a row. I know some actors get bored with long runs, but I never have." He chuckled. "Not that I won't do television for a little extra cash!"

"I'm trying to figure out what it is about acting that I love," said Rise with a sigh.

"Your choices now—let me see if I have this right—" said Landon to Rise, "joining another superhero universe or doing a two or three season drama for Netflix."

"Yes. And, which I choose will determine if I lose my agent or my manager."

"Which job sounds good to you?"

"I don't know. Neither one." It was nearly a whisper.

"Let me guess," Troy said. "You've worked all your career to have lucrative artistic choices like this. Two starring roles. You are grateful and you should be thrilled."

"I should be thrilled."

"A top agent, an effective manager." This was Landon.

"I should be thrilled." Rise rubbed his neck, looking a bit lost.

Troy asked, "Are there any parts that would thrill you just now? Thriller? Romcom? Epic adventure? Shakespeare? Broadway?"

"No," he said. "No." He sat, quietly. "I'm tired."

"Have you saved money?" Again, Troy. Practical, down to brass tacks Troy.

"Yeah. I'm good," Rise said.

"It's time for you to take a break," said Troy. "I believe you started acting too young. You've been living with other people making your decisions and shaping your life for far too long."

Landon added, "You need to learn to love your craft again. Or learn you love something else more."

Rise answered, "You've been acting as long as I have. You're not tired of your craft."

"First, I was three years older than you were when I started. You already had an impressive kid acting resume. Those three years are a big deal. You started as a kid, discovering you had a talent—then it became non-negotiable because you had to bring in the family's money. You've done three television series, which is a daily grind. Our paths have intersected, yes, but yours has been different. Very different. I personally think you need a Dirk-free life before you can make any decisions about your future. Dirk and your dad never let you make a move on your own. You are a grown-ass man now."

"But I need a manager."

"You need a manager with whom you have an equal-to-equal, grown-up relationship." Landon said quietly. "I can't tell you the number of times I've wanted to strangle Dirk."

"Not Isobel?"

"Everyone in Hollywood wants to strangle her. There, you'll have to wait in line."

"But you've been acting since you were a teenager. You still love it. You have opportunities, new opportunities—" Rise continued to Landon.

"Fabulous opportunities," added Troy.

"And you're excited about it. You love your craft."

"I'm still growing," said Landon. "You have to understand, not just my career has had a different trajectory, my background is different. When I grew up, even twenty-five years ago, having a Black father and a white mother was offensive. Just being me was an insult to some people. A mixed-race kid walking down the street or into a school classroom. In the beginning, the fact I'm light-skinned Black defined every single role I was offered. As you recall, you were a superhero. I was the Black superhero. Then the only parts I was offered were from Black people's oppressed experiences. And I did two, before I was able to look for other kinds of parts. And now, now I happen to be the right color at the right time. Who could have guessed? Now my predecessors in the industry have fought so long and so hard for opportunities that lots of folks are looking to hire people of color. And, lucky me, the skin that made both Black people and white people wary of me growing up, makes me a romantic lead! I'm at the point where I can pick and choose parts. And colorism has a good deal to do with that. Light-skinned, smaller features, and white women can feel progressive because they wouldn't kick me out of their beds. I can either be mad, or I can take the opportunity and try to show people of color POSsibilities they haven't seen before."

Langdon looked at Troy. "Sorry to be quite so forthright."

"What?" asked Troy. "You're saying my skin is dark, my features are prominent, and that might affect who hires me? I hadn't noticed. I'm shocked."

"Which means, you must be hella talented and hella smart—" Landon put forth.

"And hella lucky—" Troy added.

"To have the opportunities you've had and to make so much of them. And, while we're on the subject, please be aware that your professor's assessment was wrong. You belong in leading roles in movies and television as much as any of us do."

"I think he meant I wasn't a pretty boy, like some people here. Sorry to be so forthright."

There was a moment of silence. Then Landon burst out laughing. "Okay. I deserved that."

I glanced at the time. "I've got to get back," I said, stretching.

"Me, too," said Troy. "Can I help clean up?"

"Naw, what are houseguests for, anyhow?" asked Rise. "We have to earn our keep somehow."

As he spoke, Hannah's phone buzzed with a text, which she read. Tears sprang to her eyes. She looked away, trying to get a grip.

We all sat, waiting for her to speak.

"I'm sorry. It's bad news about a parishioner."

"So sorry," asked Landon. "Would it help to talk about it?"

She shook her head.

"I'm sorry," I said. I knew how deeply these things affected my friend.

She nodded mutely. Then she headed outside, where the rain had let up.

Rise stood and started clearing off the coffee table. I went to stand close to him. "Besides all the professional stuff coming down, are you okay here? I didn't see Con's car."

"Con went to get some sleep. It's been a godsend that Sally hired security by the road. It means Con has gotten more sleep than they have since we left L.A. Things aren't usually this intense."

I hesitated, but said, "Speaking of that, I am worried about you. Would you do me a favor and think about talking to State Police Investigator Mike Spaulding? He's a friend. I trust him. The crazy things that are happening center around you. It could be, with Betina out of the picture and others thinking you're gone, you're momentarily in the clear. Or not. But we owe it to Marissa, and LeAnn, to find out what happened, don't you think? And we owe it to you not to let you be the next victim."

"I hear you. And I know you are suggesting it because you care about me. So, thanks."

"There's a lot going on now, I know."

"There's a lot."

I went back to the living room. Landon had joined Hannah outside on the bench. Troy stood ready to leave with me. Together we headed out.

It was no longer drizzling, but as wind rustled the trees, they flung droplets with abandon.

Hannah and Landon sat together on the bench, Landon having put his jacket down to keep them dry. Were they...praying? Landon did say his mother was a priest, and, well, praying was kind of Hannah's stock-in-trade.

"Should I grab an umbrella?"

"I'm good if you are," said Troy.

"I'm not a fan of carrying things. I always forget them later."

"Then, let's be on our way," he said. He crooked his elbow and I put my arm through his.

As we left the property, Con was pulling up. I was relieved.

We walked quickly due to the wind and spattering of rain. It felt good to have another ally from the olden days. "I'll be very glad if you move here," I said.

"I'll be glad to be living near you."

"Also, can't wait to meet Janeen and your children. I can't believe one of us actually has a family. Well done, you trailblazer, you."

We reached MacTavish's Seaside Cottages in record time. "Have fun," my friend wished me.

"Hope the Q and A about the new theater goes well. I'll try to come by."

Marta had arrived early and was nearly done with set-up. "Should we open?" she asked.

"Sure. We're not usually closed for Sunday lunch, so let's see if anyone has missed us."

I stood behind the bar and started creating a new drink recipe. I decided it would be fun to create a drink to celebrate the fact that Rise and Troy and now Landon, were in town. Doing so quieted my mind. I love putting flavors together in my mind, and then trying them in real life to see if it came close to something scrumptious.

I remembered a famous quote by chef Thomas Keller, who had a renowned dish called Oysters and Pearls, featuring oysters and tapioca. After it was on his menu, someone asked him how he came up with it, and how it tasted to him.

"I've never tasted it," Keller replied. "I know it tastes good. You don't need to stick your hand in fire to know it's hot."

I liked to hold that as my ideal. But, unlike Chef Keller, I did have to taste to see how ingredients melded.

But try as I might, I couldn't clear my mind completely. The seriously terrifying question remained: who killed Marissa and Betina?

Common sense led me to consider those who came into town at the time of the deaths. It could be coincidence they both died right when the film festival happened, but a pretty big one. Or maybe Betina killed Marissa, like she'd tried to kill me, and then attempted to commit suicide? But what about that other friend of Rise's, LeAnn Astor, from the Pasadena Playhouse? That had been several years ago. Perhaps it was unrelated. Perhaps Rise's friends had really bad luck.

Perhaps it was dangerous to know him or hang out with him.

Well, yeah, it had been.

How long had Betina been stalking him? Could she have been the killer back in Los Angeles, also?

Was close to Rise a dangerous place to be?

Still?

I really hoped Rise would talk to Mike. While the rest of us were still alive.

THE BOYS ARE BACK IN TOWN

Ingredients

1/2 oz of dry vermouth
1 1/2 oz Benedictine
1 1/2 oz absinthe
Blood oranges, if available, for garnish. Regular oranges
may be substituted.

Method

Dehydrated blood oranges
With food dehydrator: slice oranges very thin and place
in dehydrator on 125 degrees for 12 hours. Check
throughout the day to see the progression of dehydration.
Some fruits dehydrate more quickly than others.
Using an oven: slice oranges very thin and spray a non-
stick pan with cooking oil or place parchment paper on
pan. Preheat oven to 225. Lay slices flat on pan and bake
for 2 1/2 or 3 hours, making sure to check oranges peri-
odically.
To speed drying, flip them over about halfway through
baking.

Cocktail

Method

In a cocktail mixing glass, add ice and all 3 liquor ingredi-
ents.
Stir ingredients lightly together.
Strain cocktail mixture into martini glass or coupe glass.

Float dried Blood Orange or regular orange on top of
cocktail for garnish.

189

19
THE BAND PLAYED ON

I DID A reconnaissance run through the lobby during the presentation by Jerry Raker and Troy. It was well attended. Leave it to Jerry to offer heaping plates of appetizers as well as nice wine choices for those who attended.

I wished I could stay to hear the whole talk.

Back in the bar, Marta and I finally had some time to catch up. We agreed that, despite the excitement of the festival, a lot of people, especially our female friends, seemed to be having a hard time right now. I was especially thinking about Hannah and Teresa with her new baby. Not to mention Betina and Marissa and Olive, also not having a great time. And Rachel Hunt, who had recently broken up with Philip—though she seemed to have landed on her feet.

"You know what we should do?" asked Marta.

"What?"

"The festival is over tomorrow, right? Everyone will be leaving town. Why don't we close early and throw a Girls' Night Out party?"

"And invite who?"

"Girls. Whoever we know."

"Interesting suggestion."

Marta was coming into her own, taking responsibility for the pub and coming up with inventive ideas.

Just then, Addie Moon slid onto a bar stool in front of me.

"Hi," I said. "Is the presentation finished?"

"Not quite," she said. "Jerry has a longer battery life than I do. I'm beat."

"I'm sorry I haven't gotten to talk to you more," I said. "I enjoy it when we get to check in." Marta and I looked at each other. "You're still here tomorrow evening, right? When everything is over?"

"Yeah," Addie said. "More planning with Jerry next week."

"If Marta and I threw a Girls' Night Out, here, tomorrow at seven, would you come?"

"Hell, yeah," said Addie. "Why not?"

"Okay, then," I said, and Marta did a fist pump. "Seven it is." As Marta moved on, I leaned in to Addie. "Do you have any idea why Rise has so many stalkers? Or what happened to Marissa Marisol?"

"I think the authorities are right. Rise attracts stalkers because he's way too good-looking and charismatic, but he also seems normal and decent and accessible."

"Mike Spaulding says with Betina in the hospital, he thinks the town will get back to normal."

Addie sighed. "Here's hoping. But I'm pretty sure William is still around. I think the police found him sleeping al fresco by Lake Serenity last night and moved him along. It's possible he simply lacks a ride out of town."

"Well, damn," I said.

"Once they're sure Rise is gone, they'll move along."

"Didn't the police tell Olive to leave town, no matter what?"

"I'm sure they did. When Rise gets back to L.A., he needs to get another order of protection."

"I can't even imagine living like that. To be constantly stalked. A hunted animal."

"Good thing he can afford an assistant/security."

"Yeah, I guess. I'll see you tomorrow if we don't talk before then."

Should I call Mike?

Did the stalkers truly not know that Rise was at my place?

Was Con enough protection?

Everything was calm and bright that night when I left the pub. I finally got to ride my bike home. I looked carefully for any sign of stalkers, then took off like a shot down Main Street. I took comfort in the fact I was too fast for walkers and too slow for automobiles not to show themselves. And why would anyone be following me, anyway? No one other than the gang allowed up to Sally's place knew who was at Sally's place.

As I passed the bank, its bricks looking golden under the streetlights, I caught my breath. A slim young woman lounged against the wall.

Olive?

I slowed my pace. When I looked back, she was gone.

It might not have been her. I'd passed so fast. I stopped the bike. There was a person that could possibly have been her, now walking up the street, holding hands with a tall man. Not Olive. Please have left town, Olive.

Deep breath. Continue on.

I wondered exactly when Sally and Saif were taking off for Paris. I hoped the premiere was everything she'd hoped. It was going to be mighty quiet around here once everyone left, and we locals remained with only each other to talk to.

As I pedaled past the theater, the penultimate film of the festival, *Seeing Color* by S.M. Hunt, was letting out. Most of the films sounded interesting. I hoped I could catch them later.

I saluted Chet and biked up the path. I was suddenly and unexpectedly drenched in dread. I had to convince Rise to talk to Mike. And I had to confront my dear friend, newly discovered, about not drugging me.

Hannah's car was here, but in a different spot. Now I added feeling bad for her to my litany of mood killers.

I walked my blue bike through wet grass, over the bridge, and around the house. I parked it to one side of the back terrace, and went in, ready to deal with any and all of Rise's crises.

"She's here!" Landon heralded as I dropped my bag in the kitchen and walked into the living room. "Guess what! My agent called and guess who is starring in his own secret agent series of feature films, written by a three-time Oscar winner?!"

"Regé-Jean Page?" I queried.

"Nope. Nope. Nope. Me. Little old me. We are celebrating, ladies and gents. I have been carrying a bottle of champagne around for an occasion such as this and—" He pushed buttons on his cellphone, and an impressive swell of music exploded from the device. It was a waltz. "'Casey would waltz with the strawberry blonde, and the band played on...' Look! A strawberry blonde!" Landon grabbed me and we were waltzing around the living room. His joy was infectious. And he was a hell of a great dancer. Rise didn't hesitate. He grabbed Hannah and the two of them took off, whirling and twirling. Both men had an impeccable frame, and we flew around and skirted the furniture and each other until the music changed, to another waltz, 'Top Hat, White Tie and Tails.' As we crossed each other, our partners gave each other a nod and spun Hannah and myself as Landon and Rise changed partners.

Oh, the wonderful things actors had to learn!

Whistle barked for a little while, then began dancing on her own, somehow miraculously not tripping anyone.

I looked up at Rise, he looked down at me. And for a while we were outside of time, with no troubles, beyond danger. Flying. I had longed for this two decades ago. And, finally, here we were.

The four of us continued through another waltz, when a slow song came on. I looked toward Hannah, wondering how she was taking all this. If she was uncomfortable at all, I'd break off the dancing.

She, um, wasn't uncomfortable.

I settled my head on Rise's chest—on Crispin's chest—and we slowed.

I felt his heartbeat.

We were back inside time, but every second was precious. He bent his head. I looked up. He smiled at me, a secret, shared smile, one that cloaked us in hope.

The song ended. We sat. The discouragement I'd felt walking up the hill had fallen away. Hannah also looked like she had more of her equilibrium back.

"Hannah," I said, "what are you doing tomorrow night? Actually, whatever it is, cancel it. You're coming to a Girls' Night Out at the Battened Hatch."

"A *girls'* night?" asked Rise. "What are *we*, chopped liver?"

"You're gone is what you are," I said, then looked hopefully at Hannah.

"What time? I have a church meeting at six," she replied.

"End it by seven."

"I think I can do that. Can I invite people?"

"Sure. Anyone who needs it and would enjoy it."

"What are you doing at this girls' night?" asked Landon.

"Hanging out. Dancing. Having a drink or two."

"I am not scheduled to leave town until Monday," said Rise.

Landon looked thoughtful. "Sounds like you need a DJ and a bartender or two. You shouldn't have to work your own party."

"Well, that's true. Suggestions?"

"I have been known to gig as a bartender," said Landon. "And I've seen our young man Rise here doing his worst behind a bar, also. And, if I'm there, you'd better believe I'm DJing."

"But it's *girls'* night."

"So you let two well-trained men do the work while the 'girls' have a night out."

Hannah mouthed to me, *Are you nuts?*

"Okay, okay. But, Landon, you need to be in New York City by tomorrow night."

"If I fly out by ten, I'll be fine. They'll already have my hotel room checked in and waiting."

"But...having you guys out in public? Stalkers. Gate crashers."

"Everyone thinks we're gone. And no one knows who's bartending except you two. If word gets out, I guess we know who the culprits are."

Technically, I had to say no. No one who didn't work at Mac-

Tavish's was allowed behind the bar for insurance reasons. But Landon was also right. No one would know. And Glenn MacTavish himself had let me tend that very bar before I was hired. No one died. Well, they did, but before I started making drinks.

"Okay, okay," I said. "Not a word."

Not long after, Con came to check in before settling on Sally's porch. Hannah walked them over before departing. Rise and Landon man-hugged good night, and Landon headed for his bedroom.

Rise took my hand as we headed toward the bedroom. I again closed the door against the crestfallen Pomeranian.

My heart was revving a million miles an hour.

Rise leaned down and kissed me. I kissed back. I couldn't not. I remembered that look of unabashed hope he'd worn only minutes ago.

Clothing flew off both of us, though we were still in undergarments as we sat on the bed. Which is when Rise went to the nightstand on his side of the bed. Oddly, it took me a minute to realize what he was doing.

He was back, and he leaned in to kiss me. "Here you go," he said. "Just open your mouth."

"No," I said, "*No*."

"Come on, Av. There's some fun things I want to show you...that we can do."

"I don't want drugs, Crispin."

"It's only Pernexipan. Peter Pans. They don't hurt anything. And I know the dose, the exact dose. It's fine."

"Can't we just kiss? Just make love?"

"Really?" He leaned in again, and his kiss was eager and filled with longing at the same time.

He stopped for a moment, and when he kissed me again, his tongue pushed a pill into my mouth. He held me fast, so I couldn't pull away. His mouth remained clamped over mine.

I shoved him. Shoved him again. Damn, he was bigger than me. And the muscles of his arms were like rocks. I threw him around under me, which he liked fine, and, once I was on top and our kiss broke, I spit out the remains of the Peter Pan.

Then I sat down on the end of the bed and started to cry. They were tears of fury, of confusion, of betrayal.

Rise sat up and put his arm around me. I threw it off and jumped up.

"*What is wrong with you?*" I asked, wondering how much of the Pernexipan I'd ingested. "Get out of here. I mean it. Go!"

Then I realized it was the only available bedroom, and as incensed as I was, I wasn't going to toss him out into Stalker Land.

I ran to my closet and grabbed an oversized shirt, which I pulled on. Then I ran out of the bedroom, through the kitchen and out into the evening.

There was a warm front behind the rain. Thank God. If it had been freezing, I would have been forced back inside. Instead, I went around the back of the cottage. I wanted to find somewhere to lay down before the drugs kicked in. My skin was already crackling and coming alive.

I dropped down into the grass. I had a fleeting thought that if there were stars, I might have been able to at least enjoy part of the experience. But rain clouds still roiled. My whole life was roiling.

I have no idea how long I lay there before Rise found me. I had my eyes closed, and when I opened them, he was sitting there.

"I'm sorry," he said.

"What were you thinking? I said no. Like, the word itself. Multiple times. *No.*"

"Sometimes women are scared to try it. They need a little urging. But once they do…"

"I tried it the other night. I said no."

"No one has ever said no before."

"It's because you're Rise Fucking O'Connor and if they want to sleep with you, they have to do what you want. How are you possibly not aware of that?"

"You think…really?"

"Good god. What is wrong with you?"

"Apparently, I'm tired of being Rise O'Connor. It's gotten toxic. For me, for other people. God, I'm sorry, Av."

He laid down beside me. I rolled on my side to look at him. He was only wearing a shirt and navy briefs. And he was crying.

"Look at all the misery I bring into the world. People leave their families. They upend their lives to follow me. Or, like Dirk, they give me their whole lives and if I fire them, they have no income, no means of support. I play these parts, I get offered these jobs, they're good scripts, they're great parts, but they hurt my heart. And I don't know why.

"I thought...I thought the one thing I could do well, the one way I know I can bring someone joy is making love. Letting us both feel special, rise above. So to speak."

He sat up again. "I have to fire Dirk, but I can't. I don't know how. I feel like he's my responsibility."

"Crispin...Landon is right. So is Troy. People have been using you. Your whole life. You were a kid. It wasn't your responsibility to pay the mortgage or save your mother's salon. If Dirk is a good manager, he can go find some other kid whose parents will be thrilled to know their son or daughter has been chosen by Dirk as the next Rise O'Connor. Let him go! Disney is casting more freaking shows for kids every minute!"

"That should make me feel good. But I can't imagine my life going in any direction that has happiness in it."

"Then step away."

"The industry is brutal. If you go away, chances are you won't be coming back."

"Does that matter to you? I'd say you served your time."

"It might matter. I don't know."

"I can't answer that for you. All I know is, if we get out of this week alive, and you ever, *ever* drug me without my consent, you won't be alive for long."

"I'm sorry. Truly I am. I have to discover who I am again. How to be me. I'm pretty sure, being just me won't be good enough. Suppose you finally got to go to bed with your favorite actor and he was a lousy lay?"

"Oh, dear god. Of all the things you need to worry about, that one...no. Just no."

We sat for a minute. "I'm getting cold. Should we go in?"

"Yeah." Rise helped me to my feet and I grasped him for balance as we made our way back inside the house. We fell back on the bed. "I'm so grateful you're here," said Rise. "Don't worry, I won't try anything."

Given that assurance, I snuggled against him. And even though we'd both ingested a small but noticeable amount of amphetamines, the exhaustion of stalkers and murderers and life decisions waylaid us and we passed out in each other's arms.

It wasn't until the next morning that I saw a text that had come in earlier in the evening from Investigator Spaulding. *Bad news: Betina died. Good news: we now know how. Same cause of death as Ms. Marisol. Will you be at the Battened Hatch tomorrow? I'll stop by.*

THE BAND PLAYED ON

Kimchi Gibson

Ingredients

Small dollop of Small Town Cultures turmeric kimchi ferments (smalltowncultures.faire.com)
2 1/12 oz dry gin of choice
1/4 oz dry vermouth
Dash of celery bitters

Method

Chill martini glass.
In cocktail shaker, add ice, 1/2 of small dollop of turmeric kimchi ferments, dry gin, dry vermouth and celery bitters.
Shake all ingredients together until cocktail shaker is chilled.
Strain into martini glass.
Add remainder of small dollop of kimchi to martini glass.

20
THOSE MAGIC MOMENTS

I WAS THE first one awake.

Crispin lay beside me, looking particularly strong and manly and vulnerable.

I let Whistle out, read Mike's message and pulled on a sweater and pants to head down to pick up breakfast.

When I called the Cardamom Café to put in my order, things seemed normal. But when I arrived, it was to find a throng of people on the street. It took me a minute to realize why.

The store had been vandalized, the front of the shop spray painted a myriad of colors. On the largest window were the words in red: GO BACK WHERE YOU CAME FROM.

My heart dropped.

Of course, Avantika's family was from India, but she was a long-time resident of Tranquility, even before she was widowed. She had put herself out there by running for mayor. I'm sure in many people's eyes, she stood for change, for people of different ethnicities moving to the area, for artists coming. It likely wasn't a coincidence this happened the night after Jerry Raker made his presentation.

True to the spirit and gumption of Tranquility, the line to order breakfast from the café that was growing by the minute showed that our denizens would stand up to bullying. Or terrorizing.

I was glad I'd called in my order. It was waiting for me inside. Avantika handed it to me herself. She wasn't cowed, she was energized.

"You doing okay?" I asked.

"You have to stand for something," she said. "And you don't make a difference if you don't make some people uncomfortable."

We grinned at each other. "Check your phone when you have a minute."

She nodded that she would.

I had her cell number from back when I bought her car. Once I got outside and down the block, I texted her the particulars of the Girls' Night Out, adding *Hope you can come.*

While I was at it, I texted Mike that I would indeed be working my regular hours at the pub and looked forward to seeing him there, knowing he'd likely stop in before we opened.

Then I took my overfilled bags and headed back to my place.

There are times in life you know will become forever memories, even as they're happening. For all its craziness, I was sorry this week would soon be over. I would miss Rise and Landon. I'd even miss the Chets. It would be hard to go to work and come home, then rinse, repeat. It's hard when everyone else moves on and you stay put.

Ah, well. First, breakfast.

I'd purchased an extra pistachio muffin for Chet, and he actually accepted it with gratitude. Avantika's positivity in the face of hostility put me in a good mood, and once back at the cottage, I hummed as I got out plates for the goodies.

I plugged in the teapot and went outside to await my sleepy-headed guests.

Rise appeared first. He'd showered and pulled on loose-fitting pajama pants but wore no shirt. He held a towel, which he used to continue to dry his hair. His slightly sheepish smile asked, "We good?" He must have interpreted my reply as positive, because he strode to stand behind me and put his hands on my shoulders while eyeing the plates of crepes and pastries.

"Morning, Av," he said, letting the towel settle around his bare shoulders, his chest muscles glistening. He kissed the top of my head.

It was at that particular moment, that exact one, that Philip

Young rounded the corner of the cottage. He obviously wasn't expecting the tableau with which he was presented, and he stood stock-still. "Hi," Philip said. "I came for Whistle."

When does this ever happen, the guy who dumped you showing up when you most wish he would? When? Cause just as he said that, the kitchen door banged open and my other guest walked out, shaking off the remnants of sleep, wearing shorts, t-shirt and robe. "Made myself some coffee, Av, hope you don't mind. Wow! That looks fabulous!"

As he pulled out a chair, he saw Philip. "Hello," he said. "Landon Presser." He smiled, strode over and shook Philip's hand.

Philip Young is a marvelous human being who is never at a loss for words. Never, if I live to be 112, will I forget that one remarkable occasion when he was.

Rise, still standing, followed Landon's lead, stepped over to the new arrival, shook his hand, and said, "Rise O'Connor."

Then Rise came back, ran his fingers over my shoulders, and sat next to me. "Can you sit, old man?" Rise asked Philip. "Avalon has certainly provided us with more than we can eat."

("Old man"? What movie was *that* from?)

Philip got ahold of himself and said again, "I've come for my dog."

"Gentlemen," I introduced, "this is Sally's grandson, Philip Young."

Whistle had somehow ducked into the kitchen with all the comings and goings and had inadvertently been closed in. She was now digging furiously at the door in an attempt to reach her human. I grinned at Philip and said, "It sounds like she's ready for you."

Philip followed me to the kitchen. The truth is, I have my own set of Whistle's bowls and treats and food, so there really wasn't much to pack up. I did have a leash. Whistle was so excited at Philip's return that he had to hold her while I snapped it onto her collar because she wouldn't stop dancing.

"How was Paris?" I asked, remaining nonchalant, like I had a house full of famous half-naked actors all the time.

"Good," he said.

"I'll walk you down," I said. It seemed only polite and was surely what one would do for any friend about whom one had no overwhelming feelings.

"Thanks for recommending Rachel to do the catering at the theater," Philip said.

"Sure," I said. "Are you two—?"

"We're not together," he said.

I nodded as if any answer would be okay and equal in my opinion.

As we crossed the bridge from the house where Philip had grown up, I looked and saw the car he had pulled up in below. It was a white luxury car, obviously built for speed.

"Holy crap," I said. "Is that yours?" It was a sports car, aerodynamic design with chrome details.

"Yeah," he said, and now he grinned. "I sold some paintings in Paris. It's a Porsche 911."

"Zero to sixty in…?"

"Three point five seconds. Takes turns really well."

"Holy crap. She's really pretty, too."

"Yeah," he said, a look of total awe on his face. "She is."

"Congratulations. I'm really happy for you."

I was.

He opened the passenger side door. Whistle studied the situation for only a moment before jumping in. Philip walked around, got in, and started the engine. He did a three-point turn (gorgeous red design around the taillights) and rolled as slowly as the vehicle could possibly go down the lane.

I returned for a final breakfast with my guests.

Even in the light of day, Landon still wanted to bartend and DJ the party. He contacted his pilot and was able to push his flight time back a few hours.

Rise was of the same mind about bartending. It was risky to have him out and about, of course.

"You can only come if Con does," I said. "Come to think of it, I was planning to invite them to the party, anyway. I guess calling it a Girls' Night narrows it unnecessarily. It's a Anyone-Who-Doesn't-Identify-As-A-Man night out. I'd love Con to come, but I kind of hate that they'd need to be working."

"Con and I are used to working while having fun," said Rise. "It's a thing we do."

I got ready for work, texting folks to invite them to the party as I thought of them. I was looking forward to it.

Rise came into the bedroom as I was finishing up.

"I wanted to let you know that I'm talking to Dirk today. Letting him go. It's time."

"That won't be an easy discussion."

"No, but it's past due. It will be easier knowing you and Landon are in my corner."

"Good luck."

"One more thing. Would you mind if I stay one more night? If I'm working a party, it would be easier. Con and I could leave in the morning. If that doesn't work, I could get a hotel, of course. There must be rooms opening up."

"Don't be crazy. Of course, you can stay. Tomorrow we can have a proper goodbye. When are you going to talk to Dirk?"

"As soon as I get my courage up. Say a little prayer for me if you think of it."

"Will do."

Philip's new car was like a ghost image as I crossed the bridge and hopped on my bike. If he'd sold enough paintings to be able to afford that, how many paintings had he sold? He deserved respect in the art world. He was crazy talented.

A Stitch in Time: Saving the Penguins of Australia by B.K. Sherer was the Sunday morning wrap-up film and the audience was beginning to assemble.

At MacTavish's, I stashed my bike in the storeroom, and went back to survey the pub that was my kingdom. It looked great. I was happy that Rise and Landon would have a chance to see it. It would be a fun party, even if Marta, Hannah, Con and I were the sole participants.

The autumn air was so brisk and clear that I opened the door to the smokers' porch to let it in.

Someone was knocking at the hall door.

Mike Spaulding. I let him in. Usually, if I knew he was coming, I left the door unlocked. Not this time. Subconscious at work?

"Good morning," I said. "Have a seat. Can I get you an orange juice?"

"Actually, yes. I'd like that."

"So, what's going on?"

"Someone from Betina's family is coming to i.d. the body and take it back for burial."

"Oh. I'm sorry. Truly."

"Yes, me, too."

"And she was found by Chateau Tranquility. In the woods."

"Yes. Sitting against a tree."

"Simply sitting there?"

"Simply sitting there."

"Cause of death?"

"Overdose. Same as Marissa."

"Overdose of what?" I hated the word, since it only recently applied to our friend Winsome.

"A drug called Pernexipan. Peter Pans on the street."

Dread washed through me.

Mike said, "What? What are you thinking?"

"Just...remembering finding my friend dead from an overdose."

We were quiet.

"Flashbacks can surprise you for quite a while," said Mike.

"Yeah. I guess."

"You sure that's all, Avalon?"

"That's *all*?" I asked, deflecting. "I really...can't talk any more right now. I've got to get ready to open."

"Sure. Later," he said, and put a hand, meant to be comforting, on my arm. "As always, if you think of anything..."

"Yup."

Once he was gone, all I could think of was Rise, telling me it was okay, he knew the exact dose...

THOSE MAGIC MOMENTS

Ingredients

2 oz Hpnotiq liquor
1 oz coconut rum
1 oz white rum
1 oz unsweetened coconut milk
Large dollop of coconut cream such as Coco Lopez, gently mixed until smooth (rimming)
Toasted shredded coconut (method below, used for rimming)

Method

Toasted shredded coconut:
In a small frying pan, add a half cup of shredded unsweetened coconut flakes.
Turn burner on low and gently stir the shredded coconut until it becomes a light brown color, 45 seconds to one minute. Watch carefully as coconut will brown very quickly.

Cocktail

Method

On a small plate, add dollop of coconut cream making sure that it is silky smooth. On a separate small plate add toasted coconut.
Dip a cocktail glass into coconut cream and then into shredded toasted coconut
In a cocktail shaker add ice, Hpnotiq, coconut rum, white

rum, and coconut milk and shake all ingredients together
until cocktail shaker is chilled.
Pour into cocktail glass.

21
CLOSING EARLY

WAS RISE PLANNING to kill me? I mean, simply the thought sounded crazy.

And yet...

Both Marissa and Betina were in Rise's orbit. Both died from an overdose of his recreational drug of choice.

It couldn't be Rise who killed them. Couldn't be. For one thing, he wasn't even in town the night before the film festival when Marissa died, he was in some cabin somewhere. Without a car, even. Right? As for Betina, he would have had to have found her, drugged her, and gotten over to the Chateau between my freezer incident and when Dirk and I arrived at my place, and found Rise there. Without an Uber at the ready or Philip's crazy fast car, I'm not seeing it.

Plus, Rise. My Rise. I knew him. Since he was a little kid. Issues and all.

"I know the exact dose..."

Or...was he deciding how much to give me, and whether (or when) to kill me?

I wanted to throw up.

It couldn't be true. For no other reason than he'd know he'd get caught. He was the obvious nexus. Or did he see self-sabotage as a way out of the life in which he felt stuck?

Slow down. Think. Who else in the film world thought Peter Pans were good fun?

There was still a chance the answer was Betina, that she somehow figured out Marissa was here to see Rise and offed the competition.

Think logically.

Who was close enough to Rise to likely know he enjoyed enhanced lovemaking? Who would help him get what he wanted? All I could think of were possibly Con and Dirk.

Dirk. Rise was so hesitant to fire him. Dirk had run his life since he was young. Hollywood was famous for plying its youth with uppers and downers. I could imagine a scenario in which Dirk demanded Rise work harder, longer, later.

As I was pondering, a text came in. *I did it. Fired Dirk. OMG.*

How did he take it?

Not well.

Of course, he wouldn't take it well. Rise O'Connor was Dirk's bread and butter. His virtual son, his creation, his life. Dirk likely knew everything there was to know about Rise. What exactly did he know? How exactly did he control Rise? Did he have anything over on him? Had he been waiting for this day, saving up things to blackmail his protégé with? Peter Pans were obviously illegal. Did he supply the drugs? Was he ready to plant more of them on Rise, then turn him in? Was there anything else Dirk knew, could use? Would Dirk be willing to lie to ruin Rise?

I really, really had to get a grip.

If Rise fired Dirk, and Dirk was angry, I should take him off the okayed list with the Chets. Tell them not to let Dirk back onto my property. Of course, the Chets had never given me a phone number. They'd always made me walk down in person to authorize someone. *Damn.*

I texted back to Rise, *You aren't afraid he'll do something rash, are you?*

Define rash.

Not the answer I was hoping for.

Killing someone.

I sent it and then added, *With a drug overdose.* Okay, as long as I was doing this, I might as well do it. *So he can blame you.*

No answer for several minutes. Then, *WHAT?*

"Hi," said Marta, arriving the same time as Davros and Manuela.

"Hello," I said.

"Should I make a sign saying we're closing at seven for a private party?" Marta asked.

"You should indeed."

I read back over my last email exchange. It sounded crazy, even to me.

Don't tell him where you'll be tonight. Don't tell anyone. My fingers flew.

What's going on?

I'll tell you later. Stick close to Landon and Con.

You're freaking me out.

Sorry. You've got enough going on. Forget I said anything. I'm letting my imagination run away with me. Seriously. Sorry. I can't stop thinking about Betina and Marissa. Nothing new.

I put my phone down and greeted some regular customers. The afternoon started off busy and only built from there.

I was itching to text, *Don't trust Dirk*, but this was a man Rise had known for most of his life. He certainly knew Dirk and what he was capable of better than I did.

Yet he'd been hesitant, even afraid, of firing Dirk.

Let it go, Avalon.

The lunch rush took off around me, and I let myself be carried away.

I was surprised mid-afternoon when Hannah stopped by. Sundays are busy for her. She wore her black skirt and shirt and jacket along with her white priest's collar. It reminded me of the first time I'd seen her, eating right here in this pub with the rest of Tranquility's Chamber of Commerce. I'd been impressed that anyone still wore pantyhose.

"Hi," she said.

"Hi," I said. "You aren't here to say you can't make it tonight, are you?"

"Nope. On my way between meetings, and I wanted to sit for a minute, and talk to my favorite barkeep."

"Any time. What's up?"

She pulled up a photo and turned around her phone. It was a new daddy, looking at a tiny baby. The dad wore a silly grin. The infant studied him intently. She was too young to smile, but she had a look of knowing she was home.

"Adorable," I said. "Sophie?"

"Yes." She made a swiping motion, and I went to the other photos, of the mom cradling the newborn, then the little brothers crammed together in a chair, baby in their laps. They were entranced.

"Teresa and Matt. Stopped in to see them. Turns out they already have two mortgages on their home."

"Oh, no," I said. "That can't be good. Do they have anywhere to go if they lose their house? Family nearby?"

"No. People are already saying they shouldn't have had a third child. But little Sophie was so wanted. They could have skated by, if not for the complications."

"I'm sorry," I said. "Sorry for them. And I know how these things lodge inside you."

"There has to be something I can do. There has to be a way. They're such a loving and hardworking family. I don't understand how religious people can take an unyielding stand against abortion, then let the child's family lose everything the minute they're born. It seems to me that healthcare is a necessary part of 'right to life.'"

"I agree."

"I know you don't have long to talk. I needed to vent before my next meeting."

"Come by any time."

Hannah gave a grateful smile. "Thanks. And—thanks for including me with your guests this week. What a hoot."

"A hoot?"

"Can't think of a better word."

"Okay," I said, leaning forward. "I have a question for you, one you'll never tell anyone I ever asked."

"Ready."

"Could Rise O'Connor kill someone?"

Hannah started to laugh but saw my expression. "You're serious."

"First response. Off the cuff."

"Of course not. Unless—" She leaned in, nearly meeting me in the middle. "Unless something happened when you two were alone? Did he try something? To hurt you?"

"No. No, nothing like that. It's that...it turns out Rise's recreational drug of choice is the same one that killed Betina and Marissa Marisol, the young girl in the movie theater."

"Oh." She sat back. "If everyone who used some sort of recreational drug was a killer, funerals would be my main gig. I come down definitively in the 'Rise O'Connor isn't a murderer' camp."

That cheered me. Hannah, for all her annoying optimism, had a good head on her shoulders and routinely saw corners of the human condition few others did. She'd met more than one killer in her day. Her certainty relieved me.

The supper crowd was light. Film festival folks were checking out and heading home. Everyone was a bit spent.

Until 7 p.m. when we cleared everyone out and the party started.

I'd told Marta I was letting two visiting men in to bartend and DJ. When Landon and Rise showed up, I thought she might faint.

"Could you show Rise where everything is behind the bar?" I asked. "Oh and show Landon our music set-up."

While I was at it, I made up pitchers of an alcoholic and non-alcoholic harvest cocktail, so the men didn't have to mix every cocktail one at a time.

As long as I'm collecting unforgettable moments, I'm going to add every minute of those three hours. Partly because I knew Landon would be leaving straight from the pub to the airport, and Rise would leave early the next day.

Mostly because it was the most fun possible. Hannah was there, and brought friends, Addie Moon brought film people; Gillian Petrakov, an Olympic medalist ice skater, brought her wife and Olympic people. Avantika brought friends who really knew how to dance. I'd invited Rachel Hunt, too, and she'd invited some of her best friends from Tranquility...well, you get the idea. Con, was there of course, having a good time, but not letting their guard down. They kept an eye on the door where we admitted partygoers.

I did, too.

Perhaps my favorite moment came shortly after seven when I was able to say, "Folks, there are currently two actors being sought the world over by their fans, but these gentlemen seem to have disappeared. I'm happy to announce they heard we could use some bartenders this evening. *But you may not tell anyone they are here. No texting, no social media of any kind. Please.* It is a matter of urgency. This ban is lifted as of ten a.m. tomorrow morning. If you have itchy fingers and can't abide by this, please leave now."

Oddly, no one did.

"Alrighty then, one final rule: no photos of them behind the bar. Otherwise, come order a drink or at least stop up and say hello to Rise O'Connor and Landon Presser!"

Hooting and hollering.

Landon said, into the mic, "You mean DJ ImPRESSer!" He started with 'Long, Cool Woman in a Red Dress,' and went on to play songs from many eras up to modern day. Everyone danced. Most of us needed to expend some energy and banish some nerves, and we sure did that. Every single person I saw on the dance floor was happy to be there. It struck me that they were all new friends to me as of this year, but they felt like old friends.

I even danced with Rachel Hunt.

I wish Philip could have seen that.

The magical night was just starting to wind down when Landon motioned to me from behind the bar. He and I stepped back unobtrusively. "My car is here. I'm heading out," he said. "Thanks again for a great few days. I am on Eastern Standard Time and newly energized."

"You're very welcome."

"I feel like an honorary member of the Salty Gang."

"You are. Friends forever. Come back any time."

"And you have my number, should anything come up."

"I do."

He took me in a warm embrace. "One last favor. After I'm gone, at the end of the evening, will you give this to Hannah?"

It was a sealed envelope bearing the return address of MacTavish's, which he'd undoubtedly gotten from the front desk.

"Will do."

"Bye, Av. Take care of the young man."

"I'll try my best."

With that, I took him to exit through the kitchen. And he was gone.

Half an hour later, we announced closing. All of us who worked at the Battened Hatch transformed into closing up fairies. When I saw Hannah getting ready to go, I gave her the envelope and went back to closing chores.

Next thing I knew, Hannah was sitting alone at a table, tears streaking her cheeks.

I went and sat across from her. "What is it?"

A piece of hotel stationary sat on the table. She pushed it towards me.

Dear Hannah, I wanted you to know I have been in contact with the billing department at the hospital and Teresa's and Sophie's bill is taken care of. Also, my accountant will be in touch with their mortgage lenders on Monday to get things straightened out. I'd like this to be anonymous. -Landon

Hannah said, "He once told me he'd rather give enough to really help fewer people than to give a Band-Aid that wouldn't last to many more."

Well, damn.

"Sometimes prayers are answered." Yes, it was me who said that.

Hannah wiped her eyes and waved at her waiting friends. "Okay. Heading out. We'll talk tomorrow. Great party."

"Sure thing."

Soon everyone was gone, except me, Rise and Con.

Rise and Con sat amiably at the bar as I cashed out. "We did well tonight," I said. "Great bartending."

Rise laughed. "I could have made twice as many drinks if I didn't need to pose for a selfie with the recipient of every order. But I had a good time. This is a beautiful pub, Avalon. I can see why you love it here."

"Really?"

"Yeah. Really."

"All right, I'm done. We can go. Except, I haven't given a thought to how we get home. Shall I call an Uber?"

Con and Rise exchanged glances. Con stood and wandered away.

Rise said, "Actually, I was hoping I could prevail upon you to take a moonlight stroll with me."

"A moonlight stroll?"

"Yup. I'm leaving in the morning, and I know my behavior hasn't been the best. I'd like us to part on a positive note."

"Crispin, you don't have to..."

"I want to. Please. Come."

It's funny how seldom we humans actually look straight into each other's eyes. Crispin looked into mine. "Please."

"Of course."

He grinned and took my hand.

Then we walked behind Con through the hotel lobby just like normal people and out the front door where the limo waited for us. Castor opened the back door for Rise and me. Con got into the passenger's seat. And we took off into the night.

CLOSING EARLY

Harvest Punch (with alcohol)

Ingredients

Large cocktail pitcher
2 cans of dry hard apple cider from your area (support local)
1 bottle of dry champagne
2 cups orange juice
2 cups apple cider
1 cup apple mash
1/4 cup cranberries
1 green apple sliced thin
1 orange sliced thin
4 cinnamon sticks

Apple Mash

Ingredients

3 apples sweet and tart peeled and cut into small cubes
1 cup sugar
1/4 tsp ground ginger
1/4 tsp ground all spice
2 tbsp ground cinnamon
Dash ground black pepper
1 small orange cut into slices
Juice of one fresh lemon
1 cup orange juice
3 cups water

Method

Pour all ingredients into medium saucepan. Keep on medium to low heat until apples have become soft, about 35-45 minutes, making sure to stir occasionally.
Turn off heat and let sit until room temperature. Pour into container and keep in refrigerator. Retain the cooking liquids as you will use in cocktail.

Cocktail

Method

Pour all liquids into large cocktail pitcher and add all fruits and cinnamon sticks stirring together gently with a large serving spoon.
Put an ice bucket on the side. Do not add ice to large cocktail pitcher as this will water down the Harvest Punch. Set up glasses on the side.
To serve, fill glass with ice, then pour punch into each glass, finishing with a dollop of fruit.

Harvest Punch (Non-Alcoholic)

Ingredients

Large cocktail pitcher
2 bottles of non-alcoholic sparkling cider or wine
1 cup orange juice
2 cups apple flat apple cider
1 cup apple mash (recipe above)
1/4 cup cranberries
1 green apple sliced thin
1 orange sliced thin

4 cinnamon sticks

Method

Pour all liquids into large cocktail pitcher, then add the
fruit and cinnamon sticks. Stir gently with a large serving
spoon.
Put ice an ice bucket on the side. Do not add ice to large
cocktail pitcher as this will water down the Harvest
Punch. Set up glasses on the side.
To serve, fill glass with ice, then pour punch, finishing
with a dollop of fruit.

22

HARVEST MOON

THE LAST FEW days had been so rainy I hadn't realized the moon was inching towards full. Tonight there was not a cloud in the sky, and the Harvest Moon illuminated the road through the mountains as we drove out of town.

I know this because the limo had a moonroof.

Rise said, "Would you like some champagne?"

I'd had one drink during the party, mostly because I wanted to use our celebrity bartenders, but I'm not actually a big drinker—and I was in charge, even if I was partying.

Now I wasn't.

"Sure."

Apparently, Rise had this excursion well-planned. There was a bottle of champagne on ice, which he opened with expertise. He poured two flutes and handed me one.

"To old friends."

"Old friends."

Our glasses clinked.

"It's so beautiful around here, Av," he said.

"It really is."

An idea came to him, and he pushed the button to open the moonroof. "Come on."

He stood up, champagne in hand. I joined him. We'd left town, and the mountain roads were windy and dark. Castor drove carefully but still fast enough that I felt like a dog hanging its head outside the window. We quickly popped back down.

Crispin put on some music, settled onto the bench seat in the back, and opened his arms. I sat against him and he pulled me close. I was ready to relax. I could easily have fallen asleep.

We rode for another five minutes before the limo turned up a smaller road. At the turn was a forty-foot statue of a moose, with two small spotlights for emphasis. We rode on for another few minutes, then made a turn and slowed down, eventually coming to a stop. Crispin nudged me and we climbed out.

I knew exactly where we were: Starlight Falls, a popular hiking trail that made a mile loop along the Ausable River past a beautiful waterfall. But at night?

As Rise checked in with Castor and Con, I walked forward. The parking lot was situated on a bluff high above the river. While the lot had two streetlights, the river was so far below and cloaked by darkness that I only knew it was there by the sound of rushing water.

"Come on." Crispin offered his hand and I took it.

Castor and Con were outside the limo, leaning against the hood. Castor was having a smoke. The trail we were taking was a loop; from where they sat, Con could see anyone who followed us.

Crispin turned on his phone flashlight and we headed toward the trail.

At one point, the trail came out from beneath the trees and ran along the river. Moonlight illuminated the path. Our eyes adjusted enough that Crispin turned off his phone. A wooden split-rail fence ran along the river so no one would tumble over by accident. There was a small solar light every hundred feet or so, enough to lure you forward.

Full-throated owls bandied calls back and forth over the persistent hum of crickets.

It was magical.

The parking lot had been empty, so it was no surprise that we walked alone. We didn't talk, we simply enjoyed nature's music, the friendly moon and the power of the river rushing below us.

The sound of water crashing grew louder as we approached the waterfall. And then there it was, and it was stirring. Fifty feet high, and lights placed strategically behind the water gave it an unearthly glow as the river cascaded from the mountain bluff above to the deep, rocky pool below.

Sometimes nature encapsulates you in its grandeur in such a way you never want to escape. Crispin and I stood, awestruck. Then he wrapped his arms around me, and still we stood, entranced by the mist of the falls and encased in a moment far beyond time.

Eventually, Crispin took my hand and we walked forward and onto the return path, until we were far enough away that we could hear each other when we spoke. At that point he turned and took both my hands in his.

"This week has unexpectedly been a week of many decisions. Having you and Landon and Con and Troy to talk to has helped me see my way forward more clearly. In fact, I had a long talk with Landon, who pointed out that I need to rid myself of a number of crutches. My plan is to check into rehab, to get my mind clear without Dirk or Isobel or Peter Pans. To be me.

"Then I plan to take a break, and maybe go on an extended vacation with my mom up to Victoria, Canada, maybe, to spend time with her before her dementia worsens.

"But this is a long way around of saying..." Here, he got nervous. He took a step away from me and went down on one knee.

"Avalon, will you be my person? I don't want to ask you to commit to marrying me, you might find out I'm too much of a fixer-upper. But, for now? When I'm done with rehab, can we go away together? Sometimes with my mom, but mostly just us? Somewhere beautiful, where we can just be away. I've got money saved. We can hang out. Just live."

"You mean...leave Tranquility? Leave my life here?"

"I know it's asking a lot. But we could reorient ourselves. See what we want to do with the rest of our lives."

I'm not often stunned and speechless, but...

"Crispin, we've been together a few days!'

"Twenty years," he corrected.

"True. True."

What to say? What to think?

"You know I love you. Like, I really love you," I started. "And it's a good plan to go and untangle everything your dad and Dirk and the industry has done with you, and you with it. I'm all for it. And, yes, please yes, spend this precious time with your mother."

"I need you, Av. I need your strength and good common sense to get me through this. I really, really do."

"Crispin. This is sudden. I love my life here. I love my new friends and my job. I love that I did it myself—so I know what you mean, about standing on your own two feet. But I…I…"

He stood, as I struggled for words.

"I'm not ready to give up my journey to be part of yours. I'm not seeing yet how the journey would be ours, I'm only seeing how it would be yours with me along for the ride.

"That doesn't mean I don't love you, that I haven't always loved you. It doesn't mean I won't want us to journey together in the future. It only means that right now, my journey is still here. But—when you've done what you need to do on your own, and figured things out, you know where to find me."

Now he was at a loss for words.

Finally, he said, "So, this isn't no, forever, no."

"It isn't no, forever. Only for now."

One thing he'd have to get better at, my Crispin, was hearing no.

"You'll still be my best friend."

"I will."

"And maybe more."

"Maybe."

We walked slowly back to the waiting car. Con and Castor got in without asking any questions. Crispin and I got into the back and sat leaning together back into town.

Castor dropped off Con, Rise and me on Cherry Lane and we walked up into Mill Pond, past Sally's house to my house. No Whistle, of course, which I found disappointing. Con came in with us, and I offered them the bedroom that had been Landon's. They declined, washed their face and brushed their teeth and headed over the bridge to keep watch on Sally's porch for the last time.

Crispin and I got ready for bed. He stood in the middle of the bedroom floor, waiting for me. We hugged.

"Can we make love one more time, to say good-bye?"

"Just us?"

"Just us. No Peter Pan."

"Good-bye *for now*," I added.

"For now."

And so Crispin and I made love. We really made love.

Afterwards, we fell asleep holding each other, with tears running down our cheeks.

HARVEST MOON

Cranberry Curd Sparkling Sangria

Ingredients

- 1 dollop homemade cranberry curd (recipe below)
- 1 oz orange liqueur (preferably Grand Marnier)
- 4 oz sparkling white wine
- Fresh citrus peel
- Fresh cranberries
- Cranberry curd
- 2 1/2 cups fresh cranberries
- 1/2 cup water
- 3 egg yolks
- 1 whole egg
- 3/4 cup of sugar
- 4 tablespoons unsalted butter, cut into small cubes

Method

In a small saucepan, combine cranberries and water. Keep covered, on medium heat until cranberries pop and the liquid comes to a low boil or bubbling point, about 10 to 15 minutes.

Turn off heat.

Take the cooked, broken down cranberries and pass through a metal mesh strainer, making sure to use a spatula and press the liquid through. Clean bottom of strainer for usable purée.

In separate bowl, whisk the 3 egg yokes with 1 whole egg until combined. Then whisk in sugar.

Put cranberry mixture back into saucepan and slowly mix
in the egg and sugar mixture. Whisk until creamy.
Turn on medium heat for 8 to 10 minutes until curd
thickens and has a nice nap on the back of a wooden
spoon.
Remove saucepan from heat. Slowly add butter one cube
at a time while mixing.
Strain into bowl and place in fridge for an hour or two
until completely cooled

Cocktail

Method

In cocktail shaker, add ice, a large dollop of homemade
cranberry curd and orange liqueur. Shake ingredients
together and pour into a Collins glass
Fill remainder of glass with a small amount of ice and
then top off with sparkling white wine.
Garnish with fresh citrus peel and cranberries

$$23$$

UNPLUGGED

I FORGOT TO plug in my phone the night before. I'd been a bit distracted.

So I plugged it in on Monday morning to charge while I went to fetch breakfast. Our last one together.

I called in an order for three crepes, figuring I'd give Con one, whether they wanted it or not. It had all kinds of healthy stuff in it. Right up their alley.

The order wasn't quite ready when I arrived, but I was more than happy to chat with Avantika and a couple of other women who'd been at the Battened Hatch the night before.

I blocked out knowledge that Rise was leaving within a couple of hours and I didn't know when, or really if, I'd see him again.

I grabbed the bag when my order was up, pushed out the front door, and almost ran into Mike Spaulding who stood squarely in my path just outside the doorway. He stepped to one side and grabbed my arm, pulling me with him.

"You'd tell me if Rise O'Connor was still in town, right?" he asked. He flicked his phone and turned it around to show the photo an attendee had posted of Rise and Landon at the Battened Hatch the night before. "Right?"

I glanced at my watch. 10:15. Damn. The moratorium was over. More photos were sure to be cropping up.

"If Landon Presser and Rise O'Connor want to run a party at my bar, I'm supposed to say no?"

"You're supposed to call me."

"Suppose I know for certain Rise had nothing to do with the murders?"

"If that is true, you call me because *you obviously know* a *hell of a lot* you aren't mentioning."

We looked at each other. He didn't look emotional and like I'd betrayed our friendship. He looked professional and angry and like someone I didn't know.

"I didn't tell you because you were suspicious of him, you told me not to trust him, but I do trust him and I know he wouldn't do it and I didn't want you to ruin his career if word got out that police were questioning him about a murder."

Mike stared at me like I was from Mars. "How little do you know me?" he asked.

"He's leaving town today, he might already be gone. But if he's around, I can see if he'll talk to you. But not at State Police HQ. I'll see if he'll come to my place at noon. Would that work?"

"Let him know it's important, and it will mean a lot to the families of the deceased if we can end this."

"It will mean a lot to Rise, also. He is living in fear."

"Then we should be working together."

"Let me eat breakfast and shower. I'll text you as soon as I hear back."

"Avalon." He sounded put out.

"Mike."

I walked in the direction of my cottage.

He stood on the sidewalk watching me go.

Damn. First, Rise *should* talk to him. They should work together. But if he didn't want to talk, he and Con could be gone in half an hour, long before noon.

I felt oddly like I was harboring a fugitive, instead of an actor hoping for a new life.

I was so wrapped up in my thoughts that it took me a moment to realize that someone was ahead of me on Cherry Lane, heading for the clearing at a good clip.

It was Olive.

I grabbed for my phone, which was charging at my place. *Damn.*

I started running, to catch up with her. Perhaps she didn't know for certain that Rise was here. She disappeared around the corner. She was stalking forward with determination, that was for certain.

By the time I turned the corner, Olive had come to a stop. She looked from Sally's place to mine, not certain which residence to choose.

The screen door on Sally's porch opened and slammed shut.

Con strode across the drive.

Instead of being disappointed or worried, Olive's countenance brightened. If Con was near, so was Rise.

Con said, "Olive, he's not here."

Olive said, "Oh, I think he is. And he's expecting me."

"He's not, and this is private property. You've got to go before I call the police."

Olive pulled a gun.

I had no phone to call 911. I turned and ran for the guardhouse to get a Chet. Finally, they'd be good for something!

No Chet was sitting outside or gardening or looking out the window. I banged on the door.

No one answered.

I pulled on it, pounding.

The house was empty. Of course it was. The Chets were not hired to keep me safe, or Rise.

Sally and Saif had left for Paris.

Damn! The quickest thing would be to get to my phone, but how? Maybe I could talk to Olive. Maybe she'd remember me, would listen to me.

I ran back up the lane and around the corner and found Olive and Con in the same positions.

"Olive, you haven't broken the law yet. If you put the gun down, we can make this all go away." Con was dead calm.

Olive's laugh was shrill. "Why would I want it to go away? I'm going to love someone or I'm going to kill someone. I'm going to do something, be somebody. I'm not going to go away and be nobody."

Should I call out to her? She seemed irrational. Would she turn around and shoot me?

Break the pattern, break the pattern. Do something unexpected.

"Hi, Olive, I brought some breakfast," I said cheerfully. "Would you like some?"

She spun around. "It's me, Avalon. Do you like crepes?"

Con ran down the hill towards the girl.

It only took Olive a moment to compute what was going on. She apparently was high functioning.

She whirled, saw Con much closer than before, planted her feet, held out her arms, and pulled the trigger.

The gun's retort reverberated through the glen. Olive went flying backwards, landing on her butt.

Con kept coming forward.

Olive caught her breath and regained her determination. She sat up, pointed at Con, and shot again.

This time, the bullet came mighty close.

Con kept coming.

What could I do? How do you handle someone with a gun who can't shoot straight? Did I have a hope in hell of disarming her? Seemed like you couldn't count on her not to shoot you, if only by accident. But come on! If your self-described job title is stalker, and you'd outfitted yourself with a firearm, wasn't it at least your job to learn to use it properly?

Damn. I couldn't let her keep shooting at Con. I had to jump her from the back.

As I positioned myself to run, an engine gunned behind me.

The white limousine roared into the glen and did a three-quarter turn.

Con stopped in their tracks. Olive stood and whirled around.

Castor opened his window. "Are you Olive?" he asked. "Rise O'Connor sent me to get you."

Olive stood, slack-jawed.

"Are you free right now?" Castor asked. "Can you come?"

A visible change came over Olive. "Yes. Are you for real?"

"Have you not seen me drive Rise around? This is his limo. He sent me to fetch you."

Castor got out of the car and went around to open the back door. "Can you come, or shall I tell him you said no?"

Olive started to shake. This was not part of her plan. He could be fooling her. But it's what she'd dreamed of for years.

"Where is he?"

"I can't tell you, you know that. He's hidden. But he sends me for his friends."

I was still determined to get to my phone, to call 911. I walked calmly around the side of the limo, past the open door. "Are you sure he didn't send you for *me*?" I asked, trying to make Castor's offer seem legitimate. "I bought breakfast. I thought he might want breakfast."

Castor was standing, locking eyes with Olive. "Are you coming, or not?"

"I'm coming."

"Put the gun down. You have to know Rise doesn't like guns. I won't tell him about this. Just drop it. You can get it later."

To her credit, Olive didn't drop the gun, which could still have caused a tragedy. She stooped and set it carefully on the ground. Then she walked toward the limo.

All I could think was, *Thank God for Castor*. He could lure her into the car and lock it.

If she would get in.

Olive threw her shoulders back and walked proudly to where Castor stood, cap in hand, holding the back limo door open for her.

She stooped to enter the limo. From where I stood, I could see her give the driver a conspiratorial smile.

To my surprise, Castor stepped into the back of the limousine and whispered something to her. Her eyes widened. She nodded.

He opened the hidden compartment where I'd seen Rise get the script from Isobel and the other small packet. It made sense now. I knew what was in the packet.

Castor put something into Olive's hand.

"Do it now so you'll be ready," he said. He climbed back out of the car. "You don't actually need water. They'll melt beneath your tongue." He winked at her.

I stood, transfixed. In Olive's hand were four pills, considerably larger than the ones Rise had used. What was Castor doing? That was enough to poison a horse.

"Olive! Don't take them!" I lunged forward, and dove into the limo. She saw me coming, gave a smile of triumph, and put all four pills into her mouth. She let herself plunk onto the back bench seat.

"Spit them out! That's too much!" I plead, kneeling on the floor in front of her.

"Rise likes to get high when he makes love." She smirked at me, believing she was the chosen one.

"No! Not like that!" I said.

Then the door closed behind me. I looked out the window to see Castor lock the doors with his key fob.

No.

I lunged across and tried the door. It was well and truly locked.

Castor walked around the car to the driver's seat and entered through the open door, which he closed behind him. We were all locked in together. He started the motor. And we rolled out.

No, no, no.

"Olive, spit them out!" I said. "It's too much. It might kill you."

"You poor, jealous little thing," she said.

And she opened her mouth to let me see they had nearly all dissolved. I dived for her, hoping to what? Use a finger to sweep the rest from her mouth? But I wasn't quick enough. She clamped her mouth shut.

"Ooooh," she said for my benefit, "I'm feeling gooood." She dropped back against the seat, writhing a bit for emphasis.

As Castor drove down Cherry Lane, Philip and Whistle turned in by the now-vacated guardhouse. As we drove past, I banged on my window. Philip looked up, and when he realized it was me, he was surprised. "Help," was all I could mouth before we drove past.

The look on his face was one of confusion and concern. Then he was gone, and Castor shaded the windows, so I could see out, somewhat, but no one outside could see in.

"Oh my god," said Olive, "You have to try these. Heaven is taking over my body. It's filling me up, like punch. From my toes...to my knees...to my...oh, Rise..."

Oh, fuck.

We turned onto Main Street for half a block, then made a right up the hill to the road that ran parallel. The car drove fast along residential roads.

The front panel wasn't fully open, but the speaker was on. "Castor!" I said. "Stop! Let me out!"

He barely glanced back. He had his phone out and was dialing. It wasn't on speaker, but through the phone I heard the distant ring of another. I took a breath. Maybe it was the police. Maybe he was taking us to State Police Headquarters to let them deal with Olive.

It didn't seem likely.

"Hello, Daddy?"

"Callie? You picked up! I thought I was going to have to leave a message!"

"What is it? Why are you calling?"

"I have something to tell you and I need you to listen very carefully."

"I'm late, I'm walking out the door. Maybe you can call back and leave a voicemail."

"In my apartment. There's a safe in my bedroom. The combination is your birthday. Got that?"

"Safe at your place. My birthday." She was still sounding nonchalant and a bit irritated.

"It's all in there. All the information about bank accounts.

They're Swiss. It's your money. All of it. I've saved it all for you. I wrote instructions how to get it. The account is in your name, so there's no taxes or anything. It's yours, free and clear. You don't even need to tell the cops."

"What are you talking about?"

"Calista, I...love you. You and Emilia and your mom. No matter what you hear. I did everything for you."

"Everything, what everything?"

We were at the intersection that led out of town. He turned right at the first light, left at the next, and headed into the mountains.

A strange gurgling sound came from the woman beside me. "Olive? Olive?" I shook her.

She barely registered. One eye opened an eighth of an inch. "Come on in," she said.

Would it help if I put my finger down her throat and made her throw up? Probably not. The pills had already dissolved under her tongue, they were in her blood stream, not in her stomach.

"Callie. Callie, this is important. Go over to my place right now and get the information out of the safe. Drop what you're doing and go over before the apartment is sealed."

"Sealed? What? Why would it be sealed?"

"Just do it. Now. It's important. That money is yours, it's nobody else's business. Have a good life. Use it wisely to set yourself up. And know your father has always loved you. No matter what you hear about me. And tell your mother I loved her, too."

He'd become less emotional throughout the call. By the time he hung up, his tone was flat.

His apartment would only be sealed if he was dead.

And if there was a crime involved.

I was in the back seat of a crime in process.

We were driving quickly, passing the Olympic ski jumping complex. I knew the State Police often used the parking lot to hide as a speed trap for unsuspecting tourists. How could I get their attention?

The moon roof!

I dove for the button. It started to open. Maybe even if they didn't see me, I could climb out. How hurt would I get, tumbling from a limo going over sixty miles per hour?

Pretty hurt.

But I could stand up and wave at passing cars to call for help.

That plan lasted six inches worth of open before Castor locked the roof.

As we roared past the complex, I at least put my hands up through the opening to wave at anyone who might see. No one paid any attention. Limo people joyriding.

Olive was passed out now.

Think. What was in the car, or what did Olive have that might help?

A phone. Olive had to have a phone.

She wore leggings and a flowy top. Not there. I grabbed her purse and unzipped it, then held it upside down and emptied its contents onto the seat beside her.

Bingo.

I picked it up. The home screen was locked, of course. Fortunately, she'd set up facial recognition. I let the phone recognize her. She had three percent power. What was wrong with her, anyway? asked the person whose dead phone was charging back by the bed where Rise likely still slept. With shaking hands, I dialed 911.

The phone rang once, then dropped the call.

Before it was completely dead, I tried a text. The phone number that came to mind was Philip's. I remembered the concern on his face as we drove by. I typed, *Headed out of town. Call 911. He's going to kill us.*

I hit send. I couldn't even tell if it went through.

For no reason at all, except it was becoming clear that Castor was about to kill himself and take me with him, I texted my final words: *I love you.*

The partition was still partly open.

"Castor," I said, "Please don't do this. There has to be another way. This will haunt your daughter and your wife forever. Please."

He didn't answer.

"At least let me and Olive out. Pull over for one second and we'll get out."

"Why should that bitch live when my Ellie died?"

"I have no answer. Olive clearly needs help. You were brilliant getting her into the car before she hurt anyone."

He didn't answer.

"Let me out, then, please. I'm sorry about Ellie, I'm so sorry. You know I am."

"It's your own fault, sticking your nose in, getting into the car. I'm sorry, you are different, but fate intervened."

"You know that's not true. Did fate intervene with Ellie? You're going to cause my family the same grief! You couldn't save her, but you can save me! Let me out."

He closed the panel.

He made a right-hand turn and gunned the engine as we passed the forty-foot statue of a moose. I knew where we were going. And I knew what would happen there.

We're headed for the overlook at Starlight Falls. We're going to drive off.

I hit send. I don't think the text went. The phone went black. It was dead.

UNPLUGGED

Spiked Raspberry Iced Maple Latte

Ingredients

1 oz Chambord
1 oz vodka
1 1/2 oz heavy cream
2 oz ice coffee
1 teaspoon of local maple syrup
Fresh raspberries for garnish

Method

In cocktail shaker, add ice and all ingredients.
Shake together until cocktail shaker is cold on the outside.
Pour into Collins glass.
Add fresh raspberries for garnish

24

OVER THE CLIFF

I REMEMBERED CASTOR talking about Princess Diana and the night she died. I'd read somewhere that she likely would have survived if she'd been wearing a seatbelt.

Does a seatbelt help when you launch off a cliff into a raging river?

Maybe only for the first part of that journey.

I crawled over to Olive. Was she still breathing? I couldn't tell. Hot tears streaked my cheeks as I pulled her into the back corner seat of the limo and clumsily pulled the seatbelt across her. It took a crazy minute for it to snap.

She fell forward against it.

As she did, I heard a siren in the distance. Then another.

It could be a fire truck or an ambulance or a police car chasing a speeder.

We passed two cars going the other way from the Falls parking lot. I put my hands through the gap in the moon roof and waved, but nothing. It didn't matter if they did see me. It was too late to call 911 and get a party started, if there wasn't one started already.

I sat on the back seat in the corner across from Olive and buckled my own three-point seatbelt. I rested my head and stared at the small patch of sky above me. I'd enjoyed this world. I loved the sky, in all its iterations. *Thanks for the sky, God.*

It occurred to me that when we hit the river, it would normally take a while for water to seep in and fill the vehicle. Instead, since the moon roof was partially open, the limo would fill with water, posthaste.

Oh, well, why waste more time waiting to die? It's not like I could open windows or doors to get out.

If we were even alive or conscious after going off that bluff. How high was it, anyway? Five hundred feet? And the Ausable River was at its deepest and widest below. Plenty of room for a limousine to join the flow.

The sirens were louder.

Maybe the police were coming, after all.

My heart lurched. Could it be true? Could they save us?

Castor took the limo to top speed. We were almost there. Even if the police did catch up to us, likely all they could do would be to give us an escort to drive off the bluff into the river that would kill us.

My mother would be devastated. *I'm so sorry, Mom. I thought I had time to figure stuff out. I thought we had plenty of time to reconcile.*

My cousin Reggie would be devastated. Hannah would be devastated.

My father would know I was in Hell and it was on him because he hadn't been able to save me.

At least there was that.

I saw them then, the flashing lights, as the state police cars moved out of the woods on the road behind us. There was another park service road into the parking lot, but it was a long, curvy drive. Even if police cruisers went that way, they'd never have time to head us off.

And what would they do, anyway? Park across the top of the bluff? Castor was so calm and determined, I had no doubt he'd ram that car into the river with us.

I'm sorry, Mom. I'm sorry.

God, forgive me for hating my dad. I don't actually hate You, I hate the version of You my dad is selling.

I'd know soon enough if my dad was right.

But maybe he wasn't. Maybe I'd see Winsome, and Mormor.

As we broke through the final trees into the parking lot, the police veered closer.

But not close enough. They'd follow us to our departure.

Thanks to dash cams, there'd be dramatic footage. I hoped, for my family's sake, it wouldn't end up on the news.

One car, a red Toyota, was parked facing the bluff where we'd parked the night before, but there was plenty of room beside it for us to drive past.

I'm sorry, Olive, I tried to save us.

Maybe she was already gone.

Or maybe this was her dream exit. Have a limo come to take her to Rise and never come back. Their names linked forever, as she wished.

Sadly, my name would be linked to this fiasco, too.

It was very odd knowing I was sitting here, perfectly fine, and within moments I would be not fine. Not fine at all.

I sat back and looked up.

Thank you again for the sky.

I closed my eyes.

There was a crash. A huge thunk, coming from Olive's side of the car, only farther forward. My seatbelt cut into me as my body was jerked into the door.

There was grinding. We were being pushed forward, but more sideways. Sideways.

Animated body language from the driver. Someone had rammed the front of the limo and was forcing it to turn.

Castor turned the steering wheel. The tires spun.

We were shoved into the back of the Toyota.

Body language that indicated swearing from the front. He tried to back up, since he couldn't go forward or to the left. The pressure of the car driving into us abated. Castor tried to back up fast to ram the gas pedal for the final leap. But the car that hit us had apparently backed up, hit their gas pedal, and rammed us again.

The front of the limo was a mess.

Castor saw the writing on the wall.

He opened the door of the limousine and stepped out. He didn't bother to stop the car or close his door.

Four state police vehicles made a circle behind us. The occupants of the first police vehicle got out, prepared to somehow capture Castor.

Sorry, too late.

Castor walked to the edge of the precipice. He stood looking straight ahead for one second. Then he calmly took a step off.

Castor had left the limo in drive, and we were moving.

A state police officer saw us and ran for the car.

Depending on what we hit, we would either go sailing off the cliff farther down or hit a tree.

The officer jumped in and got situated only in time to slow us down before we hit the tree.

I sat back, reeling from this final impact, trying to catch my breath.

The officer took a moment, put her head down on the steering wheel for a second, put the car into park and removed the key. Then she hit the back door lock release.

I still sat. Slowly I reached around to find the release for my seatbelt. It hurt as it slid off me.

The back door opened. "Don't move," said a voice with some authority. "The ambulance is on its way."
I felt whiplashed and battered, certainly, but I didn't have a broken neck.

The rest I didn't care about. I got out of that car.

As I did, I looked across the parking lot to see who had saved us.

And there sat Philip by the remains of his beautiful brand-new Porsche 911.

OVER THE CLIFF

Cocktail Verte

Ingredients

1 oz green Chartreuse
1 oz gin
2 oz pear juice
2 dashes lemon bitters
Fresh lemon peel (for garnish)
Fresh sliced pears (for garnish)
Chilled martini glass

Method

In cocktail shaker add ice, green Chartreuse, gin, pear juice, lemon bitters.
Shake all ingredients together until cocktail shaker is cold.
Strain into coupe or martini glass.
Add fresh lemon peel and fresh pear for garnish

25

INTO THE SUNSET

OLIVE, PHILIP AND I were dispersed to three different ambulances, likely depleting Tranquility's store. I have insurance now since my job is manager level at MacTavish's. Lucky me. X-rays and CT scans to prove I had nothing broken, only whiplash. They insisted on admitting me for 24 hours for observation, in case a blood vessel had burst in my brain or something.

Investigator Spalding took my statement at the hospital. I had an interesting story to tell, if I do say so myself. It involved Rise O'Connor only tangentially, although I admitted I'd known Rise since we were kids and he stayed at my place. The investigator had already taken a statement from Rise, in the presence of his attorney, Con. Yep, they were personal assistant, security, and attorney. Best hire ever, in my opinion. Rise's statement, although not mainly about me, included the fact we'd been romantically involved. I conceded we had.

The glare Mike gave me for withholding this piece of information could have raised me off the ground and choked me if he was a Jedi. What did he expect? Rise was an old friend, yet Mike told me not to trust him. It seemed as though Mike had it out for Rise. Whose side did Mike expect me to be on?

Police in Los Angeles had already gone to Castor's apartment. I secretly hoped Callie had gotten the stuff about her bank account out of the safe.

Inspector Spaulding said they'd likely want to talk to me more, as the story unfolded.

As he prepared to leave the room, I said, "You know, if there are any screenplays on his computer, or in his apartment, they might want to take a look."

Con and Rise came to say good-bye in my hospital room on their way to the airport.

"Thanks," said Con. "You were about to wrestle Olive to the ground."

"Had to do something."

Olive had been admitted to the hospital, but it didn't look good.

I repeated the story of the last limo ride for Con and Rise. They were shocked by Castor's actions, that there was a killer among them, in their inner circle, for so long without anyone guessing. They were horrified by his actions and shaken by his death. His body was found slightly downriver the day after he jumped.

"This seems like the perfect time for me to take a career break. Even Isobel has to understand why I need time off."

"It's time to head for the airport," said Con. "I'll wait in the hall." As they left, they added to me, "Oh, and great party. Thanks."

The door closed.

"This isn't how I pictured our farewell," said Rise. "Thank you for everything. Everything. You could have been killed trying to save Olive."

"She terrified you for years. But she was still a person. And maybe could have been helped."

"Yeah. I wish she'd gotten a chance."

I was sitting in the room's chair. I stood and went to Rise. He gave me a gentle embrace.

"You're headed to deal with your life's crutches?" I asked.

"That's the plan."

"Then you'll spend time with your mom."

"Also the plan. You're sure you won't join me?"

"Yes, I'm sure. But you know where I am."

"I do." He took my hand. Our fingers entwined. "Love you, Av."

"Love you, Crispin. Friends for life."

Crispin leaned down and gave me a parting kiss. The moment was bittersweet.

"Friends for life." He pulled away. "I guess this meeting of the Salty Gang is adjourned."

"As we ride into the sunset," we said together.

"Into the sunset." He gave a brief salute, opened the door, and stepped back out of my life.

Mike Spaulding came back the next morning as I was waiting to be discharged.

"How did you know about the screenplay?" he asked.

"At one point, I was in the front seat of the limo talking to Castor, and he told me about how entitled a lot of the starlets acted. I said he could probably write a book and he said, 'or a screenplay.' I knew he'd been in the business, so thought maybe…"

"Well, you were right. Not a screenplay, exactly, but a treatment for one. It will take us a while to see how grounded in reality it is. The premise seems to be that two young girls are hit by a car, one has a rich dad and goes to the best hospital and survives, one has a poor dad and doesn't. The poor dad becomes an avenging angel and murders young women he feels are too entitled. At the end, he kills the rich dad."

"Wow."

"Circumstances of his fictional deaths seem to match those of LeAnn Astor and Marissa Marisol. There are indications he felt protective of Rise O'Connor and possibly killed the two stalkers in the spur of the moment because he had means and opportunity.

"Castor was apparently a known drug dealer and was active in that world. Likely he used those drugs for his murders—as well as his main source of income."

Holy smokes. Just…holy smokes.

An hour later, Hannah gave me a ride home. We sat together having a cup of tea on my terrace, our comforting ritual.

"Sorry to get you involved in all this," I said.

"Hey," she said. "Never a dull moment."

"We have to figure out where to go to apply for some more of those. Dull moments, I mean."

"Yeah. We do."

One thing about living near a waterfall is that you don't hear people coming over the bridge. I was more than a little surprised when Rise's former manager, Dirk Fortney, rounded the corner of the house. He had worked himself into a rage.

"Where is he? I know he's here!"

Hannah and I gave him our best blank looks.

"If the 'him' is Rise, nope."

"His phone isn't working. He's not available through Isobel. He's not at his house in L.A. He's vanished. He has to be here."

"You can look around," I said. "He's not. You're two days late and two dollars short."

Dirk actually stomped through my cottage, flinging doors open and not closing them. It took all of three minutes. He stomped back out.

"I'm going to find him, and I'm going to kill him."

"Again, late with the drama," I said. "That ship has sailed."

"Well, where is he? Where has he gone? You must know!"

"I don't. Truly, I don't. But there is a plan for you. Want to sit down and hear about it?"

Dirk's compact body was still shaking. His suit looked like he'd traveled a long distance while wearing it.

"What?"

I motioned to a chair. "Coffee? Tea?"

"What?" But he sat.

"From what I understand, here's your next move. You go back to L.A., you find the scion of a wealthy family who wants to be the next Rise O'Connor, and you say, 'I can do that.'"

"What?"

"You'll demand such a good fee that you become wealthy while re-Rising. But do us a favor and take on a kid a couple years older than Rise was. And leave his nose alone."

Dirk stared at me.

"Where is he?"

Hannah and I both shook our heads. The fact she wore a priest's collar made him accept we were telling the truth.

He stood up and stormed back off.

"Dramatic exit, stage left," I said.

Olive was still alive when I left the hospital, but she died the next day, on Wednesday. I had the eerie feeling she'd say her quest was fulfilled.

By Thursday, I decided I felt well enough to go back to work, if I pre-fortified my body with ibuprofen.

I took a cup of coffee and stepped out onto my terrace that morning. I was too full of electricity to sit still, so I decided to stroll around the suddenly very empty property. I ended up across the bridge sitting on the white bench.

Sally's place was unoccupied, and I knew the 'guardhouse' was, as well. It's funny, because I was used to Sally being gone, and the little crooked guardhouse had sat empty for months. The place only seemed vacant because I'd grown used to Con on Sally's porch, revolving Chets below, Rise and Landon having breakfast on the patio. And Whistle, of course, dancing happily at my feet.

As if conjured, a little auburn dog magically appeared, ran barking up the slope, stood on her two back feet, and begged for me to pick her up.

"Whistle! What are you doing here?"

Her human walked into the glade. He wore khakis and a white muslin shirt. His jet-black hair was long and tousled. He exuded Philip-ness.

"Hey," I said.

"Hey," he responded.

He traversed the hill.

"Do you want to sit?"

"Sure." He turned around and lowered himself gingerly next to me.

"Cracked ribs," he explained.

"I'm so sorry. Are you all right? Other than that?"

"Yes. Or I will be. Had a killer headache from the airbag deploying. It's better. Nothing on the CT scan."

"Thank you. Times a million. I mean it. You saved my life."

"We're even. Last time, you saved mine."

"How did you get to that parking lot in time?"

"That back entrance. It's a long windy road. I had a car that takes curves exceptionally well."

"So you must have gotten my texts."

He looked back at the stream. "Yeah."

The air was thick between us. I hadn't meant to send that middle text. Or maybe I had.

Philip cleared his throat. "Let me say this. Don't interrupt, or I won't get through it."

"Okay."

"I'm sorry about what happened with you and me and Rachel. But Avalon..." He stopped and gathered his emotions. "I knew I loved you. God, how I love you. And when we...when we...that night..."

I nodded that I knew the night he was referring to.

"My whole life had changed. But I'd been with Rachel for two years. We meant a lot to each other. Our relationship had run its course, and she was leaving town. It was time. But it was hard for both of us. We hadn't officially broken up. We hadn't said our good-byes. She deserved that. Our relationship deserved that. I felt I needed to disentangle, giving Rachel the respect she deserved before I could officially begin ours.

"I blew it. I...you and me...we...if only I could have waited two days. Two days, until she left. But God, I loved you and you were right there and..."

"I get the picture," I said. "I remember."

We lapsed into silence.

"What we had was so new. When Rachel was here, at Gran's

party, I didn't feel I could just drop her, publicly. You and I...it was our first day. Rachel and I were breaking up. I just needed time.

"I'm not that suave guy who can balance two women. I don't know how to do that. I don't *want* to know how. I don't want to be that guy. And I blew it."

"Words," I said. "You could have used your words. 'I'm sorry' is not 'I need time.' It's not 'I love you, give me time to respectfully break up with Rachel.'"

"You're right. I know that now."

"It hurt. A lot." It had almost killed me.

"God, Avalon, I'm so sorry. I just...did you mean what you texted me when you were in the limo?"

"*I love you*. You mean that one?"

"Yes."

I looked up at him. "Yeah. I found out it's hard to lie, even to yourself, when you're on the way to your death."

"Is there anything I can do to win you back? Any kind of atonement?"

"Atonement?"

"Pay for my crimes. Wipe the slate clean." It was as if he remembered where those words came from. "We are on Sally's spanking bench. But you'd have to wait till my ribs heal."

I burst out laughing. "First of all, you're brave to want to try this relationship again. Somehow you end up in the hospital, and usually broken ribs is the least of it. Second, and speaking of this very bench, don't tempt me.

"But third, I think the sacrifice of a Porsche 911 more than fulfills any necessary expiation. You saved my life."

"And you do love me? You really do?"

"God help me, I do. Do you...love me?"

"God help me, yes. I can't stop. I've tried."

Philip reached over and held my hand.

"Yeah. I've tried, too. No luck."

Together we sat.

"So why were Landon Presser and Rise O'Connor up here with you?" he finally asked, "And why did they have so few clothes on?"

"Who was the beautiful woman in Paris, in love with the talented painter all summer?"

Phillip looked surprised at my assumption, which I took to mean it was correct. "I tried to quit you," he said. "I really tried."

"I tried, too."

"Here we sit."

"Here we sit."

He squeezed my hand and I squeezed back.

INTO THE SUNSET

Ingredients

Dry sparkling rosé wine
1 oz dry gin
1/4 oz simple syrup
Fresh lemon juice and peel

Method

In champagne flute add simple syrup, followed by gin and
fresh squeeze of lemon.
Slowly top off with sparkling rosé.
Add fresh lemon peel for garnish.

ACKNOWLEGEMENTS

With 2020 hindsight, 2020 was a difficult year. The losses were great, starting with daily life as we knew it. There are no words deep enough to mourn those lost to COVID-19 or scorching enough to describe the loss of loved ones to outrage over alternate versions of what is true.

Perhaps I shouldn't mention such things here, but storytelling is my way to process the world around me, and that is partly what this book became. One of the positives about a worldwide pandemic and being stuck at home was that we were given time to discover what was, and is, important to us.

For me, and for Avalon, friends are at the top of the list. I belong to Creators Haven—a group of female artists, thinkers and clergy who go on retreats to make art and strengthen each other. (If you enjoyed this book, you'd likely fit right in.) During lockdown, a group of us met twice a day, five days a week via Zoom, and, much to our surprise, crazy amounts of art got made and friendships deepened. I send undying gratitude to Barb Sherer, Mary Ann O'Roark, Sharrata Hunt, Anne Harkness, Suzy Webber, Judy Malloy, Melissa Hinnen, Valerie Paul Watson, Jean Stephenson, Karen Valentin, and Crystal Paul Watson, sisters in lockdown. They were present for stages of writing I don't usually share, and likely heard my resistance to "the cards, I have to do the cards," more times than they cared to.

Thanks to those who gave inspiration at readings as things progressed: Debra McArthur, Wendy Welch, Christine Farrell, Deborah Lee, Melissa Paul, Theresa Paul, Claire Woodley, Stacey Duensing, Lisa Cullen, Wendy Paige Paul and Laura Paul Reynolds.

As always, thanks to my husband, Robert Owens Scott, who was suddenly at home 24/7, and it turns out we like each other a lot. Whew. He's a trusted first reader, as are Barb and Sharrata. Many thanks. You made the story better.

A shout out to my son, Jonathan Scott, with whom I learned bartending many moons ago, and daughter Linnéa Scott, my advisor in just about everything.

Thanks to my talented editor Elizabeth Ward, my designer Phillip Gessert, and my proofreader, Gillian Freed, and, as always, the brilliant Bob Venables who creates the covers.

Much gratitude to Sarah and Marc Galvin from the Bookstore Plus in Lake Placid for supplying and sending out signed copies, Andy Flynn, editor of the Lake Placid News as well as the We are Lake Placid podcast (find Jamielynn and my podcast there). He is dedicated to keeping journalism alive.

I recommend you check out the Adirondack Film Society (AdirondackFilmSociety.org) which "advances the art and appreciation of film and filmmaking in the Adirondack region." They have a film festival in Lake Placid each October, but without the dead bodies. Likely preferable.

Has a TV show you love ever ended, or you've finished streaming a series or reading a book and you're sad because you're really going to miss those characters? This time more than most, I'm feeling a bit silly, because once I finished writing this story, I really missed these guys. For months they lived in my head and walked around and said unexpected and often funny or raucous things. I came to know and love them and spent more time with them than almost anyone. They were great comrades—especially "the boys." Now they've moved on to have their own life in the world.

Which brings me here. Thanks very much to you for reading this book. A storyteller is nothing without an audience. Now that you've read this book, I feel as if we have friends in common. If you did enjoy it and would be willing to write a review online, it would be appreciated. It can be as short as, "I liked it!" If you'd be willing to help spread the word by telling your friends, better yet. Things like that truly help authors find their audience, which is why we tell stories and how we can keep doing it.

Cheers!

Sharon Linnéa
Warwick, New York
July 2021

S HARON LINNÉA (AUTHOR) is the author of the bestselling
Chasing Eden and the Eden Thrillers with B.K. Sherer, as well
as *These Violent Delights*, a movie mystery. She has written award-
winning biographies of Raoul Wallenberg, and Hawaii's Princess
Ka'iulani and a dozen other titles. She is a TIPS certified bartender.
SharonLinnea.com and BartendersGuidetoMurder.com

JAMIELYNN BRYDALSKI (RECIPES) grew up with a love
and passion for the art of food. After studying hospitality at Paul
Smith college, she fell in love with the art of crafting specialty cocktails while travelling the world. She bartended in Lake Placid, New
York, for 11 years. She runs the Buffalo Cocktail Company.

START READING AVALON'S
NEXT ADVENTURE

DEATH FROM BEYOND

1

ALL HALLOWS' EVE EVE

S HE SAT DOWN at the bar at 9:14 PM on the last Friday in October, a tall woman, with large hazel eyes, a long nose, a chiseled chin, paperwhite skin, and thick black hair. She wore an ecru shirt topped by an olive green jacket.

"I need some liquid courage," she said.

"You've come to the right place." I plunked down our Scary October Cocktail menu.

"The problem is, I can't drink alcohol. Doesn't mix with my meds."

"Got you covered." I turned over the cocktail menu to the mocktail side. The list was equally as long. "I'm afraid you'll have to provide the courage yourself."

"I'll try the Fall Fiesta," she said, choosing a cider-based libation.

"Coming up."

It was Halloween weekend and the Battened Hatch was crazy busy. The Adirondack town of Tranquility went all-out for the holiday; in fact, it had been named Best Halloween Town by an upscale travel magazine. Folks flooded in. The Visitors Bureau concentrated on events for kids—parades, daytime trick or treating on Main Street, scavenger hunts. If you wanted witchy doings, you still had to head for Salem, Massachusetts. Or parties here to which I was not invited.

"Visiting for the holiday?" I asked, setting down the drink. "Would you like to see a food menu?"

"No, thanks. And I'm only kind of visiting. I grew up here. There's a mini high school reunion tomorrow. My class was always weird. Instead of meeting up on Labor Day or some other three-day weekend, we did stuff on Halloween."

"Oh, wow. I'm always of two minds about reunions. Is your family still in town?"

"Yes. Hence my need for alcohol."

"Which you were smart enough not to drink." I smiled and offered my hand, which was engulfed in her own. "Avalon."

"Sandy."

As we shook, I recognized the scent she wore: lily of the valley. It was one of my two signature scents. "Diorissimo?" I asked.

She stared at me, then a small smile crept onto her face. "How did you know?"

Certainly no one would accuse me of knowing my designer perfumes. But I did recognize this one. "Lily of the valley. Hardly anyone uses the fragrance in perfume anymore."

"It was in our backyard, growing up. In the spring we had a volleyball net up. My friends and I spent many happy hours there."

"It was in the garden behind my mormor's brownstone in Brooklyn. They were planted closest to the house, in the shade. Every year, my grandmother spoke of how it grew outside the family homesteads in Tennessee and Småland, Sweden. She's gone now—that whole generation is—but it makes me feel close to her, even for a while."

"It reminds me of the happy parts of growing up," Sandy said.

We took a second to smile.

It was then I noticed a pin she was wearing, a small pink flower with a scroll that said *Sensitive Badass*.

"Doubleclicks," I said, nodding at it.

"You know the band?"

"Yeah. That's a good song. Who these days doesn't feel like a badass—albeit a sensitive one?"

"You got that right."

"Let me know if you need anything else," I said, pulling myself back to work.

Drink orders were stacking up. Halloween is a big creative cocktail holiday, unlike, say, Easter, when mimosas are your best bet. Tonight, the large carved bar behind me was glowing with an array of two hundred bottles; those in the center were being used almost as frequently as those in the well. I remembered the first time I saw it. While the rest of the Scottish pub is paneled with cherry wood, the bar itself is mahogany. It must have cost a fortune. Mahogany darkens over time. The carved wood wore its age and care impressively.

Marta, my assistant manager and co-bartender, swung back through the kitchen with a green plastic rack filled with glasses from the dishwasher. Marta used to think of herself as Goth. Now she wore the same clothing, which had miraculously morphed into bartender black. She's eighteen, just graduated from high school, and taking a gap year to save money before going to art school. I honestly didn't know what the Battened Hatch would do without her next year.

She stowed the glasses and we both got to work.

"Hey, Marta," said Sandy.

"Hey…"

"Sandy."

"Sandy," said Marta.

"You work here?"

"Yes," Marta smiled, holding up a martini glass.

"Cool," said Sandy.

As the evening wore on, I watched Sandy out of the corner of my eye. Like virtually everyone who sat alone at the bar, she was checking her phone. She was naturally charismatic, with a twinkle in her eye, but there was something on her mind. She exuded an odd mixture of confidence and hesitation. She'd be perfectly cast in a Neil Gaiman series: ruler of some fascinating realm, who could tell plenty of interesting stories to a therapist. Or to a bartender. Maybe, if she was from here, she'd return when I had time to chat.

It's funny how when you meet someone who will impact your

life, you seldom know it. But sometimes, as happened that night, there is a connection, a silent buzzer that goes off, and you aren't surprised when your lives become somehow intertwined.

Meanwhile, three ghosts and a woman dressed like Princess Leia in the Jabba the Hutt scene pressed in towards the bar for orders. This far north in New York State, nights were already dipping down into the thirties. Even inside, Princess Leia had to be freezing. She tossed her head haughtily towards any male person who smiled her way.

Around 9:45, a young man, maybe five-eight with a long-sleeved pullover and short hair, sidled up to the end of the bar. He held the hand of a wafer-thin woman of the same age, who followed behind. They both looked too young to drink.

"Hey. Marta," he beckoned. She looked up, finished the potion she was mixing, and went over.

"Hey, Toby."

"You're coming Sunday, right?"

"I don't know."

"Come on. This is the last year we're all going to be around, probably."

"I'm still thinking. But maybe."

"Get Colin to come. He's always the best."

"I'll see."

Toby did a two-fingered salute and headed back out of the Hatch. Which is what we call the Battened Hatch when we're busy. The actual name, still on the pub sign outside, is That Ship Has Sailed. It's inside MacTavish's Seaside Cottage, a Scottish hotel that has never had cottages or been seaside. Whoever named the inn, I've long been a fan. I've managed the bar since I arrived in town in May and found the last bartender murdered, then stayed to find out why.

"Who was that?" I murmured to Marta.

"That was Toby and his girlfriend. He wants me and my friend Colin to go with them to investigate Appleton Lodge on Monday."

She used the soda gun to finish a Collins. She looked straight ahead as she said, "It's supposed to be haunted."

"Okay," I said.

"They go every year."

"And you don't?"

"Why would I go looking for ghosts?"

I chuckled. Marta was a sensitive, meaning dead people found her. She was learning to control her gift, but I could see why she didn't want to go into overload.

"Why don't they go on Halloween?" It seemed like a natural time for exploring haunted venues.

"The other two lodges attached to Appleton burned down mysteriously, so the cops always watch it super carefully on times like Halloween. Then, the day after, they don't."

"Got it." I could see how Marta would be hesitant to go. The large, rambling Adirondack-style inn had been empty for years. Probably everyone in town wondered if it was haunted. I could see how visiting it could entice local explorers.

Halloween was on a Saturday this year, which was tomorrow. Tonight was crazy enough that Marta and I fell into a time warp. The only time I looked up was when Sandy paid with cash and I had to make change. "Hey, listen," she said, seeming nervous. "Is there a chance...I could leave my suitcase here...and pick it up in an hour?"

"In an hour?"

"My folks live on Ivy Circle, just off Maple. It's close enough I can walk, but I don't think I can drag a suitcase all the way up. I'll get my dad to drive down and pick it up." When I paused, she said, "I asked the lobby bellman. He said the hotel is so full, if I'm not a guest, no can do."

"Sure. Stick it in the back hall there, past the bathrooms. It should be safe enough."

"Thank you very much," said Sandy. She got up and dragged the brown suitcase I hadn't realized was at her feet towards the bathrooms.

I turned back to work.

Oddly, our clients didn't voice objection to us closing at eleven, our regular time. Maybe they had other places to go, or perhaps they were saving their Halloween energy for the next day. They all paid up, we closed out quickly, and my crew headed out happily enough that I knew they were going to continue celebrating. I never cared how they celebrated—as long as they were back in working form the next day.

I stood alone looking at the streamers of black and orange along the walls, mentally counting the hours until I could rip them down. Not a fan of streamers, crepe, or orange and black.

As I turned out the lights in the back hall, I saw that the brown suitcase was still there. It was well past an hour since Sandy left. Likely she and her family had been distracted and she'd come back for it tomorrow.

I put on my coat, hat, and gloves and locked the inside door—although Hugo, the night janitor, was heading over to start cleaning.

An expectant buzz tinged the frigid air even though the streets were emptying. I walked down Tranquility's homey Main Street and turned up Maple, the same street Sandy would have turned up earlier. It climbed at a steep angle. Three cul-de-sacs branched off to the right. The first was Forest, the second, Orchard, the last, Ivy Circle. As I climbed that hill, north winds picked up, warning empty tree boughs of a hard night to come. I was glad to turn right onto Forest. It sat quiet and dark, interior lights glowing discreetly behind windows of well-built older homes, each surrounded by an acre or more of woodland. I walked the road to one especially solid residence at the end of the dead-end street. It was one story, Craftsman-style, its painted wooden porch empty. Dark windows on either side of the front door seemed to signal no one was home.

I knew someone was.

I didn't go up the driveway but walked past it and started through the dead leaves on the left side of the house. It was the more level side of the property. Still, I knew enough to step carefully and go from tree to tree, steadying myself by holding onto trunks in the murky darkness, swirling leaves crackling like cellophane beneath my feet.

Finally rounding the back of the house, I came upon a profusion of illumination spilling from tall windows. Escaping strains of Rachmaninoff's "Symphonic Dances" filtered, nearly muted, into the woods from inside the panes.

Before me sat an artist's studio, attached to a back hallway of the dwelling. It was like another country. Intensive warm light, huge canvases with dancing colors, careful strokes, slashes, blues, green, browns, yellows, in shades of colors only artists know: cadmium chartreuse, India yellow, alizarin crimson, cerulean, phthalo emerald.

And a tall young man, wearing thick painter's pants and no shirt, focused like a laser, like a train through Siberia, or Smaug guarding treasure. The strokes of his brush were purposeful, masterful, almost violent. The muscles of his back and his arms were firm and tensed in service to the work, gingerbread skin glistening with perspiration. His thick black hair was a tousled mess.

I stood and watched Philip work until the wind's constant assault shook me. I realized how irritated he'd be if I froze to death and my body was found in his yard and he had to stop work to deal with it.

I made my way back, again from tree to tree. Gray flakes of early snow zipped past but nothing stuck. Thankful to be back on the road, I walk-jogged down to Main Street, then up to the employee parking lot, where I turned on my Subaru and cleared the frosted windows while waiting for the heater and my seat to warm up. I drove back down Main Street, now devoid of traffic but bursting with toy witches and cauldrons and promises of the next day's treats.

The dirt lane from the main road up into my little glade was frozen firm. I parked in a makeshift spot down below just in case it got slick overnight.

The living room lamp I'd left on in my cottage served as a beacon. I walked up the path easily, past my landlady's lodge, then grasped the railing tightly as I crossed the footbridge. The back patio was somewhat sheltered. My arrival cued the motion-activated light, which helped as I punched in the code to unlock the back door.

"Hi, Whistle," I said to the little Pomeranian at my feet. I let her out to relieve herself, and we both happily returned to the warmth of the house.

"Yeah, I saw him," I said. I made a cup of tea, and the small dog and I went into the living room, where I turned on the gas logs in the fireplace and pulled a soft white throw over my lap. My watch declared midnight. "Happy Halloween," I said, as the little dog settled in. I knew it was going to be another lonely night.

That is what I knew. Here is what I did not know until much later:

That Sandy shivered the half block down Main Street, then turned to trudge up the hill through the biting wind, until she came to the top, to Ivy Circle. That her parents were having a party and though it was late, the street was lined with cars. That the house in which she grew up, a lovely three-story dwelling, had light pouring from each window, golden light, like in the fairy tales. The pine tree in the front yard had a string of golden twinkle lights and the outline of a horn of plenty sat at each window. Her parents did not celebrate Halloween. There were no witches or ghosts. It was a harvest gathering.

As she climbed the front steps, the door opened and a middle-aged couple in heavy coats and carrying a tin of cookies took their leave. "Goodbye! Goodbye! Thanks for the lovely time!"

Sandy waited until they'd departed before she started up the steps.

I did not know that her father saw her first and started to ask,

"What are you doing here?" when her mother saw clearly who it was, then said, "I need you GONE," and slammed the door.

I didn't know Sandy stood behind the garage, shivering, watching old family friends depart the house, get into their cars, and leave.

When her fingers stabbed with cold even through her gloves, she wandered back to the main road, walked down to Main Street, and retraced her steps to MacTavish's Seaside Cottage. The bar was locked, but the lights were on. She sat unobtrusively in the lobby and watched a couple, late arrivals, check in at reception, others stopping to ask what around this town was still open—didn't they know this was Friday night?

When Hugo, a sturdy, balding man who did the cleaning, opened the door from the pub dragging his floor polisher, she told him she needed to grab her suitcase. Hugo knew there was a suitcase in the back hall because he'd cleaned around it. He let her in and dragged the shiny steel contraption across to the janitor's closet and prepared for his next room. He remembered letting someone into the pub, so he went back, opened the door, and called out to see if she was still there. No one answered. Convinced she'd gotten her bag and left, he locked the door.

I didn't know that Sandy shrunk into the back hallway, hoping he wouldn't come in. He didn't. She heard the door lock.

Grateful for the warmth, and exhausted, she took off her coat and made herself a bed. She opened her suitcase, found a shirt, and used it as a pillow. She did her best to pull the coat up around her as a blanket as well as a mattress. She found it worked best if she rolled onto her side.

She didn't want to give in to tears, but they streaked her face as she finally let her body relax and passed out into sleep. I also didn't know that she was awakened the next morning by the noisy sound of the adjoining kitchen preparing to serve hungry, impatient tourists the breakfast that came with their expensive winter stay packages, in Pepper's, the restaurant overlooking the lake.

She got up and changed into a pink sweater and ecru pants—her best outfit—and went into the pub's bathroom, injecting her meds, doing her makeup, and getting ready for the day. When she was done, she closed up the suitcase and left it like a sentinel in the back hallway. She put on her coat, hat, and gloves.

She looked through the window from the pub into the kitchen, by now controlled chaos, and chose her path. Then she pushed through and walked quickly out the back door into the bright Halloween morning. She went around to the hotel's front door. She smiled and talked to Rusty, the doorman, who welcomed her as a newly arriving guest. She crossed the lobby and got herself a cup of coffee and a hot cookie. Then she wandered down a hall towards the meeting rooms where there were plenty of benches to sit and wait until it was time to meet her classmates up the street at the high school for the first welcome event for their reunion.

I did not know that no one would admit seeing her alive after the reunion—that no one would ever pick up that brown suitcase.

ALL HALLOWS' EVE EVE

Fall Fiesta

Ingredients

2 oz apple cider
½ oz pomegranate liqueur
1 oz Bourbon
Sprinkle of fresh ground cinnamon
Ginger beer
Cinnamon stick
Fresh pomegranate seeds
Ice
Mule mug

Method

Fill mule mug with ice.
In cocktail shaker, add ice, apple cider, pomegranate liqueur, Bourbon, and ground cinnamon. Shake all ingredients together.
Strain contents of cocktail shaker into mule mug. Top with ginger beer.
Add fresh pomegranate seeds and cinnamon stick for garnish.

9 781933 608365